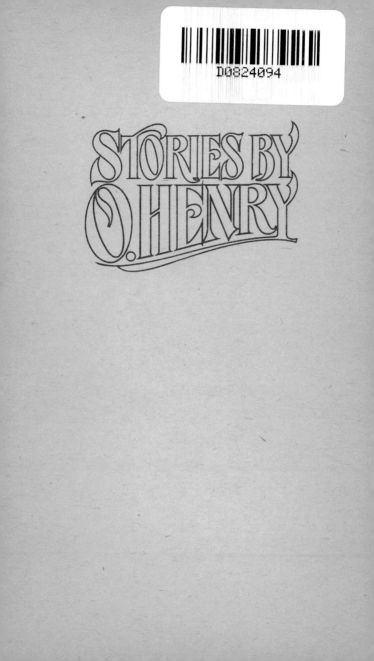

STORIES BY
O. HENRY

D0824094

STORIES BY O. HENRY

A TOM DOHERTY ASSOCIATES BOOK
NEW YORK

This is a work of fiction. All the characters and events portrayed in this book are fictional, and any resemblance to real people or incidents is purely coincidental.

STORIES BY O. HENRY

All new material in this edition is copyright
© 1988 by Tom Doherty Associates, Inc.

A TOR Book

Published by Tom Doherty Associates, Inc.
49 West 24th Street
New York, N.Y. 10010

ISBN: 0-812-50502-6 Can. ISBN: 0-812-50503-4

First Tor edition: July 1989

Printed in the United States of America

0 9 8 7 6 5 4

Contents

The Life of O. Henry

William Sydney Porter ("O. Henry") was born September 11, 1862, near Greensboro, North Carolina. At twenty, he moved to Texas. Jailed in 1896 for bank embezzlement, he served three years and three months of his five-year sentence. He died in New York City on June 5, 1910, after a decade during which he wrote the several hundred stories that have made his reputation.

The most popular short-story writer in American history grew up in a shattered world—the pattern that would convulse, bedevil, and eventually end his short life already emerging. An elusive and mysterious figure, he exaggerated and fabulated so much about his life that contradictions abound. One can still read biographical articles that state that he moved to Texas because he had tuberculosis and that he eventually died of it, though there's no evidence for the first claim, and his death came from cirrhosis of the liver and diabetes, the legacy of nine years of drinking two bottles of whiskey a day.

Will Porter's mother died, before he could have remembered her, at the devastating end of the Civil War and a whole Southern way of life. Previously a successful physician, his father withdrew to "his barn with his perpetual motion machines and his bottle, oftentimes sleeping as much as one half of the time." Young Will was well educated by his forceful aunt, "Miss Lina," who ran a private primary school. Though he seems to have had no other formal education, he came to have a vast knowledge of English literature, and he probably employed a larger vocabulary than any other American writer; he picked up Spanish, French, and German somewhere along the way. From seventeen to twenty, Will worked as a pharmacist in his uncle's drugstore, where, as his stories would eventually reveal, he began his study of human foibles and regional speech. While he read incessantly, he had also become a charming and dreamy young man, one who easily called forth favors, loans, and protection from friends—and forgiveness when he failed to act responsibly.

After two years on a Texas ranch, as houseguest of the Richard Hall family, Will moved on in 1884 to the Joseph Harrell family home in Austin, where he lived two years, reading, writing sketches, and developing his considerable talent as a cartoonist. On July 1, 1887, he eloped with nineteen-year-old Athol Estes, who had tuberculosis, marrying against her parents' will. He now worked briefly as a bookkeeper and then, through the favor of Richard Hall who headed the office, as a draftsman in the Texas Land Office. His first son died in 1888. Margaret was born the next year, but Athol's health suffered and she did not ever fully recover.

In 1891 Will became a teller at the First National Bank of Austin, and in 1894 wrote, drew, and published a weekly humor magazine, *The Rolling Stone*, which survived for a year, losing some of his and friends' money, and quite probably that of First National as well. In any case, shortages appeared in his accounts in December, when he had to resign; indictment followed in July, 1895. Again friends helped, and the Grand Jury no-billed him. He became a feature writer for the *Houston Post*, turning out successful sketches and short stories for six months until bank examiners revived the charge against him. He was arrested in February, 1896, released on his friends' bond and borrowed money for his defense—which he then used to flee to New Orleans and finally to Honduras, where he impractically hoped Athol and Margaret might join him. After five months he received a package from Athol into which a friend had secretly slipped a note reading, "Athol packed this with temperature 105. Will, come home." Which he did. He was permitted to remain free until Athol's death a few months later. His most famous story, "The Gift of the Magi," reflects some of the poignancy of their relationship

Though he now had a story accepted by *McClure's* magazine and continued to write, Will retreated from his friends and further into himself, finding it too painful to discuss details of his case even with his lawyer. In April of 1898 he became Number 30664 in the Federal Penitentiary at Columbus, Ohio. A prison doctor later wrote he had "never known a man so deeply humiliated by prison." Margaret was not told where he was, and Will wrote her lighthearted letters about his business activities in the Northeast. For the rest of his life, he was to do all he could to conceal and deny his prison life. Working as a night druggist in the prison hospital, he wrote and published the first fourteen O. Henry stories: "Porter entered prison an amateur, but he came out three years later as O. Henry, the professional literary artist." It is impossible to imagine a more arduous apprenticeship.

No other author had so sure a command of the regional speech and realities of so many ordinary human beings. No one celebrated more their right to triumph and tragedy. The book that first won him clear popular and critical acclaim for his tales of New Yorkers, *The Four Million,* was titled so in mocking contrast to the then famous list of New York's most prestigious families, The 400. Every bit of ill-spent life—Honduras, New Orleans, Texas, New York City, all the way back to his uncle's drugstore—fed the stories. When William Porter was rushed dying to New York City's Polyclinic Hospital a decade later, he told the attendant who asked for his name, "Call me Dennis. My name will be Dennis in the morning." The physician who opened him said he had the most enlarged and conjested heart he had ever seen.

—Justin Leiber

Foreword

O. Henry isn't popular with the English literature professors these days, though occasionally one may still sneak a couple of his stories into "introduction to literature" anthologies for high school students. ("After all," Professor Profundity mutters, "they are *very* short and kids think they are 'neat' until they are taught better in college. Since high school students in these TV days have the attention span, sophistication, and taste of pig's loosed on the slop bucket, O. Henry will be just their speed." He pauses reflectively, guiltily remembering just how much he enjoyed O. Henry so very long ago. "They do stick in your mind, though, like the catchiest of advertising jingles—ninety percent of middle-aged Americans have 'The Gift of the Magi' printed somewhere deep down in their brains, stuck there like summer camp songs long after Hawthorne and Melville have washed away.")

In the last decade of his life and the two decades after his death in 1910, O. Henry was possibly more widely read and enjoyed than any other American writer, his works translated and acclaimed through the world for their compact, intricate structure and emotional punch, for his extraordinary vocabulary and his effortlessly fanciful and skillful use of it. No other author seemed so able, with a few deft lines, to pull forth a smile or a tear of startled emotion, and, with those same lines, capture the language and way of life of so many regions of the U.S. In the 1920s, *Encyclopedia Britannica* summarized a consensus that "some of the greatest native endow-

ments a writer can have were undeniably his; of him, as
much as of any modern writer, it can be said that he had
'no talent, only genius.' ''

The current *Britannica*, however, dismissively comments, ''often had surprise endings, a device that came
to be identified with his name, and cost him critical favor
when its vogue had passed.'' While it is true that the
critics counsel against surprise endings, the sharp decline
in O. Henry's critical reputation has much more to it than
that. (After all, surprise endings that rest on various
incredibly wonderful coincidences are standard in the
classics. To give one example, Shakespeare produces one
of literature's most outrageously coincidental surprise endings when he contrives it so that the witches' apparently
reassuring first act prophesy in fact dooms Macbeth; in
act five, Birnam Wood does, incredibly, *move* to Dunsinane
Castle, and Macbeth, who cannot be killed ''by one of
woman born,'' faces in the last lines of the play a man
whose birth, we are suddenly told, required the surgical
intervention of a male doctor.)

O. Henry wrote short shorts, stories around 5,000
words. He also wrote ''sketches'' of much the same
length, meaning a brief, atmospheric picture of a compelling and revealing human scene, capped with some ironic
comment (like some of the short sections of Ernest Hemingway's still highly acclaimed *In Our Time*; Hemingway
owes a lot to O. Henry). But O. Henry's reputation
ultimately has to rest on the short short, which unlike the
sketch, has in miniature the beginning, middle, and intri-
cately prepared, powerfully surprising climax of longer
works like *Macbeth* or many of Charles Dicken's novels.
Given its length, the short short cannot detail compli-
cated character development, any more than a haiku
poem or a rapidly penciled sketch of a face. Contrary
to the critics, this doesn't have to mean the use of
trite ethnic, class, or regional stereotypes (Picasso,
Daumier, and Goya did marvelous drawings in which a
few lines somehow mount up to a face). The husband

and wife in "The Gift of the Magi" aren't *caricatures*.

If their story is *not* already printed on your brain, read it now, before reading the rest of this introduction.

Back?

"The Gift of the Magi" is the perfect O. Henry short short. Like shades of Athol and Will, the poor but loving couple have but two valued possessions, her beautiful long hair and his family's gold watch. Next day is Christmas. Gulping, Della sells her hair to buy an expensive platinum fob worthy of Jim's watch. When Jim comes home and is given the fob, he presents her with the expensive tortoiseshell combs she dreamed of, all the while taking in her shorn head. He gently says only, "Let's put our presents away and keep 'em a while. They're too nice to use just at present. I sold the watch to get the money to buy your combs."

With that one-liner, the story is complete, the ingenious symmetry to two lines of action dove-tailing marvelously. All that follows is the magical coda paragraph which allows the reader to savor the sentimental paradox of foolish wisdom. (In "The Skylight Room," *everything* happens in the final line.)

"Unrealistic, fantastic coincidence——bah! humbug!" protests Professor Profundity. How can we reply?

Of course, it *is* extraordinarily unlikely that there actually were a James and Della Dillingham Young who did and said exactly what O. Henry relates, from platinum fob and tortoiseshell, jewel-rimmed combs and all, down to the last detail.

But so what? *All fiction*, however "realistic," is *fiction* and didn't happen. If it did, if O. Henry got it all, down to the last detail, from the police blotter and interviews, then it's a newspaper report, not fiction.

"Okay, okay," says Professor Profundity. "But the point is that realistic fiction depicts the *sort* of thing that happens in the real world, not the miraculous coincidence that is central to the Magi story."

Professor Profundity, one suspects had little knowledge of gambling, statistical theory, or the kind of evidence that leads people (incorrectly) to believe in psychic phenomena. Given a long run of events, the marvelously coincidental *has to happen*. If you roll some dice twice, your chances of getting snake eyes both times are one in nine hundred and ninety-six (a marvelous coincidence). If you roll them two thousand times, naturally, the chances of two snake eyes in a row are slightly better than even. What if you roll two million times? Then the "marvelous coincidence" of two snake eyes in a row becomes something that almost certainly has to occur.

Take O. Henry's four million New Yorkers. Isn't it close to certain that there will be, around Christmas, one poor but loving couple, each with a prized possession and each sacrificing, unknown to the other, that possession (feeling, project, avocation, etc.) in order to get something to enhance the value of the other's beloved whatever-it-is?

"I suppose so," replies Profundity, "but for every such case there will be hundreds of cases where it does not go that way—where one but not the other makes the sacrifice, and so on. How much more realistic, so to speak, if Della sells her hair and, having sold the watch to buy whiskey and a box of cigars, Jim staggers in and punches out Della because her hair is gone. Or, how about a version in which Della sells her hair and uses the proceeds to buy Jim an up-to-date wristwatch, for she, quite mistakenly and rather stupidly self-servingly, believes that Jim must be secretly ashamed of 'this dumb old watch' (through ignorance, she pays fifty times what she should for a cheap, promotional wristwatch); Jim arrives, having sold his watch to buy a life insurance policy, and he laughs so hard at what she's done that he goes into cardiac arrest. Or, the whole story goes as in O. Henry, but then, after the chop and too many drinks, Jim turns on Della and shouts, 'I *sold* my father's watch for *your hair*, you dumb broad'—which shows us another aspect of Will and Athol's relationship."

Had enough? I could, of course, let the professor run on, but the point is clear. O. Henry crystalized, in the briefest and therefore clearest and most universal way, something that taps our deepest sense of the ideal possibilities of human love. Our minds are built to see, in a flash of revelation, what the ancient philosopher Plato argued: that acts of physical sacrifice, done from the spirit of love, really do make one better and happier, and deepen and ennoble a loving relationship, even if—indeed *especially if*—chance arranges it so that the physical sacrifices do not bring the intended *physical* rewards.

Of course, when we face the bleary, noisy, near endless confusion of "real" life (something sprawling "realistic" novels used to strive to simulate), archetypical truths are buried in the confusion. In his economy, brevity, and artifice, O. Henry returns us to some of them. That's why you have "The Gift of the Magi" indelibly printed on your brain. You'll soon have more, O. Henry's gifts.

—Justin Leiber

The Gift of the Magi

One dollar and eighty-seven cents. That was all. And sixty cents of it was in pennies. Pennies saved one and two at a time by bulldozing the grocer and the vegetable man and the butcher until one's cheeks burned with the silent imputation of parsimony that such close dealing implied. Three times Della counted it. One dollar and eighty-seven cents. And the next day would be Christmas.

There was clearly nothing to do but flop down on the shabby little couch and howl. So Della did it. Which instigates the moral reflection that life is made up of sobs, sniffles, and smiles, and sniffles predominating.

While the mistress of the home is gradually subsiding from the first stage to the second, take a look at the home. A furnished flat at $8 per week. It did not exactly beggar description, but it certainly had that word on the lookout for the mendicancy squad.

In the vestibule below was a letter-box into which no letter would go, and an electric button from which no mortal finger could coax a ring. Also appertaining thereunto was a card bearing the name "Mr. James Dillingham Young."

The "Dillingham" had been flung to the breeze during a former period of prosperity when its possessor was being paid $30 per week. Now, when the income was shrunk to $20, the letters of "Dillingham" looked blurred, as though they were thinking seriously of contracting to a modest and unassuming D. But whenever Mr. James

Dillingham Young came home and reached his flat above he was called "Jim" and greatly hugged by Mrs. James Dillingham Young, already introduced to you as Della. Which is all very good.

Della finished her cry and attended to her cheeks with the powder rag. She stood by the window and looked out dully at a gray cat walking a gray fence in a gray backyard. Tomorrow would be Christmas Day, and she had only $1.87 with which to buy Jim a present. She had been saving every penny she could for months, with this result. Twenty dollars a week doesn't go far. Expenses had been greater than she had calculated. They always are. Only $1.87 to buy a present for Jim. Her Jim. Many a happy hour she had spent planning for something nice for him. Something fine and rare and sterling—something just a little bit near to being worthy of the honor of being owned by Jim.

There was a pier-glass between the windows of the room. Perhaps you have seen a pier-glass in an $8 flat. A very thin and very agile person may, by observing his reflection in a rapid sequence of longitudinal strips, obtain a fairly accurate conception of his looks. Della, being slender, had mastered the art.

Suddenly she whirled from the window and stood before the glass. Her eyes were shining brilliantly, but her face had lost its color within twenty seconds. Rapidly she pulled down her hair and let it fall to its full length.

Now, there were two possessions of the James Dillingham Youngs in which they both took a mighty pride. One was Jim's gold watch that had been his father's and his grandfather's. The other was Della's hair. Had the Queen of Sheba lived in the flat across the airshaft, Della would have let her hair hang out the window some day to dry just to depreciate Her Majesty's jewels and gifts. Had King Solomon been the janitor, with all his treasures piled up in the basement, Jim would have pulled out his watch every time he passed just to see him pluck at his beard from envy.

So now Della's beautiful hair fell about her rippling and shining like a cascade of brown waters. It reached below her knee and made itself almost a garment for her. And then she did it up again nervously and quickly. Once she faltered for a minute and stood still while a tear or two splashed on the worn red carpet.

On went her old brown jacket; on went her old brown hat. With a whirl of skirts and with the brilliant sparkle still in her eyes, she fluttered out the door and down the stairs to the street.

Where she stopped and sign read: "Mme. Sofronie. Hair Goods of All Kinds." One flight up Della ran, and collected herself, panting. Madame, large, too white, chilly, hardly looked the "Sofronie."

"Will you buy my hair?" asked Della.

"I buy hair," said Madame. "Take yer hat off and let's have a sight at the looks of it."

Down rippled the brown cascade.

"Twenty dollars," said Madame, lifting the mass with a practised hand.

"Give it to me quick," said Della.

Oh, and the next two hours tripped by on rosy wings. Forget the hashed metaphor. She was ransacking the stores for Jim's present.

She found it at last. It surely had been made for Jim and no one else. There was no other like it in any of the stores, and she had turned all of them inside out. It was a platinum fob chain simple and chaste in design, properly proclaiming its value by substance alone and not by meretricious ornamentation—as all good things should do. It was even worthy of The Watch. As soon as she saw it she knew that it must be Jim's. It was like him. Quietness and value—the description applied to both. Twenty-one dollars they took from her for it, and she hurried home with the 87 cents. With that chain on his watch Jim might be properly anxious about the time in any company. Grand as the watch was, he sometimes looked at it on the sly on account of the old leather strap that he used in place of a chain.

When Della reached home her intoxication gave way a little to prudence and reason. She got out her curling irons and lighted the gas and went to work repairing the ravages made by generosity added to love. Which is always a tremendous task, dear friends—a mammoth task.

Within forty minutes her head was covered with tiny, close-lying curls that made her look wonderfully like a truant schoolboy. She looked at her reflection in the mirror long, carefully, and critically.

"If Jim doesn't kill me," she said to herself, "before he takes a second look at me, he'll say I look like a Coney Island chorus girl. But what could I do—oh! what could I do with a dollar and eighty-seven cents?"

At 7 o'clock the coffee was made and the frying-pan was on the back of the stove hot and ready to cook the chops.

Jim was never late. Della doubled the fob chain in her hand and sat on the corner of the table near the door that he always entered. Then she heard his step on the stair way down on the first flight, and she turned white for just a moment. She had a habit of saying little silent prayers about the simplest everyday things, and now she whispered: "Please God, make him think I am still pretty."

The door opened and Jim stepped in and closed it. He looked thin and very serious. Poor fellow, he was only twenty-two—and to be burdened with a family! He needed a new overcoat and he was without gloves.

Jim stopped inside the door, as immovable as a setter at the scent of quail. His eyes were fixed upon Della, and there was an expression in them that she could not read, and it terrified her. It was not anger, nor surprise, nor disapproval, nor horror, nor any of the sentiments that she had been prepared for. He simply stared at her fixedly with that peculiar expression on his face.

Della wriggled off the table and went for him.

"Jim, darling," she cried, "don't look at me that way. I had my hair cut off and sold it because I couldn't have lived through Christmas without giving you a present. It'll grow out again—you won't mind, will you? I just had to do it. My hair grows awfully fast. Say 'Merry Christmas!' Jim, and let's be happy. You don't know what a nice—what a beautiful, nice gift I've got for you."

"You've cut off your hair?" asked Jim, laboriously, as if he had not arrived at that patent fact yet even after the hardest mental labor.

"Cut it off and sold it," said Della. "Don't you like me just as well, anyhow? I'm me without my hair, ain't I?"

Jim looked about the room curiously.

"You say your hair is gone?" he said, with an air almost of idiocy.

"You needn't look for it," said Della. "It's sold, I tell you—sold and gone, too. It's Christmas Eve, boy. Be good to me, for it went for you. Maybe the hairs of my head were numbered," she went on with a sudden serious sweetness, "but nobody could ever count my love for you. Shall I put the chops on, Jim?"

Out of his trance Jim seemed quickly to wake. He enfolded his Della. For ten seconds let us regard with discreet scrutiny some inconsequential object in the other direction. Eight dollars a week or a million a year—what is the difference? A mathematician or a wit would give you the wrong answer. The magi brought valuable gifts, but that was not among them. This dark assertion will be illuminated later on.

Jim drew a package from his overcoat pocket and threw it upon the table.

"Don't make any mistake, Dell," he said, "about me. I don't think there's anything in the way of a haircut or a shave or a shampoo that could make me like my girl any less. But if you'll unwrap that package you may see why you had me going a while at first."

White fingers and nimble tore at the string and paper. And then an ecstatic scream of joy; and then, alas! a quick feminine change to hysterical tears and wails, necessitating the immediate employment of all the comforting powers of the lord of the flat.

For there lay The Combs—the set of combs, side and back, that Della had worshipped for long in a Broadway window. Beautiful combs, pure tortoise shell, with jewelled rims—just the shade to wear in the beautiful vanished hair. They were expensive combs, she knew, and her heart had simply craved and yearned over them without the least hope of possession. And now, they were hers, but the tresses that should have adorned the coveted adornments were gone.

But she hugged them to her bosom, and at length she was able to look up with dim eyes and a smile and say: "My hair grows so fast, Jim!"

And then Della leaped up like a little singed cat and cried, "Oh, oh!"

Jim had not yet seen his beautiful present. She held it out to him eagerly upon her open palm. The dull precious metal seemed to flash with a reflection of her bright and ardent spirit.

"Isn't it a dandy, Jim? I hunted all over town to find it. You'll have to look at the time a hundred times a day now. Give me your watch. I want to see how it looks on it."

Instead of obeying, Jim tumbled down on the couch and put his hands under the back of his head and smiled.

"Dell," said he, "let's put our Christmas presents away and keep 'em a while. They're too nice to use just at present. I sold the watch to get the money to buy your combs. And now suppose you put the chops on."

The magi, as you know, were wise men—wonderfully wise men—who brought gifts to the Babe in the manger. They invented the art of giving Christmas presents. Being wise, their gifts were no doubt wise ones, possibly bearing the privilege of exchange in case of duplication. And here I have lamely related to you the uneventful chronicle of two foolish children in a flat who most unwisely sacrificed for each other the greatest treasures of their house. But in a last word to the wise of these days let it be said that of all who give gifts these two were the wisest. Of all who give and receive gifts, such as they are wisest. Everywhere they are wisest. They are the magi.

The Social Triangle

At the stroke of six Ikey Snigglefritz laid down his goose. Ikey was a tailor's apprentice. Are there tailors' apprentices nowadays?

At any rate Ikey toiled and snipped and basted and pressed and patched and sponged all day in the steamy fetor of a tailor-shop. But when work was done Ikey hitched his wagon to such stars as his firmament let shine.

It was Saturday night, and the boss laid twelve begrimed and begrudged dollars in his hand. Ikey dabbled discreetly in water, donned coat, hat and collar with its frazzled tie, and chalcedony pin, and set forth in pursuit of his ideals.

For each of us, when our day's work is done, must seek our ideal, whether it be love or pinochle or lobster à la Newburg, or the sweet silence of the musty bookshelves.

Behold Ikey as he ambles up the street beneath the roaring "El" between the rows of reeking sweatshops. Pallid, stooping, insignificant, squalid, doomed to exist forever in penury of body and mind, yet, as he swings his cheap cane and projects the noisome inhalations from his cigarette you perceive that he nurtures in his narrow bosom the bacillus of society.

Ikey's legs carried him to and into that famous place of entertainment known as the Café Maginnis—famous because it was the rendezvous of Billy McMahan, the greatest man, the most wonderful man, Ikey thought, that the world had ever produced.

8

Billy McMahan was the district leader. Upon him the Tiger purred, and his hand held manna to scatter. Now, as Ikey entered, McMahan stood, flushed and triumphant and mighty, the centre of a huzzaing concourse of his lieutenants and constituents. It seems there had been an election; a signal victory had been won; the city had been swept back into line by a resistless besom of ballots.

Ikey slunk along the bar and gazed, breath-quickened, at his idol.

How magnificent was Billy McMahan, with his great, smooth, laughing face; his gray eye, shrewd as a chicken hawk's; his diamond ring, his voice like a bugle call, his prince's air, his plump and active roll of money, his clarion call to friend and comrade—oh, what a king of men he was! How he obscured his lieutenants, though they themselves loomed large and serious, blue of chin and important of mien, with hands buried deep in the pockets of their short overcoats! But Billy—oh, what small avail are words to paint for you his glory as seen by Ikey Snigglefritz!

The Café Maginnis rang to the note of victory. The white-coated bartenders threw themselves featfully upon bottle, cork and glass. From a score of clear Havanas the air received its paradox of clouds. The leal and the hopeful shook Billy McMahan's hand. And there was born suddenly in the worshipful soul of Ikey Snigglefritz an audacious, thrilling impulse.

He stepped forward into the little cleared space in which majesty moved, and held out his hand.

Billy McMahan grasped it unhesitatingly, shook it and smiled.

Made mad now by the gods who were about to destroy him, Ikey threw away his scabbard and charged upon Olympus.

"Have a drink with me, Billy," he said familiarly, "you and your friends?"

"Don't mind if I do, old man," said the great leader, "just to keep the ball rolling."

The last spark of Ikey's reason fled.

"Wine," he called to the bartender, waving a trembling hand.

The corks of three bottles were drawn; the champagne bubbled in the long row of glasses set upon the bar. Billy McMahan took his and nodded, with his beaming smile at Ikey. The lieutenants and satellites took theirs and growled "Here's to you." Ikey took his nectar in delirium. All drank.

Ikey threw his week's wages in a crumpled roll upon the bar.

"C'rect," said the bartender, smoothing the twelve one-dollar notes. The crowd surged around Billy McMahan again. Some one was telling how Brannigan fixed 'em over in the Eleventh. Ikey leaned against the bar a while, and then went out.

He went down Hester Street and up Chrystie, and down Delancey to where he lived. And there his women folk, a bibulous mother and three dingy sisters, pounced upon him for his wages. And at his confession they shrieked and objurgated him in the pithy rhetoric of the locality.

But even as they plucked at him and struck him Ikey remained in his ecstatic trance of joy. His head was in the clouds; the star was drawing his wagon. Compared with what he had achieved the loss of wages and the bray of women's tongues were slight affairs.

He had shaken the hand of Billy McMahan.

Billy McMahan had a wife, and upon her visiting cards was engraved the name "Mrs. William Darragh McMahan." And there was a certain vexation attendant upon these cards; for, small as they were, there were houses in which they could not be inserted. Billy McMahan was a dictator in politics, a four-walled tower in business, a mogul, dread, loved and obeyed among his own people. He was growing rich; the daily papers had a dozen men on his trail to chronicle his every word of

wisdom; he had been honored in caricature holding the
Tiger cringing in leash.

But the heart of Billy was sometimes sore within him.
There was a race of men from which he stood apart but
that he viewed with the eye of Moses looking over into
the promised land. He, too, had ideals, even as had Ikey
Snigglefritz; and sometimes, hopeless of attaining them,
his own solid success was as dust and ashes in his mouth.
And Mrs. William Darragh McMahan wore a look of
discontent upon her plump but pretty face, and the very
rustle of her silks seemed a sigh.

There was a brave and conspicuous assemblage in the
dining saloon of a noted hostelry where Fashion loves to
display her charms. At one table sat Billy McMahan and
his wife. Mostly silent they were, but the accessories
they enjoyed little needed the indorsement of speech.
Mrs. McMahan's diamonds were outshone by few in the
room. The waiter bore the costliest brands of wine to
their table. In evening dress, with an expression of gloom
upon his smooth and massive countenance, you would
look in vain for a more striking figure than Billy's.

Four tables away sat alone a tall, slender man, about
thirty, with thoughtful, melancholy eyes, a Van Dyke
beard and peculiarly white, thin hands. He was dining on
filet mignon, dry toast and apollinaris. That man was
Cortlandt Van Duyckink, a man worth eighty millions,
who inherited and held a sacred seat in the exclusive
inner circle of society.

Billy McMahan spoke to no one around him, because
he knew no one. Van Duyckink kept his eyes on his plate
because he knew that every one present was hungry to
catch his. He could bestow knighthood and prestige by a
nod, and he was chary of creating a too extensive nobility.

And then Billy McMahan conceived and accomplished
the most startling and audacious act of his life. He rose
deliberately and walked over to Cortlandt Van Duyckink's
table and held out his hand.

"Say, Mr. Van Duyckink," he said, "I've heard you

was talking about starting some reforms among the poor people down in my district. I'm McMahan, you know. Say, now, if that's straight I'll do all I can to help you. And what I says goes in that neck of the woods, don't it? Oh, say, I rather guess it does.''

Van Duyckink's rather somber eyes lighted up. He rose to his lank height and grasped Billy McMahan's hand.

"Thank you, Mr. McMahan," he said, in his deep, serious tones. "I have been thinking of doing some work of that sort. I shall be glad of your assistance. It pleases me to have become acquainted with you."

Billy walked back to his seat. His shoulder was tingling from the accolade bestowed by royalty. A hundred eyes were now turned upon him in envy and new admiration. Mrs. William Darragh McMahan trembled with ecstasy, so that her diamonds smote the eye almost with pain. And now it was apparent that at many tables there were those who suddenly remembered that they enjoyed Mr. McMahan's acquaintance. He saw smiles and bows about him. He became enveloped in the aura of dizzy greatness. His campaign coolness deserted him.

"Wine for that gang!" he commanded the waiter, pointing with his finger. "Wine over there. Wine to those three gents by that green bush. Tell 'em it's on me. D——n it! Wine for everybody!"

The waiter ventured to whisper that it was perhaps inexpedient to carry out the order, in consideration of the dignity of the house and its custom.

"All right," said Billy, "if it's against the rules. I wonder if 'twould do to send my friend Van Duyckink a bottle? No? Well, it'll flow all right at the caffy to-night, just the same. It'll be rubber boots for anybody who comes in there any time up to 2 A.M."

Billy McMahan was happy.

He had shaken the hand of Cortlandt Van Duyckink.

*　　*　　*

The big pale-gray auto with its shining metal work looked out of place moving slowly among the push carts and trash-heaps on the lower east side. So did Cortlandt Van Duyckink, with his aristocratic face and white, thin hands, as he steered carefully between the groups of ragged, scurrying youngsters in the streets. And so did Miss Constance Schuyler, with her dim, ascetic beauty, seated at his side.

"Oh, Cortlandt," she breathed, "isn't it sad that human beings have to live in such wretchedness and poverty? And you—how noble it is of you to think of them, to give your time and money to improve their condition!"

Van Duyckink turned his solemn eyes upon her.

"It is little," he said, sadly, "that I can do. The question is a large one, and belongs to society. But even individual effort is not thrown away. Look, Constance! On this street I have arranged to build soup kitchens, where no one who is hungry will be turned away. And down this other street are the old buildings that I shall cause to be torn down and there erect others in place of those death-traps of fire and disease."

Down Delancey slowly crept the pale-gray auto. Away from it toddled coveys of wondering, tangle-haired, barefooted, unwashed children. It stopped before a crazy brick structure, foul and awry.

Van Duyckink alighted to examine at a better perspective one of the leaning walls. Down the steps of the building came a young man who seemed to epitomize its degradation, squalor and infelicity—a narrow-chested, pale, unsavory young man, puffing at a cigarette.

Obeying a sudden impulse, Van Duyckink stepped out and warmly grasped the hand of what seemed to him a living rebuke.

"I want to know you people," he said, sincerely. "I am going to help you as much as I can. We shall be friends."

As the auto crept carefully away Cortlandt Van Duyckink felt an unaccustomed glow about his heart. He was near to being a happy man.

He had shaken the hand of Ikey Snigglefritz.

Schools and Schools

Old Jerome Warren lived in a hundred-thousand-dollar house at 35 East Fifty-Soforth Street. He was a downtown broker, so rich that he could afford to walk—for his health—a few blocks in the direction of his office every morning and then call a cab.

He had an adopted son, the son of an old friend named Gilbert—Cyril Scott could play him nicely—who was becoming a successful painter as fast as he could squeeze the paint out of his tubes. Another member of the household was Barbara Ross, a step-niece. Man is born to trouble; so, as old Jerome had no family of his own, he took up the burdens of others.

Gilbert and Barbara got along swimmingly. There was a tacit and tactical understanding all round that the two would stand up under a floral bell some high noon, and promise the minister to keep old Jerome's money in a state of high commotion. But at this point complications must be introduced.

Thirty years before, when old Jerome was young Jerome, there was a brother of his named Dick. Dick went West to seek his or somebody else's fortune. Nothing was heard of him until one day old Jerome had a letter from his brother. It was badly written on ruled paper that smelled of salt bacon and coffee-grounds. The writing was asthmatic and the spelling St. Vitusy.

It appeared that instead of Dick having forced Fortune to stand and deliver, he had been held up himself, and made to give hostages to the enemy. That is, as his letter disclosed, he was on the point of pegging out with a complication of disorders that even whiskey had failed to check. All that his thirty years of prospecting had netted him was one daughter, nineteen years old, as per invoice, whom he was shipping East, charges prepaid, for Jerome to clothe, feed, educate, comfort, and cherish for the rest of her natural life or until matrimony should them part.

Old Jerome was a board-walk. Everybody knows that the world is supported by the shoulders of Atlas; and that Atlas stands on a rail-fence; and that the rail-fence is built on a turtle's back. Now, the turtle has to stand on something; and that is a board-walk made of men like old Jerome.

I do not know whether immortality shall accrue to man; but if not so, I would like to know when men like old Jerome get what is due them?

They met Nevada Warren at the station. She was a little girl, deeply sunburned and wholesomely good-looking, with a manner that was frankly unsophisticated, yet one that not even a cigar-drummer would intrude upon without thinking twice. Looking at her, somehow you would expect to see her in a short skirt and leather leggings, shooting glass balls or taming mustangs. But in her plain white waist and black skirt she sent you guessing again. With an easy exhibition of strength she swung along a heavy valise, which the uniformed porters tried in vain to wrest from her.

"I am sure we shall be the best of friends," said Barbara, pecking at the firm, sunburned cheek.

"I hope so," said Nevada.

"Dear little niece," said old Jerome, "you are as welcome to my house as if it were your father's own."

"Thanks," said Nevada.

"And I am going to call you 'cousin,' " said Gilbert, with his charming smile.

"Take the valise, please," said Nevada. "It weighs a million pounds. It's got samples from six of dad's old mines in it," she explained to Barbara. "I calculate they'd assay about nine cents to the thousand tons, but I promised him to bring them along."

II

It is a common custom to refer to the usual complications between one man and two ladies, or one lady and two men, or a lady and a man and a nobleman, or—well, any of these problems—as the triangle. But they are never unqualified triangles. They are always isosceles—never equilateral. So, upon the coming of Nevada Warren, she and Gilbert and Barbara Ross lined up into such a figurative triangle; and of that triangle Barbara formed the hypotenuse.

One morning old Jerome was lingering long after breakfast over the dullest morning paper in the city before setting forth to his downtown fly-trap. He had become quite fond of Nevada, finding in her much of his dead brother's quiet independence and unsuspicious frankness.

A maid brought in a note for Miss Nevada Warren.

"A messenger-boy delivered it at the door, please," she said. "He's waiting for an answer."

Nevada, who was whistling a Spanish waltz between her teeth, and watching the carriages and autos roll by in the street, took the envelope. She knew it was from Gilbert, before she opened it, by the little gold palette in the upper left-hand corner.

After tearing it open she pored over the contents for a while, absorbedly. Then, with a serious face, she went and stood at her uncle's elbow.

"Uncle Jerome, Gilbert is a nice boy, isn't he?"

"Why, bless the child!" said old Jerome, crackling his paper loudly; "of course he is. I raised him myself."

"He wouldn't write anything to anybody that wasn't exactly—I mean that everybody couldn't know and read, would he?"

"I'd just like to see him try it," said uncle, tearing a handful from his newspaper. "Why, what—"

"Read this note he just sent me, uncle, and see if you think it's all right and proper. You see, I don't know much about city people and their ways."

Old Jerome threw his paper down and set both his feet upon it. He took Gilbert's note and fiercely perused it twice, and then a third time.

"Why, child," said he, "you had me almost excited, although I was sure of that boy. He's a duplicate of his father, and he was a gilt-edged diamond. He only asks if you and Barbara will be ready at four o'clock this afternoon for an automobile drive over to Long Island. I don't see anything to criticize in it except the stationery. I always did hate that shade of blue."

"Would it be all right to go?' asked Nevada, eagerly.

"Yes, yes, yes, child, of course. Why not? Still, it pleases me to see you so careful and candid. Go, by all means."

"I don't know," said Nevada, demurely. "I thought I'd ask you. Couldn't you go with us, uncle?"

"I? No, no, no! I've ridden once in a car that boy was driving. Never again! But it's entirely proper for you and Barbara to go. Yes, yes. But I will not. No, no, no, no!"

Nevada flew to the door, and said to the maid:

"You bet we'll go. I'll answer for Miss Barbara. Tell the boy to say to Mr. Warren, 'You bet we'll go.' "

"Nevada," called old Jerome, "pardon me, my dear, but wouldn't it be as well to send him a note in reply? Just a line would do."

"No, I won't bother about that," said Nevada, gayly. "Gilbert will understand—he always does. I never rode in an automobile in my life; but I've paddled a canoe down Little Devil River through the Lost Horse Cañon, and if it's any livelier than that I'd like to know!"

III

Two months are supposed to have elapsed.

Barbara sat in the study of the hundred-thousand-dollar house. It was a good place for her. Many places are provided in the world where men and women may repair for the purpose of extricating themselves from divers difficulties. There are cloisters, wailing-places, watering-places, confessionals, hermitages, lawyers' offices, beauty-parlors, air-ships, and studies; and the greatest of these are studies.

It usually takes a hypotenuse a long time to discover that it is the longest side of a triangle. But it's a long line that has no turning.

Barbara was alone. Uncle Jerome and Nevada had gone to the theatre. Barbara had not cared to go. She wanted to stay at home and study in the study. If you, miss, were a stunning New York girl, and saw every day that a brown, ingenuous Western witch was getting hobbles and a lasso on the young man you wanted for yourself, you, too, would lose taste for the oxidized silver setting of a musical comedy.

Barbara sat by the quartered-oak library table. Her right arm rested upon the table, and her dextral fingers nervously manipulated a sealed letter. The letter was addressed to Nevada Warren; and in the upper left-hand corner of the envelope was Gilbert's little gold palette. It had been delivered at nine o'clock, after Nevada had left.

Barbara would have given her pearl necklace to know what that letter contained; but she could not open and read it by the aid of steam, or a pen-handle, or a hair-pin, or any of the generally approved methods, because her position in society forbade such an act. She had tried to read some of the lines of the letter by holding the envelope up to a strong light and pressing it hard against the paper, but Gilbert had too good a taste in stationery to make that possible.

At eleven-thirty the theatre-goers returned. It was a delicious winter night. Even so far as from the cab to the door they were powdered thickly with the big flakes downpouring diagonally from the east. Old Jerome growled good-naturedly about villainous cab service and block-aded streets. Nevada, colored like a rose, with sapphire eyes, babbled of the stormy nights in the mountains around dad's cabin. During all these wintry apostrophes, Barbara, cold at heart, sawed wood—the only appropriate thing she could think of to do.

Old Jerome went immediately upstairs to hot-water-bottles and quinine. Nevada fluttered into the study, the only cheerfully lighted room, subsided into an armchair, and, while at the interminable task of unbuttoning her elbow gloves, gave oral testimony as to the demerits of the "show."

"Yes, I think Mr. Fields is really amusing—sometimes," said Barbara. "Here is a letter for you, dear, that came by special delivery just after you had gone."

"Who is it from?" asked Nevada, tugging at a button.

"Well, really," said Barbara, with a smile. "I can only guess. The envelope has that queer little thing in one corner that Gilbert calls a palette, but which looks to me rather like a gilt heart on a school-girl's valentine."

"I wonder what he's writing to me about," remarked Nevada, listlessly.

"We're all alike," said Barbara; "all women. We try to find out what is in a letter by studying the postmark. As a last resort we use scissors, and read it from the bottom upward. Here it is."

She made a motion as if to toss the letter across the table to Nevada.

"Great catamounts!" exclaimed Nevada. "These centrefire buttons are a nuisance. I'd rather wear buck-skins. Oh, Barbara, please shuck the hide off that letter and read it. It'll be midnight before I get these gloves off!"

"Why, dear, you don't want me to open Gilbert's

letter to you? It's for you, and you wouldn't wish any one else to read it, of course."

Nevada raised her steady, calm, sapphire eyes from her gloves.

"Nobody writes me anything that everybody mightn't read," she said. "Go on, Barbara. Maybe Gilbert wants us to go out in his car again tomorrow."

Curiosity can do more things than kill a cat; and if emotions, well recognized as feminine, are inimical to feline life, then jealousy would soon leave the whole world catless. Barbara opened the letter, with an indulgent, slightly bored air.

"Well, dear," she said, "I'll read it if you want me to."

She slit the envelope, and read the missive with swift-travelling eyes; read it again, and cast a quick, shrewd glance at Nevada, who, for the time, seemed to consider gloves as the world of her interest, and letters from rising artists as no more than messages from Mars.

For a quarter of a minute Barbara looked at Nevada with a strange steadfastness; and then a smile so small that it widened her mouth only the sixteenth part of an inch, and narrowed her eyes no more than a twentieth flashed like an inspired thought across her face.

Since the beginning no woman has been a mystery to another woman. Swift as light travels, each penetrates the heart and mind of another, sifts her sister's words of their cunningest disguises, reads her most hidden desires, and plucks the sophistry from her wiliest talk like hairs from a comb, twiddling them sardonically between her thumb and fingers before letting them float away on the breezes of fundamental doubt. Long ago Eve's son rang the door-bell of the family residence in Paradise Park, bearing a strange lady on his arm, whom he introduced. Eve took her daughter-in-law aside and lifted a classic eyebrow.

"The Land of Nod," said the bride, languidly flirting the

leaf of a palm. "I suppose you've been there, of course?"

"Not lately," said Eve, absolutely unstaggered. "Don't you think the applesauce they serve over there is execrable? I rather like that mulberry-leaf tunic effect, dear; but, of course, the real fig goods are not to be had over there. Come over behind this lilac-bush while the gentlemen split a celery tonic. I think the caterpillar-holes have made your dress open a little in the back."

So, then and there—according to the records—was the alliance formed by the only two who's-who ladies in the world. Then it was agreed that women should forever remain as clear as a pane of glass—though glass was yet to be discovered—to other women, and that she should palm herself off on a man as a mystery.

Barbara seemed to hesitate.

"Really, Nevada," she said, with a little show of embarrassment, "you shouldn't have insisted on my opening this. I—I'm sure it wasn't meant for any one else to know."

Nevada forgot her gloves for a moment.

"Then read it aloud," she said. "Since you've already read it, what's the difference? If Mr. Warren has written to me something that any one else oughtn't to know, that is all the more reason why everybody should know it."

"Well," said Barbara, "this is what it says: 'Dearest Nevada—Come to my studio at twelve o'clock to-night. Do not fail.'" Barbara rose and dropped the note in Nevada's lap. "I'm awfully sorry," she said, "that I knew. It isn't like Gilbert. There must be some mistake. Just consider that I am ignorant of it, will you, dear? I must go upstairs now, I have such a headache. I'm sure I don't understand the note. Perhaps Gilbert has been dining too well, and will explain. Good night!"

IV

Nevada tiptoed to the hall, and heard Barbara's door close upstairs. The bronze clock in the study told the hour of twelve was fifteen minutes away. She ran swiftly to the front door, and let herself out into the snowstorm. Gilbert Warren's studio was six squares away.

By aërial ferry the white, silent forces of the storm attacked the city from beyond the sullen East River. Already the snow lay a foot deep on the pavements, the drifts heaping themselves like scaling-ladders against the walls of the besieged town. The Avenue was as quiet as a street in Pompeii. Cabs now and then skimmed past like white-winged gulls over a moonlit ocean; and less frequent motor-cars—sustaining the comparison—hissed through the foaming waves like submarine boats on their jocund, perilous journeys.

Nevada plunged like a wind-driven storm-petrel on her way. She looked up at the ragged sierras of cloud-capped buildings that rose above the streets, shaded by the night lights and the congealed vapors to gray, drab, ashen, lavender, dun, and cerulean tints. They were so like the wintry mountains of her Western home that she felt a satisfaction such as the hundred-thousand-dollar house had seldom brought her.

A policeman caused her to waver on a corner, just by his eye and weight.

"Hello, Mabel!" said he. "Kind of late for you to be out, ain't it?"

"I—I am just going to the drug store," said Nevada, hurrying past him.

The excuse serves as a passport of the most sophisticated. Does it prove that woman never progresses, or that she sprang from Adam's rib, full-fledged in intellect and wiles?

Turning eastward, the direct blast cut down Nevada's speed one half. She made zigzag tracks in the snow; but she was as tough as a piñon sapling, bowed to it as gracefully. Suddenly the studio-building loomed before her, a familiar landmark, like a cliff above some well-remembered cañon. The haunt of business and its hostile neighbor, art, was darkened and silent. The elevator stopped at ten.

Up eight flights of Stygian stairs Nevada climbed, and rapped firmly on the door numbered "89." She had been there many times before, with Barbara and Uncle Jerome.

Gilbert opened the door. He had a crayon pencil in one hand, a green shade over his eyes, and a pipe in his mouth. The pipe dropped to the floor.

"Am I late?" asked Nevada. "I came as quick as I could. Uncle and me were at the theatre this evening. Here I am, Gilbert!"

Gilbert did a Pygmalion-and-Galatea act. He changed from a statue of stupefaction to a young man with a problem to tackle. He admitted Nevada, got a whiskbroom, and began to brush the snow from her clothes. A great lamp, with a green shade, hung over an easel, where the artist had been sketching in crayon.

"You wanted me," said Nevada, simply, "and I came. You said so in your letter. What did you send for me for?"

"You read my letter?" inquired Gilbert, sparring for wind.

"Barbara read it to me. I saw it afterward. It said: 'Come to my studio at twelve to-night, and do not fail.' I thought you were sick, of course, but you don't seem to be."

"Aha!" said Gilbert, irrelevantly. "I'll tell you why I asked you to come, Nevada. I want you to marry me immediately—to-night. What's a little snowstorm? Will you do it?"

"You might have noticed that I would, long ago," said Nevada. "And I'm rather stuck on the snowstorm idea, myself. I surely would hate one of those flowery church noon-weddings. Gilbert, I didn't know you had grit enough to propose in this way. Let's shock 'em—it's our funeral, ain't it?"

"You bet!" said Gilbert. "Where did I hear that

expression?'' he added to himself. ''Wait a minute, Nevada; I want to do a little 'phoning.''

He shut himself up in a little dressing-room, and called upon the lightnings of the heavens—condensed into unromantic numbers and districts.

''That you, Jack? You confounded sleepy-head! Yes, wake up; this is me—or I—oh, bother the difference in grammar! I'm going to be married right away. Yes! Wake up your sister—don't answer me back; bring her along, too—you *must*. Remind Agnes of the time I saved her from drowning in Lake Ronkonkoma—I know it's caddish to refer to it, but she *must* come with you. Yes! Nevada is here, waiting. We've been engaged quite a while. Some opposition among the relatives, you know, and we have to pull it off this way. We're waiting here for you. Don't let Agnes out-talk you—bring her! You will? Good old boy! I'll order a carriage to call for you, double-quick time. Confound you, Jack, you're all right!''

Gilbert returned to the room where Nevada waited.

''My old friend, Jack Peyton, and his sister were to have been here at a quarter to twelve,'' he explained; ''but Jack is so confoundedly slow. I've just 'phoned them to hurry. They'll be here in a few minutes. I'm the happiest man in the world, Nevada! What did you do with the letter I sent you to-day?''

''I've got it cinched here,'' said Nevada, pulling it out from beneath her opera-cloak.''

Gilbert drew the letter from the envelope and looked it over carefully. Then he looked at Nevada thoughtfully.

''Didn't you think it rather queer that I should ask you to come to my studio at midnight?'' he asked.

''Why, no,'' said Nevada, rounding her eyes.''Not if you needed me. Out West, when a pal sends you a hurry call—ain't that what you say here?—we get there first and talk about it after the row is over. And it's usually snowing there, too, when things happen. So I didn't mind.''

Gilbert rushed into another room, and came back burdened with overcoats warranted to turn wind, rain, or snow.

"Put this raincoat on," he said, holding it for her. "We have a quarter of a mile to go. Old Jack and his sister will be here in a few minutes." He began to struggle into a heavy coat. "Oh, Nevada," he said, "just look at the headlines on the front page of that evening paper on the table, will you? It's about your section of the West, and I know it will interest you."

He waited a full minute, pretending to find trouble in the getting on of his overcoat, and then turned. Nevada had not moved. She was looking at him with strange and pensive directness. Her cheeks had a flush on them beyond the color that had been contributed by the wind and snow; but her eyes were steady.

"I was going to tell you," she said, "anyhow, before you—before we—before—well, before anything. Dad never gave me a day of schooling. I never learned to read or write a darned word. Now if—"

Pounding their uncertain way upstairs, the feet of Jack, the somnolent, and Agnes, the grateful, were heard.

V

When Mr. and Mrs. Gilbert Warren were spinning softly homeward in a closed carriage, after the ceremony, Gilbert said:

"Nevada, would you really like to know what I wrote you in the letter that you received to-night?"

"Fire away!" said his bride.

"Word for word," said Gilbert, "it was this: 'My dear Miss Warren—You were right about the flower. It was a hydrangea, and not a lilac.' "

"All right," said Nevada. "But let's forget it. The joke's on Barbara, anyway!"

Shearing the Wolf

Jeff Peters was always eloquent when the ethics of his profession were under discussion.

"The only times," said he, "that me and Andy Tucker ever had any hiatuses in our cordial intents was when we differed on the moral aspects of grafting. Andy has his standards and I had mine. I didn't approve of all of Andy's schemes for levying contributions from the public, and he thought I allowed my conscience to interfere too often for the financial good of the firm. We had high arguments sometimes. Once one word led on to another till he said I reminded him of Rockefeller.

" 'I know how you mean that, Andy,' says I, 'but we have been friends too long for me to take offense, at a taunt that you will regret when you cool off. I have yet,' says I, 'to shake hands with a subpoena server.'

"One summer me and Andy decided to rest up a spell in a fine little town in the mountains of Kentucky called Grassdale. We was supposed to be horse drovers, and good decent citizens besides, taking a summer vacation. The Grassdale people liked us, and me and Andy declared a secession of hostilities, never so much as floating the fly leaf of a rubber concession prospectus or flashing a Brazilian diamond while we was there.

"One day the leading hardware merchant of Grassdale drops around to the hotel where me and Andy stopped, and smokes with us, sociable, on the side porch. We knew him pretty well from pitching quoits in the after-

27

noons in the court house yard. He was a loud, red man, breathing hard, but fat and respectable beyond all reason.

"After we talk on all the notorious themes of the day, this Murkison—for such was his entitlements—takes a letter out of his coat pocket in a careful, careless way and hands it to us to read.

" 'Now, what do you think of that?' he says laughing —'a letter like that to ME!'

"Me and Andy sees at a glance what it is; but we pretend to read it through. It was one of them old-time typewritten green goods letters explaining how for $1,000 you could get $5,000 in bills that an expert couldn't tell from the genuine; and going on to tell how they were made from plates stolen by an employee of the Treasury at Washington.

" 'Think of 'em sending a letter like that to ME!' says Murkison again.

" 'Lots of good men get 'em,' says Andy. 'If you don't answer the first letter they let you drop. If you answer it they write again asking you to come on with your money and do business.'

" 'But think of 'em writing ME!' says Murkison.

"A few days later he drops around again.

" 'Boys,' says he, 'I know you are all right or I wouldn't confide in you. I wrote to them rascals again just for fun. They answered and told me to come on to Chicago. They said telegraph to J. Smith when I would start. When I get there I'm to wait on a certain street corner till a man in a gray suit comes along and drops a newspaper in front of me. Then I am to ask how the water is, and he knows it's me and I know it's him.'

" ' 'Ah, yes,' says Andy, gaping, 'it's the same old game. I've often read about it in the papers. Then he conducts you to the private abattoir in the hotel, where Mr. Jones is already waiting. They show you brand-new real money and sell you all you want at five to one. You see 'em put it in a satchel for you and know it's there. Of course it's brown paper when you come to look at it afterward.'

" 'Oh, they couldn't switch it on me,' says Murkison. 'I haven't built up the best paying business in Grassdale without having witticisms about me. You say it's real money they show you, Mr. Tucker?''

" 'I've always—I see by the papers that it always is,' says Andy.

" 'Boys,' says Murkison, 'I've got it in my mind that them fellows can't fool me. I think I'll put a couple of thousand in my jeans and go up there and put it all over 'em. If Bill Murkison gets his eyes once on them bills they show him he'll never take 'em off of 'em. They offer $5 for $1, and they'll have to stick to the bargain if I tackle 'em. That's the kind of trader Bill Murkison is. Yes, I just believe I'll drop up Chicago way and take a 5 to 1 shot on J. Smith. I guess the water'll be fine enough.'

"Me and Andy tries to get this financial misquotation out of Murkison's head, but we might as well have tried to keep the man who rolls peanuts with a toothpick from betting on Bryan's election. No, sir; he was going to perform a public duty by catching these green goods swindlers at their own game. Maybe it would teach 'em a lesson.

"After Murkison left us me and Andy sat a while preponder ing over our silent meditations and heresies of reason. In our idle hours we always improved our higher selves by ratiocination and mental thought.

" 'Jeff,' says Andy after a long time, 'quite unseldom I have seen fit to impugn your molars when you have been chewing the rag with me about your conscientious way of doing business. I may have been often wrong. But here is a case where I think we can agree. I feel that it would be wrong for us to allow Mr. Murkison to go alone to meet those Chicago green goods men. There is but one way it can end. Don't you think we would both feel better if we was to intervene in some way and prevent the doing of this deed?'

"I got up and shook Andy Tucker's hand hard and long.

"'Andy,' says I, 'I may have had one or two hard thoughts about the heartlessness of your corporation but I retract 'em now. You have a kind nucleus at the interior of your exterior after all. It does you credit. I was just thinking the same thing that you have expressed. It would no be honorable or praiseworthy,' says I, 'for us to let Murkison go on with this project he had taken up. If he is determined to go let us go with him and prevent this swindle from coming off.'

"Andy agreed with me; and I was glad to see that he was in earnest about breaking up this green goods scheme.

"'I don't call myself a religious man,' says I, 'or a fanatic in moral bigotry, but I can't stand still and see a man who has built up a business by his own efforts and brains and risk be robbed by an unscrupulous trickster who is a menace to the public good.'

"'Right, Jeff,' says Andy. 'We'll stick right along with Murkison if he insist on going and block this funny business. I'd hate to see any money dropped in it as bad as you would.'

"Well, we went to see Murkison.

"'No, boys,' says he. 'I can't consent to let the song of this Chicago siren waft by me on the summer breeze. I'll fry some fat out of this ignis fatuus or burn a hole in the skillet. But I'd be plumb diverted to death to have you all go along with me. Maybe you could help some when it comes to cashing in the ticket to that 5 to 1 shot. Yes, I'd really take it as a pastime and regalement if you boys would go along too.'

"Murkison gives it out in Grassdale that he is going for a few days with Mr. Peters and Mr. Tucker to look over some iron ore property in West Virginia. He wires J. Smith that he will set foot in the spider web on a given date; and the three of us lights out for Chicago.

"On the way Murkison amuses himself with premonitions and advance pleasant recollections.

" 'In a gray suit,' says he, 'on the southwest corner of Wabash Avenue and Lake Street. He drops the paper, and I ask how the water is. Oh, my, my, my!' And then he laughs all over for five minutes.

"Sometimes Murkison was serious and tried to talk himself out of his cogitations, whatever they was.

" 'Boys,' says he, 'I wouldn't have this to get out in Grassdale for ten times a thousand dollars. It would ruin me there. But I know you all are all right. I think it's the duty of every citizen,' says he, 'to try to do up these robbers that prey upon the public. I'll show 'em whether the water's fine. Five dollars for one—that's what J. Smith offers, and he'll have to keep his contract if he does business with Bill Murkison.'

"We got into Chicago about 7 P.M. Murkison was to meet the gray man at half-past 9. We had dinner at a hotel and then went up to Murkison's room to wait for the time to come.

" 'Now, boys,' says Murkison, 'let's get our gumption together and inoculate a plan for defeating the enemy. Suppose while I'm exchanging airy bandage with the gray capper you gents come along, by accident, you know, and holler: "Hello, Murk!!" and shake hands with symptoms of surprise and familiarity. Then I take the capper aside and tell him you all are Jenkins and Brown of Grassdale, groceries and feed, good men and maybe willing to take a chance while away from home.'

" ' "Bring 'em along," he'll say, of course, "if they care to invest." Now, how does that scheme strike you?'

" 'What do you say, Jeff?' says Andy, looking at me.

" 'Why, I'll tell you what I say,' says I. 'I say let's settle this thing right here now. I don't see any use of wasting any more time.' I took a nickel-plated .38 out of my pocket and clicked the cylinder around a few times.

" 'You undevout, sinful, insidious hog,' says I to Murkison, 'get out that two thousand and lay it on the table. Obey with velocity,' says I, 'for otherwise alternatives are impending. I am preferably a man of mildness, but now and then I find myself in the middle of extremities. Such men as you,' I went on after he had laid the money out, 'is what keeps the jails and court houses going. You come up here to rob these men of their money. Does it excuse you?' I asks, 'that they were trying to skin you? No, sir; you was going to rob Peter to stand off Paul. You are ten times worse,' says I, 'than that green goods man. You go to church at home and pretend to be a decent citizen, but you'll come to Chicago and commit larceny from men that have built up a sound and profitable business by dealing with such contemptible scoundrels as you have tried to be to-day. How do you know,' says I, 'that that green goods man hasn't a large family dependent upon his extortions? It's you supposedly respectable citizens who are always on the lookout to get something for nothing,' says I, 'that support the lotteries and wild-cat mines and stock exchanges and wire tappers of this country. If it wasn't for you they'd go out of business. The green goods man you was going to rob,' says I, 'studied maybe for years to learn his trade. Every turn he makes he risks his money and liberty and maybe his life. You come up here all sanctified and vanoplied with respectability and a pleasing post office address to swindle him. If he gets the money you can squeal to the police. If you get it he hocks the gray suit to buy supper and says nothing. Mr. Tucker and me sized you up,' says I, 'and came along to see that you got what you deserved. Hand over the money,' says I, 'you grass-fed hypocrite.'

"I put the two thousand, which was all in $20 bills, in my inside pocket.

" 'Now get out your watch,' says I to Murkison. 'No, I don't want it,' says I. 'Lay it out on the table and you sit in that chair till it ticks off an hour. Then you can go. If you make any noise or leave any sooner we'll hand-bill you all over Grassdale. I guess your high position there is worth more than $2,000 to you.''

"Then me and Andy left.

"On the train Andy was a long time silent. Then he says: 'Jeff, do you mind my asking you a question?'

" 'Two,' says I, 'or forty.'

" 'Was that the idea you had,' says he, 'when we started out with Murkison?'

" 'Why certainly,' says I. 'What else could it have been? Wasn't it yours, too?'

"In about half an hour Andy spoke again. I think there are times when Andy don't exactly understand my system of ethics and moral hygiene.

" 'Jeff,' says he, 'some time when you have the leisure I wish you'd draw off a diagram and footnotes of that conscience of yours. I'd like to have it to refer to occasionally.' "

Conscience in Art

66 I never could hold my partner, Andy Tucker, down
to legitimate ethics of pure swindling," said Jeff
Peters to me one day.

"Andy has too much imagination to be honest. He
used to devise schemes of money-getting so fraudulent
and high-financial that they wouldn't have been allowed
in the bylaws of a railroad rebate system.

"Myself, I never believed in taking any man's dollars
unless I gave him something for it—something in the
way of rolled gold jewelry, garden seeds, lumbago lo-
tion, stock certificates, stove polish or a crack on the
head to show for his money. I guess I must have had
New England ancestors away back and inherited some of
their stanch and rugged fear of the police.

"But Andy's family tree was in different kind. I don't
think he could have traced his descent any further back
than a corporation.

"One summer while we was in the middle West,
working down the Ohio valley with a line of family
albums, headache powders and roach destroyer, Andy
takes one of his notions of high and actionable financiering.

" 'Jeff,' says he, 'I've been thinking that we ought to
drop these rutabaga fanciers and give our attention to
something more nourishing and prolific. If we keep on
snapshooting these hinds for their egg money we'll be
classed as nature fakers. How about plunging into the
fastnesses of the skyscraper country and biting some big
bull caribous in the chest?'

" 'Well,' says I, 'you know my idiosyncrasies. I prefer a square, nonillegal style of business such as we are carrying on now. When I take money I want to leave some tangible object in the other fellow's hands for him to gaze at and to distract his attention from my spoor, even if it's only a Komical Kuss Trick Finger Ring for Squirting Perfume in a Friend's Eye. But if you've got a fresh idea, Andy,' says I, 'let's have a look at it. I'm not so wedded to petty graft that I would refuse something better in the way of a subsidy.'

" 'I was thinking,' says Andy, 'of a little hunt without horn, hound or camera among the great herd of the Midas Americanus, commonly known as the Pittsburgh millionaires.'

" 'In New York?' I asks.

" 'No, sir,' says Andy, 'in Pittsburgh. That's their habitat. They don't like New York. They go there now and then just because it's expected of 'em.'

" 'A Pittsburgh Millionaire in New York is like a fly in a cup of hot coffee—he attracts attention and comment, but he don't enjoy it. New York ridicules him for "blowing" so much money in that town of sneaks and snobs, and sneers. The truth is, he don't spend anything while he is true. I saw a memorandum of expenses for a ten days' trip to Bunkum Town made by a Pittsburgh man worth $15,000,000 once. Here's the way he set it down:

R.R. fare to and from	$	21 00
Cab fare to and from hotel		2 00
Hotel bill $5 per day		50 00
Tips		5,750 00
TOTAL	$	5,823 00

" 'That's the voice of New York,' goes on Andy. 'The town's nothing but a head waiter. If you tip it too much it'll go and stand by the door and make fun of you to the hat check boy. When a Pittsburgher wants to spend money and have a good time he stays at home. That's where we'll go to catch him.'

"Well, to make a dense story more condensed, me and Andy cached out paris green and antipyrine powders and albums in a friend's cellar, and took the trail to Pittsburgh. Andy didn't have any especial prospectus of chicanery and violence drawn up, but he always had plenty of confidence that his immoral nature would rise to any occasion that presented itself.

"As a concession to my ideas of self-preservation and rectitude he promised that if I should take an active and incriminating part in any little business venture that we might work up, there should be something actual and cognizant to the senses of touch, sight, taste, or smell to transfer to the victim for the money so my conscience might rest easy. After that I felt better and entered more cheerfully into the foul play.

" 'Andy,' says I, as we strayed through the smoke along the cinderpath they all Smithfield Street, 'had you figured out how we are going to get acquainted with these coke kings and pig iron squeezers? Not that I would decry my own worth or system of drawing-room deportment, and work with the olive fork and pie knife,' says I, 'but isn't the entree nous into the salons of the stogie smokers going to be harder than you imagined?'

" 'If there's any handicap at all,' says Andy, 'it's our own refinement and inherent culture. Pittsburgh millionaires are a fine body of plain, wholehearted, unassuming, democratic men.

" 'They are rough but uncivil in their manners, and though their ways are boisterous and unpolished, under it all they have a great deal of impoliteness and discourtesy. Nearly every one of 'em rose from obscurity,' says Andy, 'and they'll live in it till the town gets to using smoke consumers. If we act simple and unaffected and don't go too far from the saloons and keep making a noise like an import duty on steel rails we won't have any trouble in meeting some of 'em socially.'

"Well, Andy and me drifted about town three or four days getting our bearings. We got to knowing several millionaires by sight.

"One used to stop his automobile in front of our hotel and have a quart of champagne brought out to him. When the waiter opened it he'd turn it up to his mouth and drink it out of the bottle. That showed he used to be a glass-blower before he made his money.

"One evening Andy failed to come to the hotel for dinner. About 11 o'clock he came into my room.

" 'Landed one, Jeff,' says he. 'Twelve millions. Oil, rolling mills, real estate and natural gas. He's a fine man; no airs about him. Make all his money in the last five years. He's got professors posting him up now on education—art and literature and haberdashery and such things.

" 'When I saw him he'd just won a bet of $10,000 with a Steel Corporation man that there'd be four suicides in the Allegheny rolling mills to-day. So everybody in sight had to walk up and have drinks on him. He took a fancy to me and asked me to dinner with him. We went to a restaurant in Diamond Alley and sat on stools and had sparkling Moselle and clam chowder and apple fritters.

" 'Then he wanted to show me his bachelor apartment on Liberty Street. He's got ten rooms over a fish market with privilege of the bath on the next floor above. He told me it cost him $18,000 to furnish his apartment, and I believe it.

" 'He's got $40,000 worth of pictures in one room, and $20,000 worth of curios and antiques in another. His name's Scudder, and he's 45, and taking lessons on the piano and 15,000 barrels of oil a day out of his wells."

" 'All right,' says I. 'Preliminary canter satisfactory. But, kay vooly, voo? What good is the art junk to us? And the oil?'

" 'Now, that man,' says Andy, sitting thoughtfully on the bed, 'ain't what you would call an ordinary scutt. When he was showing me his cabinet of art curios his face lighted up like the door of a coke oven. He says that if some of his big deals go through he'll make J. P. Morgan's collection of sweatshop tapestry and Augusta. Me., beadwork look like the contents of an ostrich's craw thrown on a screen by a magic lantern.

" 'And then he showed me a little carving,' went on Andy, 'that anybody could see was a wonderful thing. It was something like 2,000 years old, he said. It was a lotus flower with a woman's face in it carved out of a solid piece of ivory.

" 'Scudder looks it up in a catalogue and describes it. An Egyptian carver named Khafra made two of 'em for King Rameses II about the year B.C. The other one can't be found. The junkshops and antique bugs have rubbered all Europe for it, but it seems to be out of stock. Scudder paid $2,000 for the one he has.'

" 'Oh, well,' says I, 'this sounds like the purling of a rill to me. I thought we came here to teach the millionaires business, instead of learning art from 'em?'

" 'Be patient,' says Andy, kindly. 'Maybe we will see a rift in the smoke ere long.'

"All the next morning Andy was out. I didn't see him until about noon. He came to the hotel and called me into his room across the hall. He pulled a roundish bundle about as big as a goose egg out of his pocket and unwrapped it. It was an ivory carving just as he had described the millionaire's to me.

" 'I went to an old second-hand store and pawnshop a while ago,' says Andy, 'and I see this half hidden under a lot of old daggers and truck. The pawnbroker said he'd had it several years and thinks it was soaked by some Arabs or Turks or some foreign dubs that used to live down by the river.

" 'I offered him $2 for it, and I must have looked like I wanted it, for he said it would be taking the pumpernickel out of his children's mouths to hold any conversation that did not lead up to a price of $335. I finally got it for $25.

" 'Jeff,' goes on Andy, 'this is the exact counterpart of Scudder's carving. It's absolutely a dead ringer for it. He'll pay $2,000 for it as quick as he'd tuck a napkin under his chin. And why shouldn't it be the genuine other one, anyhow, that the old gypsy whittled out?'

" 'Why not, indeed?' says I. 'And how shall we go about compelling him to make a voluntary purchase of it?'

"Andy had his plan all ready, and I'll tell you how we carried it out.

"I got a pair of blue spectacles, put on my black frock coat, rumpled my hair up and became Prof. Pickleman. I went to another hotel, registered, and sent a telegram to Scudder to come to see me at once on important art business. The elevator dumped him on me in less than an hour. He was a foggy man with a clarion voice, smelling of Connecticut wrappers and naphtha.

" 'Hello, Profess!' he shouts. 'How's your conduct?'

"I rumpled my hair some more and gave him a blue glass stare.

" 'Sir,' says I. 'Are you Cornelius T. Scudder? Of Pittsburgh, Pennsylvania?'

" 'I am,' says he. 'Come out and have a drink.'

" 'I have neither the time nor the desire,' says I, 'for such harmful and deleterious amusements. I have come from New York,' says I, 'on a matter of busi—on a matter of art.

" 'I learned there that you are the owner of an Egyptian ivory carving of the time of Rameses II, representing the head of Queen Isis in a lotus flower. There were only two of such carvings made. One has been lost for many years. I recently discovered and purchased the other in a pawn—in an obscure museum in Vienna. I wish to purchase yours. Name your price.'

" 'Well, the great ice jams, Profess!' says Scudder. 'Have you found the other one? Me sell? No. I don't guess Cornelius Scudder needs to sell anything that he

wants to keep. Have you got the carving with you,
Profess?'

"I shows it to Scudder. He examines it careful all
over.

" 'It's the article,' says he. 'It's a duplicate of mine,
every line and curve of it. Tell you what I'll do,' he says.
'I won't sell, but I'll buy. Give you $2,500 for yours.'

" 'Since you won't sell, I will,' says I. 'Large bills
please. I'm a man of few words. I must return to New
York to-night. I lecture to-morrow at the aquarium.'

"Scudder sends a check down and the hotel cashes it.
He goes off with the piece of antiquity and I hurry back
to Andy's hotel, according to arrangement.

"Andy is walking up and down the room looking at
his watch.

" 'Well?' he says.

" 'Twenty-five hundred,' says I. 'Cash.'

" 'We've got just eleven minutes,' says Andy, 'to
catch the B. & O. westbound. Grab your baggage.'

" 'What's the hurry?' says I. 'It was a square deal.
And even if it was only an imitation of the original
carving it'll take him some time to find it out. He seemed
to be sure it was the genuine article.'

" 'It was,' says Andy. 'It was his own. When I was
looking at his curios yesterday he stepped out of the
room for a moment and I pocketed it. Now, will you pick
up your suit case and hurry?'

" 'Then,' says I, 'why was that story about finding
another one in the pawn—'

" 'Oh,' says Andy, 'out of respect for that conscience
of yours. Come on.' "

The Enchanted Kiss

But a clerk in the Cut-rate Drug Store was Samuel Tansey, yet his slender frame was a pad that enfolded the passion of Romeo, the gloom of Lara, the romance of D'Artagnan, and the desperate inspiration of Melnotte. Pity, then, that he had been denied expression, that he was doomed to the burden of utter timidity and diffidence, that Fate had set him tongue-tied and scarlet before the muslin-clad angels whom he adored and vainly longed to rescue, clasp, comfort, and subdue.

The clock's hands were pointing close upon the hour of ten while Tansey was playing billiards with a number of his friends. On alternate evenings he was released from duty at the store after seven o'clock. Even among his fellow men Tansey was timorous and constrained. In his imagination he had done valiant deeds and performed acts of distinguished gallantry; but in fact he was a shallow youth of twenty-three, with an over-modest demeanor and scant vocabulary.

When the clock struck ten, Tansey hastily laid down his cue and struck sharply upon the show-case with a coin for the attendant to come and receive the pay for his score.

"What's your hurry, Tansey?" called one. "Got another engagement?"

"Tansey got an engagement!" echoed another. "Not on your life. Tansey's got to get home at ten by Mother Peek's orders."

"It's no such thing," chimed in a pale youth, taking a

large cigar from his mouth; "Tansey's afraid to be late because Miss Katie might come downstairs to unlock the door, and kiss him in the hall."

This delicate piece of raillery sent a fiery tingle into Tansey's blood, for the indictment was true—barring the kiss. That was a thing to dream of; to wildly hope for; but too remote and sacred a thing to think of lightly.

Casting a cold and contemptuous look at the speaker—a punishment commensurate with his own diffident spirit—Tansey left the room, descending the stairs into the street.

For two years he had silently adored Miss Peek, worshipping her from a spiritual distance through which her attractions took on stellar brightness and mystery. Mrs. Peek kept a few choice boarders, among whom was Tansey. The other young men romped with Katie, chased her with crickets in their fingers, and "jollied" her with an irreverent freedom that turned Tansey's heart into cold lead in his bosom. The signs of his adoration were few—a tremulous "Good morning," stealthy glances at her during meals, and occasionally (Oh, rapture!) a blushing, delirious game of cribbage with her in the parlor on some rare evening when a miraculous lack of engagement kept her at home. Kiss him in the hall! Aye, he feared it, but it was an ecstatic fear such as Elijah must have felt when the chariot lifted him into the unknown.

But to-night the gibes of his associates had stung him to a feeling of forward, lawless mutiny; a defiant, challenging, atavistic recklessness. Spirit of corsair, adventurer, lover, poet, Bohemian, possessed him. The stars he saw above him seemed no more unattainable, no less high, than the favor of Miss Peek or the fearsome sweetness of her delectable lips. His fate seemed to him strangely dramatic and pathetic, and to call for a solace consonant with its extremity. A saloon was near by, and to this he flitted, calling for absinthe—beyond doubt the drink most adequate to his mood—the tipple of the roué, the abandoned, the vainly sighing lover.

Once he drank of it, and again, and then again until he

felt a strange, exalted sense of non-participation in worldly affairs pervade him. Tansey was no drinker; his consumption of three absinthe anisettes within almost as few minutes proclaimed his unproficiency in the art; Tansey was merely flooding with unproven liquor his sorrows; which record and tradition allowed to be drownable.

Coming out upon the sidewalk, he snapped his fingers defiantly in the direction of the Peek homestead, turned the other way, and voyaged, Columbus-like, into the wilds of an enchanted street. Nor is the figure exorbitant, for, beyond his store the foot of Tansey had scarcely been set for years—store and boarding-house; between these ports he was chartered to run, and contrary currents had rarely deflected his prow.

Tansey aimlessly protracted his walk, and, whether it was his unfamiliarity with the district, his recent accession of audacious errantry, or the sophistical whisper of a certain green-eyed fairy, he came at last to tread a shuttered, blank, and echoing thoroughfare, dark and unpeopled. And, suddenly, this way came to an end (as many streets do in the Spanish-built, archaic town of San Antone), butting its head against an imminent, high, brick wall. No—the street still lived! to the right and to the left it breathed through slender tubes of exit—narrow, somnolent ravines, cobble paved and unlighted. Accommodating a rise in the street to the right was reared a phantom flight of five luminous steps of limestone, flanked by a wall of the same height and of the same material.

Upon one of these steps Tansey seated himself and bethought him of his love, and how she might never know she was his love. And of Mother Peek, fat, vigilant and kind; not unpleased, Tansey thought, that he and Katie should play cribbage in the parlor together. For the Cut-rate had not cut his salary, which, sordidly speaking, ranked him star boarder at the Peeks'. And he thought of Captain Peek, Katie's father, a man he dreaded and abhorred; a genteel loafer and spendthrift, battening upon the labor of his women-folk; a very queer fish, and, according to repute, not of the freshest.

The night had turned chill and foggy. The heart of the town, with its noises, was left behind. Reflected from the high vapors, its distant lights were manifest in quivering, cone-shaped streamers, in questionable blushes of un-named colors, in unstable, ghostly waves of far, electric flashes. Now that the darkness was become more friendly, the wall against which the street splintered developed a stone coping topped with an armature of spikes. Beyond it loomed what appeared to be the acute angles of moun-tain peaks, pierced here and there by little lambent paral-lelograms. Considering this vista, Tansey at length persuaded himself that the seeming mountains were, in fact, the convent of Santa Mercedes, with which ancient and bulky pile he was better familiar from different coigns of view. A pleasant noise of singing in his ears reënforced his opinion. High, sweet, holy carolling, far and harmonious and uprising, as of sanctified nuns at their responses. At what hour did the Sisters sing? He tried to think—was it six, eight, twelve? Tansey leaned his back against the limestone wall and wondered. Strange things followed. The air was full of white, fluttering pigeons that circled about, and settled upon the convent wall. The wall blossomed with a quantity of shining green eyes that blinked and peered at him from the solid masonry. A pink, classic nymph came from an excava-tion in the cavernous road and danced, barefoot and airy, upon the ragged flints. The sky was traversed by a company of beribboned cats, marching in stupendous, aërial procession. The noise of singing grew louder; an illumination of unseasonable fire-flies danced past, and strange whispers came out of the dark without meaning or excuse.

Without amazement Tansey took note of these phe-nomena. He was on some new plane of understanding, though his mind seemed to him clear and, indeed, hap-pily tranquil.

A desire for movement and exploration seized him; he rose and turned into the black gash of street to his right. For a time the high wall formed one of its boundaries, but farther on, two rows of black-windowed houses closed it in.

Here was the city's quarter once given over to the Spaniard. Here were still his forbidding abodes of concrete and adobe, standing cold and indomitable against the century. From the murky fissure, the eye saw, flung against the sky, the tangled filigree of his Moorish balconies. Through stone archways breaths of dead, vault-chilled air coughed upon him; his feet struck jingling iron rings in staples stone-buried for half a cycle. Along these paltry avenues had swaggered the arrogant Don, had caracoled and serenaded and blustered while the tomahawk and the pioneer's rifle were already uplifted to expel him from a continent. And Tansey, stumbling through this old-world dust, looked up, dark as it was, and saw Andalusian beauties glimmering on the balconies. Some of them were laughing and listening to the goblin music that still followed; others harked fearfully through the night, trying to catch the hoof beats of caballeros whose last echoes from those stones had died away a century ago. Those women were silent, but Tansey heard the jangle of horseless bridle-bits, the whirr of riderless rowels, and, now and then, a muttered malediction in a foreign tongue. But he was not frightened. Shadows, nor shadows of sounds could daunt him. Afraid? No. Afraid of Mother Peek? Afraid to face the girl of his heart? Afraid of tipsy Captain Peek? Nay! nor of these apparitions, nor of that spectral singing that always pursued him. Singing! He would show them! He lifted up a strong and untuneful voice:

"When you hear them bells go tingalingling,"

serving notice upon those mysterious agencies that if it should come to a face-to-face encounter

> "There'll be a hot time
> In the old town
> To-night!"

How long Tansey consumed in treading this haunted byway was not clear to him, but in time he emerged into a more commodious avenue. When within a few yards of the corner he perceived, through a window, that a small confectionery of mean appearance was set in the angle. His same glance that estimated its meagre equipment, its cheap soda-water fountain and stock of tobacco and sweets, took cognizance of Captain Peek within lighting a cigar at a swinging gaslight.

As Tansey rounded the corner Captain Peek came out, and they met *vis-à-vis*. An exultant joy filled Tansey when he found himself sustaining the encounter with implicit courage. Peek, indeed! He raised his hand, and snapped his fingers loudly.

It was Peek himself who quailed guiltily before the valiant mien of the drug clerk. Sharp surprise and a palpable fear bourgeoned upon the Captain's face. And, verily, that face was one to rather call up such expressions upon the faces of others. The face of a libidinous heathen idol, small eyed, with carven folds in the heavy jowls, and a consuming, pagan license in its expression. In the gutter just beyond the store Tansey saw a closed carriage standing with its back toward him and a motionless driver perched in his place.

"Why, it's Tansey!" exclaimed Captain Peek. "How are you, Tansey? H-have a cigar, Tansey?"

"Why, it's Peek!" cried Tansey, jubilant at his own temerity. "What deviltry are you up to now, Peek? Back streets and a closed carriage! Fie! Peek!"

"There's no one in the carriage," said the Captain, smoothly.

"Everybody out of it is in luck," continued Tansey,

aggressively, "I'd love for you to know, Peek, that I'm not stuck on you. You're a bottle-nosed scoundrel."

"Why, the little rat's drunk!" cried the Captain, joyfully; "only drunk, and I thought he was on! Go home, Tansey, and quit bothering grown persons on the street."

But just then a white-clad figure sprang out of the carriage, and a shrill voice—Katie's voice—sliced the air: "Sam! Sam!—help me, Sam!"

Tansey sprang toward her, but Captain Peek interposed his bulky form. Wonder of wonders! the whilom spiritless youth struck out with his right, and the hulking Captain went over in a swearing heap. Tansey flew to Katie, and took her in his arms like a conquering knight. She raised her face, and he kissed her—violets! electricity! caramels! champagne! Here was the attainment of a dream that brought no disenchantment.

"Oh, Sam," cried Katie, when she could, "I knew you would come to rescue me. What do you suppose the mean things were going to do with me?"

"Have your picture taken," said Tansey, wondering at the foolishness of his remark.

"No, they were going to eat me. I heard them talking about it."

"Eat you!" said Tansey, after pondering a moment. "That can't be; there's no plates."

But a sudden noise warned him to turn. Down upon him were bearing the Captain and a monstrous long-bearded dwarf in a spangled cloak and red trunk-hose. The dwarf leaped twenty feet and clutched him. The Captain seized Katie and hurled her, shrieking, back into the carriage, himself followed, and the vehicle dashed away. The dwarf lifted Tansey high above his head and ran with him into the store. Holding him with one hand, he raised the lid of an enormous chest half filled with cakes of ice, flung Tansey inside, and closed down the cover.

The force of the fall must have been great, for Tansey lost consciousness. When his faculties revived his first

sensation was one of severe cold along his back and
limbs. Opening his eyes, he found himself to be seated
upon the lime-stone steps still facing the wall and convent of Santa Mercedes. His first thought was of the
ecstatic kiss from Katie. The outrageous villainy of Captain Peek, the unnatural mystery of the situation, his
preposterous conflict with the improbable dwarf—these
things roused and angered him, but left no impression of
the unreal.

"I'll go back there to-morrow," he grumbled aloud,
"and knock the head off that comic-opera squab. Running out and picking up perfect strangers, and shoving
them into cold storage!"

But the kiss remained uppermost in his mind. "I might
have done that long ago," he mused. "She liked it, too.
She called me 'Sam' four times. I'll not go up that street
again. Too much scrapping. Guess I'll move down the
other way. Wonder what she meant by saying they were
going to eat her!"

Tansey began to feel sleepy, but after a while he
decided to move along again. This time he ventured into
the street to his left. It ran level for a distance, and then
dipped gently downward, opening in a vast, dim, barren
space—the old Military Plaza. To his left, some hundred
yards distant, he saw a cluster of flickering lights along
the Plaza's border. He knew the locality at once.

Huddled within narrow confines were the remnants of
the once-famous purveyors of the celebrated Mexican
national cookery. A few years before, their nightly en-
campments upon the historic Alamo Plaza, in the heart of
the city, had been a carnival, a saturnalia that was re-
nowned throughout the land. Then the caterers numbered
hundreds; the patrons thousands. Drawn by the coquet-
tish *señoritas*, the music of the weird Spanish minstrels,
and the strange piquant Mexican dishes served at a hundred competing tables, crowds thronged the Alamo Plaza
all night. Travellers, rancheros, family parties, gay
gasconading rounders, sight-seers and prowlers of poly-

glot, owlish San Antone mingled there at the centre of
the city's fun and frolic. The popping of corks, pistols,
and questions; the glitter of eyes, jewels, and daggers;
the ring of laughter and coin—these were the order of the
night.

But now no longer. To some half-dozen tents, fires,
and tables had dwindled the picturesque festival, and
these had been relegated to an ancient disused plaza.

Often had Tansey strolled down to these stands at
night to partake of the delectable *chili-con-carne*, a dish
evolved by the genius of Mexico, composed of delicate
meats minced with aromatic herbs and the poignant *chili
colorado*—a compound full of singular savor and a fiery
zest delightful to the Southron's palate.

The titillating odor of this concoction came now, on
the breeze, to the nostrils of Tansey, awakening in him
hunger for it. As he turned in that direction he saw a
carriage dash up to the Mexicans' tents out of the gloom
of the Plaza. Some figures moved back and forward in
the uncertain light of the lanterns, and then the carriage
was driven swiftly away.

Tansey approached, and sat at one of the tables covered with gaudy oilcloth. Traffic was dull at the moment.
A few half-grown boys noisily fared at another table; the
Mexicans hung listless and phlegmatic about their wares.
And it was still. The night hum of the city crowded to the
wall of dark buildings surrounding the Plaza, and subsided to an indefinite buzz through which sharply perfo-
rated the crackle of the languid faces and the rattle of
fork and spoon. A sedative wind blew from the south-
east. The starless firmament pressed down upon the earth
like a leaden cover.

In all that quiet Tansey turned his head suddenly, and
saw, without disquietude, a troop of spectral horsemen
deploy into the Plaza and charge a luminous line of
infantry that advanced to sustain the shock. He saw the
fierce flame of cannon and small arms, but heard no
sound. The careless victuallers lounged vacantly, not

deigning to view the conflict. Tansey mildly wondered to what nations these mute combatants might belong; turned his back to them and ordered his *chili* and coffee from the Mexican woman who advanced to serve him. This woman was old and careworn; her face was lined like the rind of a cantaloupe. She fetched the viands from a vessel set by the smouldering fire, and then retired to a tent, dark within, that stood near by.

Presently Tansey heard a turmoil in the tent; a wailing, broken-hearted pleading in the harmonious Spanish tongue, and then two figures tumbled out into the light of the lanterns. One was the old woman; the other was a man clothed with a sumptuous and flashing splendor. The woman seemed to clutch and beseech from him something against his will. The man broke from her and struck her brutally back into the tent, where she lay, whimpering and invisible. Observing Tansey, he walked rapidly to the table where he sat. Tansey recognized him to be Ramon Torres, a Mexican, the proprietor of the stand he was patronizing.

Torres was a handsome, nearly full-blooded descendant of the Spanish, seemingly about thirty years of age, and of a haughty, but extremely courteous demeanor. To-night he was dressed with signal magnificence. His costume was that of a triumphant *matador*, made of purple velvet almost hidden by jeweled embroidery. Diamonds of enormous size flashed upon his garb and his hands. He reached for a chair, and, seating himself at the opposite side of the table, began to roll a finical cigarette.

"Ah, Meester Tansee," he said, with a sultry fire in his silky, black eye, "I give myself pleasure to see you this evening. Meester Tansee, you have many times come to eat at my table. I theenk you a safe man—a verree good friend. How much would it please you to leeve forever?"

"Not come back any more?" inquired Tansey.

"No; not leave—*leeve;* the not-to-die."

"I would call that," said Tansey, "a snap."

Torres leaned his elbows upon the table, swallowed a mouthful of smoke, and spake—each word being projected in a little puff of gray.

"How old do you theenk I am, Meester Tansee?"

"Oh, twenty-eight or thirty."

"Thees day," said the Mexican, "ees my birthday. I am four hundred and three years of old to-day."

"Another proof," said Tansey, airily, "of the healthfulness of our climate."

"Eet is not the air. I am to relate to you a secret of verree fine value. Listen me, Meester Tansee. At the age of twenty-three I arrive in Mexico from Spain. When? In the year fifteen hundred nineteen, with the *soldados* of Hernando Cortez. I come to thees country seventeen fifteen. I saw your Alamo reduced. It was like yesterday to me. Three hundred ninety-six year ago I learn the secret always to leeve. Look at these clothes I wear—at these *diamantes*. Do you theenk I buy them with the money I make with selling the *chili-con-carne*, Meester Tansee?"

"I should think not," said Tansey, promptly. Torres laughed loudly.

"*Válgame Dios!* but I do. But it not the kind you eating now. I make a deeferent kind, the eating of which makes men to always leeve. What do you think? One thousand people I supply—*diez pesos* each one pays me the month. You see! ten thousand *pesos* everee month! *Qué diablos!* how not I wear the fine *ropo!* You see that old woman try to hold me back a little while ago? That ees my wife. When I marry her she is young—seventeen years—*bonita*—. Like the rest she ees become old and—what you say!—tough? I am the same—young all the time. To-night I resolve to dress myself and find another wife befitting my age. This old woman try to scr-r-ratch my face. Ha! Ha! Meester Tansee—same way they do *entre los Americanos*."

"And this health-food you spoke of?" said Tansey.

"Hear me," said Torres, leaning over the table until

he lay flat upon it; "eet is the *chili-con-carne* made not from the beef or the chicken, but from the flesh of the *señorita*—young and tender. That ees the secret. Everee month you must eat it, having care to do so before the moon is full, and you will not die any times. See how I trust you, friend Tansee! To-night I have bought one young ladee—veree pretty—so *fina, gorda, blandita!* To-morrow the *chili* will be ready. *Ahora si!* One thousand dollars I pay for thees young ladee. From an *American* I have bought—a veree tip-top man—*el Capitán Peek*— *Qué es, Señor?*"

For Tansey had sprung to his feet, upsetting the chair. The words of Katie reverberated in his ears: "They're going to eat me, Sam." This, then, was the monstrous fate to which she had been delivered by her unnatural parent. The carriage he had seen drive up from the Plaza was Captain Peek's. Where was Katie? Perhaps already—

Before he could decide what to do a loud scream came from the tent. The old Mexican woman ran out, a flashing knife in her hand. "I have released her," she cried. "You shall kill no more. They will hang you—*ingrato-encantador!*"

Torres, with a hissing exclamation, sprang at her.

"Ramoncito!" she shrieked, "once you loved me."

The Mexican's arm raised and descended. "You are old," he cried; and she fell and lay motionless.

Another scream; the flaps of the tent were flung aside, and there stood Katie, white with fear, her wrists still bound with a cruel cord.

"Sam!" she cried, "save me again!"

Tansey rounded the table, and flung himself, with superb nerve, upon the Mexican. Just then a clangor began; the clocks of the city were tolling the midnight hour. Tansey clutched at Torres, and, for a moment, felt in his grasp the crunch of velvet and the cold facets of the glittering gems. The next instant, the bedecked caballero turned in his hands to a shrunken, leather-visaged, white-bearded, old, old screaming mummy, sandalled, ragged, four hundred and three. The Mexican woman was crawling to her feet, and laughing. She shook her brown hand in the face of the whining *viejo*.

"Go, now," she cried, "and seek your señorita. It was I, Ramoncito, who brought you to this. Within each moon you eat of the life-giving *chili*. It was I that kept the wrong time for you. You should have eaten *yesterday* instead of *tomorrow*. It is too late. Off with you, *hombre!* You are too old for me!"

"This," decided Tansey, releasing his hold of the graybeard, "is a private family matter concerning age, and no business of mine."

With one of the table knives he hastened to saw asunder the fetters of the fair captive; and then, for the second time that night he kissed Katie Peek—tasted again the sweetness, the wonder, the thrill of it, attained once more the maximum of his incessant dreams.

The next instant an icy blade was driven deep between his shoulders; he felt his blood slowly congeal; heard the senile cackle of the perennial Spaniard; saw the Plaza rise and reel till the zenith crashed into the horizon—and knew no more.

When Tansey opened his eyes again he was sitting upon those self-same steps gazing upon the dark bulk of the sleeping convent. In the middle of his back was still the acute, chilling pain. How had he been conveyed back there again? He got stiffly to his feet and stretched his cramped limbs. Supporting himself against the stonework he revolved in his mind the extravagant adventures that had befallen him each time he had strayed from the steps that night. In reviewing them certain features strained his .credulity. Had he really met Captain Peek or Katie or the unparalleled Mexican in his wanderings—had he really encountered them under common-place conditions and his over-stimulated brain had supplied the incongruities? However that might be, a sudden, elating thought caused him an intense joy. Nearly all of us have, at some point in our lives—either to excuse our own stupidity or pla-

cate our consciences—promulgated some theory of fatal-
ism. We have set up an intelligent Fate that works by
codes and signals. Tansey had done likewise; and now he
read, through the night's incidents, the finger-prints of
destiny. Each excursion that he had made had led to the
one paramount finale—to Katie and that kiss, which
survived and grew strong and intoxicating in his memory. Clearly, Fate was holding up to him the mirror that
night, calling him to observe what awaited him at the end
of whichever road he might take. He immediately turned,
and hurried homeward.

Clothed in an elaborate, pale blue wrapper, cut to fit,
Miss Katie Peek reclined in an arm-chair before a waning
fire in her room. Her little, bare feet were thrust into
house-shoes rimmed with swan's down. By the light of a
small lamp she was attacking the society news of the
latest Sunday paper. Some happy substance, seemingly
indestructible, was being rhythmically crushed between
her small white teeth. Miss Katie read of functions and
furbelows, but she kept a vigilant ear for outside sounds
and a frequent eye upon the clock over the mantel. At
every footstep upon the asphalt sidewalk her smooth,
round chin would cease for a moment its regular rise and
fall, and a frown of listening would pucker her pretty
brows.

At last she heard the latch of the iron gate click. She
sprang up, tripped swiftly to the mirror, where she made
a few of those feminine, flickering passes at her front
hair and throat which are warranted to hypnotize the
approaching guest.

The door-bell rang. Miss Katie, in her haste, turned
the blaze of the lamp lower instead of higher, and hastened noiselessly downstairs into the hall. She turned the
key, the door opened, and Mr. Tansey sidestepped in.

"Why, the i-de-a!" exclaimed Miss Katie, "is this
you, Mr. Tansey? It's after midnight. Aren't you ashamed

to wake me up at such an hour to let you in? You're just *awful!*"

"I was late," said Tansey, brilliantly.

"I should think you were! Ma was awfully worried about you. When you weren't in by ten, that hateful Tom McGill said you were out calling on another—said you were out calling on some young lady. I just despise Mr. McGill. Well, I'm not going to scold you any more, Mr. Tansey, if it *is* a little late—Oh! I turned it the wrong way!"

Miss Katie gave a little scream. Absent-mindedly she had turned the blaze of the lamp entirely out instead of higher. It was very dark.

Tansey heard a musical, soft giggle, and breathed an entrancing odor of heliotrope. A groping light hand touched his arm.

"How awkward I was! Can you find your way—Sam?"

"I—I think I have a match, Miss K-Katie."

A scratching sound; a flame; a glow of light held at arm's length by the recreant follower of Destiny illuminating a tableau which shall end the ignominious chronicle—a maid with unkissed, curling, contemptuous lips slowly lifting the lamp chimney and allowing the wick to ignite; then waving a scornful and abjuring hand toward the staircase—the unhappy Tansey erstwhile champion in the prophetic lists of fortune, ingloriously ascending to his just and certain doom, while (let us imagine) half within the wings stands the imminent figure of Fate jerking wildly at the wrong strings, and mixing things up in her usual able manner.

The Lonesome Road

Brown as a coffee-berry, rugged, pistoled, spurred, wary, indefeasible, I saw my old friend, Deputy-Marshal Buck Caperton, stumble, with jingling rowels, into a chair in the marshal's outer office.

And because the courthouse was almost deserted at that hour, and because Buck would sometimes relate to me things that were out of print, I followed him in and tricked him into talk through knowledge of a weakness he had. For, cigarettes rolled with sweet corn husk were as honey to Buck's palate; and though he could finger the trigger of a forty-five with skill and suddenness, he never could learn to roll a cigarette.

It was through no fault of mine (for I rolled the cigarettes tight and smooth), but the upshot of some whim of his own, that instead of to an Odyssey of the chaparral, I listened to—a dissertation upon matrimony! This from Buck Caperton! But I maintain that the cigarettes were impeccable, and crave absolution for myself.

"We just brought in Jim and Bud Granberry," said Buck. "Train robbing, you know. Held up the Aransas Pass last month. We caught 'em in the Twenty-Mile pear flat, south of the Nueces."

"Have much trouble corralling them?" I asked, for here was the meat that my hunger for epics craved.

"Some," said Buck; and then, during a little pause, his thoughts stampeded off the trail. "It's kind of queer about women," he went on, "and the place they're supposed to occupy in botany. If I was asked to classify them I'd say they was a human loco weed. Ever see a bronc that had been chewing loco? Ride him up to a puddle of water two feet wide, and he'll give a snort and fall back on you. It looks as big as the Mississippi River to him. Next trip he'd walk into a cañon a thousand feet deep thinking it was a prairie-dog hole. Same way with a married man.

"I was thinking of Perry Rountree, that used to be my sidekicker before he committed matrimony. In them days me and Perry hated indisturbances of any kind. We roamed around considerable, stirring up the echoes and making 'em attend to business. Why, when me and Perry wanted to have some fun in a town it was a picnic for the census takers. They just counted the marshal's posse that it took to subdue us, and there was your population. But then there came along this Mariana Good-night girl and looked at Perry sideways, and he was all bridle-wise and saddle-broke before you could skin a yearling.

"I wasn't even asked to the wedding. I reckon the bride had my pedigree and the front elevation of my habits all mapped out, and she decided that Perry would trot better in double harness without any unconverted mustang like Buck Caperton whickering around on the matrimonial range. So it was six months before I saw Perry again.

"One day I was passing on the edge of town, and I see something like a man in a little yard by a little house with a sprinkling-pot squirting water on a rosebush. Seemed to me, I'd seen something like it before, and I stopped at the gate, trying to figure out its brands. 'Twas not Perry Rountree, but 'twas the kind of a curdled jellyfish matrimony had made out of him.

"Homicide was what that Mariana had perpetrated. He was looking well enough, but he had on a white collar and shoes, and you could tell in a minute that he'd speak polite and pay taxes and stick his little finger out while drinking, just like a sheep man or a citizen. Great sky-

rockets! but I hated to see Perry all corrupted and Willie-
ized like that.

"He came out to the gate and shook hands; and I says,
with scorn, and speaking like a paroquet with the pip:
'Beg pardon—Mr. Rountree, I believe. Seems to me I
sagatiated in your associations once, if I am not mistaken.''

" 'Oh, go to the devil, Buck,' says Perry, polite, as I
was afraid he'd be.

" 'Well, then,' says I, 'you poor, contaminated ad-
junct of a sprinkling-pot and degraded household pet,
what did you go and do it for? Look at you, all decent
and unriotous, and only fit to sit on juries and mend the
wood-house door. You was a man once. I have hostility
for all such acts. Why don't you go in the house and
count the tidies or set the clock, and not stand out here in
the atmosphere? A jackrabbit might come along and bite
you.'

" 'Now, Buck,' says Perry, speaking mild, and some
sorrowful, 'you don't understand. A married man has got
to be different. He feels different from a tough old
cloudburst like you. It's sinful to waste time pulling up
towns just to look at their roots, and playing faro and
looking upon red liquor, and such restless policies as them.'

" 'There was a time,' I says, and I expect I sighed
when I mentioned it, 'when a certain domesticated little
Mary's lamb I could name was some instructed himself
in the line of pernicious sprightliness. I never expected,
Perry, to see you reduced down from a full-grown pesti-
lence to such a frivolous fraction of a man. Why,' says I,
'you've got a necktie on; and you speak a senseless kind
of indoor drivel, that reminds me of a storekeeper or a
lady. You look to me like you might tote an umbrella and
wear suspenders, and go home of nights.'

" 'The little woman,' says Perry, 'has made some
improvements, I believe. You can't understand, Buck. I
haven't been away from the house at night since we was
married.'

"We talked on a while, me and Perry, and, as sure as

I live, that man interrupted me in the middle of my talk to tell me about six tomato plants he had growing in his garden. Shoved his agricultural degradation right up under my nose while I was telling him about the fun we had tarring and feathering that faro dealer at California Pete's layout! But by and by Perry showed a flicker of sense.

" 'Buck,' says he, "I'll have to admit that it is a little dull at times. Not that I'm not perfectly happy with the little woman, but a man seems to require some excitement now and then. Now, I'll tell you; Mariana's gone visiting this afternoon, and she won't be home till seven o'clock. That's the limit for both of us—seven o'clock. Neither of us ever stays out a minute after that time unless we are together. Now, I'm glad you came along, Buck,' says Perry, 'for I'm feeling just like having one more rip-roaring razoo with you for the sake of old times. What you say to us putting in the afternoon having fun?—I'd like it fine,' says Perry.

"I slapped that old captive range-rider half across his little garden.

" 'Get your hat, you old dried-up alligator,' I shouts, 'you ain't dead yet. You're part human, anyhow, if you did get all bogged up in matrimony. We'll take this town to pieces and see what makes it tick. We'll make all kinds of profligate demands upon the science of cork pulling. You'll grow horns yet, old muley cow,' says I, punching Perry in the ribs, 'if you trot around on the trail of vice with your Uncle Buck.'

" 'I'll have to be home by seven, you know,' says Perry again.

" 'Oh, yes,' says I, winking to myself, for I knew the kind of seven o'clocks Perry Rountree got back by after he once got to passing repartee with the bartenders.

"We goes down to the Gray Mule saloon—that old 'dobe building by the depot.

" 'Give it a name,' says I, as soon as we got one hoof on the footrest.

" 'Sarsaparilla,' says Perry.

"You could have knocked me down with a lemon peeling.

" 'Insult me as much as you want to,' I says to Perry, 'but don't startle the bartender. He may have heart-disease. Come on, now; your tongue got twisted. The tall glasses,' I orders, 'and the bottle in the left hand corner of the ice-chest.'

" 'Sarsaparilla,' repeats Perry, and then his eyes get animated, and I see he's got some great scheme in his mind he wants to emit.

" 'Buck,' he says, all interested, 'I'll tell you what! I want to make this a red-letter day. I've been keeping close at home, and I want to turn myself a-loose. We'll have the highest old time you ever saw. We'll go in the back room here and play checkers till half-past six.'

"I leaned against the bar, and I says to Gotch-eared Mike, who was on watch:

" 'For God's sake don't mention this. You know what Perry used to be. He's had the fever, and the doctor says we must humor him.'

" 'Give us the checker-board and the men, Mike,' says Perry. 'Come on, Buck, I'm just wild to have some excitement.'

"I went in the back room with Perry. Before we closed the door, I says to Mike:

" 'Don't ever let it straggle out from under your hat that you seen Buck Caperton fraternal with sarsaparilla or *persona grata* with a checkerboard, or I'll make a swallow-fork in your other ear.'

"I locked the door and me and Perry played checkers. To see that poor old humiliated piece of household bric-à-brac sitting there and sniggering out loud whenever he jumped a man, and all obnoxious with animation when he got into my king row, would have made a sheep-dog sick with mortification. Him that was once satisfied only when he was pegging six boards at keno or giving the faro dealers nervous prostration—to see him pushing them checkers about like Sally Louisa at a school-children's party—why, I was all smothered up with mortification.

"And I sits there playing the black men, all sweating for fear somebody I knew would find it out. And I thinks to myself some about this marrying business, and how it seems to be the same kind of a game as that Mrs. Delilah played. She give her old man a hair cut, and everybody knows what a man's head looks like after a woman cuts his hair. And then when the Pharisees came around to guy him he was so 'shamed he went to work and kicked the whole house down on top of the whole outfit. 'Them married men,' thinks I, 'lose all their spirit and instinct for riot and foolishness. They won't drink, they won't buck the tiger, they won't even fight. What do they want to go and stay married for?' I asks myself.

"But Perry seems to be having hilarity in considerable quantities.

" 'Buck old hoss,' says he, 'isn't this just the hell-roaringest time we ever had in our lives? I don't know when I've been stirred up so. You see, I've been sticking pretty close to home since I married, and I haven't been on a spree in a long time.'

" 'Spree!' Yes, that's what he called it. Playing checkers in the back room of the Gray Mule! I suppose it did seem to him a little immoral and nearer to a prolonged debauch than standing over six tomato plants with a sprinkling pot.

"Every little bit Perry looks at his watch and says:

" 'I got to be home, you know, Buck, at seven.'

" 'All right,' I'd say. 'Romp along and move. This here excitement's killing me. If I don't reform some, and loosen up the strain of this checkered dissipation I won't have a nerve left.'

"It might have been half-past six when commotions began to go on outside in the street. We heard a yelling and a six-shootering, and a lot of galloping and maneuvers.

" 'What's that?' I wonders.

" 'Oh, some nonsense outside,' says Perry. 'It's your move. We just got time to play this game.'

" 'I'll just take a peep through the window,' says I,
'and see. You can't expect a mere mortal to stand the
excitement of having a king jumped and listen to an
unidentified conflict going on at the same time.'

"The Gray Mule saloon was one of them old Spanish
'dobe buildings, and the back room only had two little
windows a foot wide, with iron bars in 'em. I looked out
once, and I see the cause of the rucus.

"There was the Trimble gang—ten of 'em—the worst
outfit of desperadoes and horse-thieves in Texas, coming
up the street shooting right and left. They was coming
right straight for the Gray Mule. Then they got past the
range of my sight, but we heard 'em ride up to the front
door, and then they socked the place full of lead. We
heard the big looking-glass behind the bar knocked all to
pieces and the bottles crashing. We could see Gotch-
eared Mike in his apron running across the plaza like a
coyote, with the bullets puffing up the dust all around
him. Then the gang went to work in the saloon, drinking
what they wanted and smashing what they didn't.

"Me and Perry both knew that gang, and they knew
us. The year before Perry married, him and me was in
the same ranger company—and we fought that outfit
down on the San Miguel, and brought back Ben Trimble
and two others for murder.

" 'We can't get out,' says I. 'We'll have to stay in
here till they leave.'

"Perry looked at his watch.

" 'Twenty-five to seven,' says he. 'We can finish that
game. I got two men on you. It's your move, Buck. I got
to be home at seven, you know.'

"We sat down and went on playing. The Trimble gang
had a roughhouse for sure. They were getting good and
drunk. They'd drink a while and holler a while, and then
they'd shoot up a few bottles and glasses. Two or three
times they came and tried to open our door. Then there
was some more shooting outside, and I looked out the
window again. Ham Gossett, the town marshal, had a

posse in the houses and stores across the street, and was trying to bag a Trimble or two through the windows.

"I lost that game of checkers. I'm free in saying that I lost three kings that I might have saved if I had been corralled in a more peaceful pasture. But that drivelling married man sat there and cackled when he won a man like an unintelligent hen picking up a grain of corn.

"When the game was over Perry gets up and looks at his watch.

" 'I've had a glorious time, Buck,' says he, 'but I'll have to be going now. It's a quarter to seven, and I got to be home by seven, you know.'

"I thought he was joking.

" 'They'll clear out or be dead drunk in half an hour or an hour,' says I. 'You ain't that tired of being married that you want to commit any more sudden suicide, are you?' says I, giving him the laugh.

" 'One time,' says Perry, 'I was half an hour late getting home. I met Mariana on the street looking for me. If you could have seen her, Buck—but you don't understand. She knows what a wild kind of a snoozer I've been, and she's afraid something will happen, I'll never be late getting home again. I'll say good-bye to you now, Buck.'

"I got between him and the door.

" 'Married man,' says I. 'I know you was christened a fool the minute the preacher tangled you up, but don't you never sometimes think one little think on a human basis? There's ten of that gang in there, and they're pizen with whisky and desire for murder. They'll drink you up like a bottle of booze before you get halfway to the door. Be intelligent, now, and use at least wild-hog sense. Sit down and wait till we have some chance to get out without being carried in baskets.'

" 'I got to be home by seven, Buck,' repeats this hen-pecked thing of little wisdom, like an unthinking poll parrot. 'Mariana,' says he, ' 'll be looking out for me.' And he reaches down and pulls a leg out of the checker

table. 'I'll go through this Trimble outfit,' says he, 'like
a cottontail through a brush corral. I'm not pestered any
more with desire to engage in rucuses, but I got to be
home by seven. You lock the door after me, Buck. And
don't you forget—I won three out of them five games.
I'd play longer, but Mariana——'

" 'Hush up, you old locoed road runner,' I interrupts.
'Did you ever notice your Uncle Buck locking doors
against trouble? I'm not married,' says I, 'but I'm as big
a d—n fool as any Mormon. One from four leaves three,'
says I, and I gathers out another leg of the table. 'We'll
get home by seven,' says I, 'whether it's the heavenly one
or the other. May I see you home?' says I, 'you sarsaparilla-
drinking, checker-playing glutton for death and destruction.'

"We opened the door easy, and then stampeded for
the front. Part of the gang was lined up at the bar; part of
'em was passing over the drinks, and two or three was
peeping out the door and window taking shots at the
marshal's crowd. The room was so full of smoke we got
halfway to the front door before they noticed us. Then I
heard Berry Trimble's voice somewhere yell out:

" 'How'd that Buck Caperton get in here?' and he
skinned the side of my neck with a bullet. I reckon he
felt bad over that miss, for Berry's the best shot south of
the Southern Pacific Railroad. But the smoke in the
saloon was some too thick for good shooting.

"Me and Perry smashed over two of the gang with our
table legs, which didn't miss like the guns did, and as we
run out the door I grabbed a Winchester from a fellow
who was watching the outside, and I turned and regulated
the account of Mr. Berry.

"Me and Perry got out and around the corner all right.
I never much expected to get out, but I wasn't going to
be intimidated by that married man. According to Perry's
idea, checkers was the event of the day, but if I am any
judge of gentle recreations that little table-leg parade
through the Gray Mule saloon deserved the head-lines in
the bill of particulars.

" 'Walk fast,' says Perry, 'it's two minutes to seven, and I got to be home by——'

" 'Oh, shut up,' says I. 'I had an appointment as chief performer at an inquest at seven, and I'm not kicking about not keeping it.'

"I had to pass by Perry's little house. His Mariana was standing at the gate. We got there at five minutes past seven. She had on a blue wrapper, and her hair was pulled back smooth like little girls do when they want to look grown-folksy. She didn't see us till we got close, for she was gazing up the other way. Then she backed around, and saw Perry, and a kind of look scooted around over her face—danged if I can describe it. I heard her breathe long, just like a cow when you turn her calf in the lot, and she says: 'You're late, Perry.'

" 'Five minutes,' says Perry, cheerful. 'Me and old Buck was having a game of checkers.'

"Perry introduces me to Mariana, and they ask me to come in. No, sir-ee. I'd had enough truck with married folks for this day. I says I'll be going along, and that I've spent a very pleasant afternoon with my old partner—'especially,' says I, just to jostle Perry, 'during that game when the table legs came all loose.' But I'd promised him not to let her know anything.

"I've been worrying over that business ever since it happened," continued Buck. "There's one thing about it that's got me all twisted up, and I can't figure it out."

"What was that?" I asked, as I rolled and handed Buck the last cigarette.

"Why, I tell you: When I saw the look that little woman give Perry when she turned round and saw him coming back to the ranch safe—why was it I got the idea all in a minute that that look of hers was worth more than the whole caboodle of us—sarsaparilla, checkers, and all, and that the d—n fool in the game wasn't named Perry Rountree at all?"

The Rose of Dixie

When *The Rose of Dixie* magazine was started by a stock company in Toombs City, Georgia, there was never but one candidate for its chief editorial position in the minds of its owners. Col. Aquila Telfair was the man for the place. By all the rights of learning, family, reputation, and Southern traditions, he was its foreordained, fit, and logical editor. So, a committee of the patriotic Georgia citizens who had subscribed the founding fund of $100,000 called upon Colonel Telfair at his residence, Cedar Heights, fearful lest the enterprise and the South should suffer by his possible refusal.

The colonel received them in his great library, where he spent most of his days. The library had descended to him from his father. It contained ten thousand volumes, some of which had been published as late as the year 1861. When the deputation arrived, Colonel Telfair was seated at his massive white-pine centre-table, reading Burton's "Anatomy of Melancholy." He arose and shook hands punctiliously with each member of the committee. If you were familiar with *The Rose of Dixie* you will remember the colonel's portrait, which appeared in it from time to time. You could not forget the long, carefully brushed white hair, the hooked, high-bridged nose, slightly twisted to the left; the keen eyes under the still black eyebrows; the classic mouth beneath the drooping white mustache, slightly frazzled at the ends.

The committee solicitously offered him the position of managing editor, humbly presenting an outline of the field that the publication was designed to cover and mentioning a comfortable salary. The colonel's lands were growing poorer each year and were much cut up by red gullies. Besides, the honor was not one to be refused.

In a forty-minute speech of acceptance, Colonel Telfair gave an outline of English literature from Chaucer to Macaulay, re-fought the battle of Chancellorsville, and said that, God helping him, he would so conduct *The Rose of Dixie* that its fragrance and beauty would permeate the entire world, hurling back into the teeth of the Northern minions their belief that no genius or good could exist in the brains and hearts of the people whose property they had destroyed and whose rights they had curtailed.

Offices for the magazine were partitioned off and furnished in the second floor of the First National Bank building; and it was for the colonel to cause *The Rose of Dixie* to blossom and flourish or to wilt in the balmy air of the land of flowers.

The staff of assistants and contributors that Editor-Colonel Telfair drew about him was a peach. It was a whole crate of Georgia peaches. The first assistant editor, Tolliver Lee Fairfax, had had a father killed during Pickett's charge. The second assistant, Keats Unthank, was the nephew of one of Morgan's Raiders. The book reviewer, Jackson Rockingham, had been the youngest soldier in the Confederate army, having appeared on the field of battle with a sword in one hand and a milk-bottle in the other. The art editor, Roncesvalles Sykes, was a third cousin to a nephew of Jefferson Davis. Miss Lavinia Terhune, the colonel's stenographer and typewriter, had an aunt who had once been kissed by Stonewall Jackson. Tommy Webster, the head office boy, got his job by having recited Father Ryan's poems, complete, at the commencement exercises of the Toombs City High School. The girls who wrapped and addressed the magazines were members of old Southern families in Reduced Circumstances. The cashier was a scrub named Hawkins,

from Ann Arbor, Michigan, who had recommendations
and a bond from a guarantee company filed with the
owners. Even Georgia stock companies sometimes realize that it takes live ones to bury the dead.

Well, sir, if you believe me, *The Rose of Dixie*
blossomed five times before anybody heard of it except
the people who buy their hooks and eyes in Toombs
City. Then Hawkins climbed off his stool and told on
'em to the stock company. Even in Ann Arbor he had
been used to having his business propositions heard of at
least as far away as Detroit. So an advertising manager
was engaged—Beauregard Fitzhugh Banks—a young man
in a lavender necktie, whose grandfather had been in the
Exalted High Pillow-slip of the Kuklux Klan.

In spite of which *The Rose of Dixie* kept coming out
every month. Although in every issue it ran photos of
either the Taj Mahal or the Luxembourg Gardens, or
Carmencita or La Follette, a certain number of people
bought it and subscribed for it. As a boom for it, Editor-
Colonel Telfair ran three different views of Andrew Jackson's old home, "The Hermitage," a full-page engraving
of the second battle of Manasses, entitled "Lee to the
Rear!" and a five-thousand-word biography of Belle Boyd
in the same number. The subscription list that month
advanced 118. Also there were poems in the same issue
of Leonina Vashti Haricot (penname), related to the Hari-
cots of Charleston, South Carolina, and Bill Thompson,
nephew of one of the stockholders. And an article from a
special society correspondent describing a tea-party given
by the swell Boston and English set, where a lot of tea
was spilled overboard by some of the guests masquerad-
ing as Indians.

One day a person whose breath would easily cloud a
mirror, he was so much alive, entered the office of *The
Rose of Dixie*. He was a man about the size of a real-
estate agent, with a self-tied tie and a manner that he
must have borrowed conjointly from W. J. Bryan,
Hackenschmidt, and Hetty Green. He was shown into the

editor-colonel's *pons asinorum*. Colonel Telfair rose and began a Prince Albert bow.

"I'm Thacker," said the intruder, taking the editor's chair—"T. T. Thacker, of New York."

He dribbled hastily upon the colonel's desk some cards, a bulk manila envelope, and a letter from the owners of *The Rose of Dixie*. This letter introduced Mr. Thacker, and politely requested Colonel Telfair to give him a conference and whatever information about the magazine he might desire.

"I've been corresponding with the secretary of the magazine owners for some time," said Thacker, briskly. "I'm a practical magazine man myself, and a circulation booster as good as any, if I do say it. I'll guarantee an increase of anywhere from ten thousand to a hundred thousand a year for any publication that isn't printed in a dead language. I've had my eye on *The Rose of Dixie* ever since it started. I know every end of the business from editing to setting up the classified ads. Now, I've come down here to put a good bunch of money in the magazine, if I can see my way clear. It ought to be made to pay. The secretary tells me it's losing money. I don't see why a magazine in the South, if it's properly handled, shouldn't get a good circulation in the North, too."

Colonel Telfair leaned back in his chair and polished his gold-rimmed glasses.

"Mr. Thacker," said he, courteously but firmly, "*The Rose of Dixie* is a publication devoted to the fostering and the voicing of Southern genius. Its watchword, which you may have seen on the cover, is 'Of, For, and By the South.' "

"But you wouldn't object to a Northern circulation, would you?" asked Thacker.

"I suppose," said the editor-colonel, "that it is customary to open the circulation lists to all. I do not know. I have nothing to do with the business affairs of the magazine. I was called upon to assume editorial control of it, and I have devoted to its conduct such poor literary talents as I may possess and whatever store of erudition I may have acquired.''

"Sure," said Thacker. "But a dollar is a dollar anywhere. North, South, or West—whether you're buying codfish, goober peas, or Rocky Ford cantaloupes. Now, I've been looking over your November number. I see one here on the desk. You don't mind running over it with me?

"Well, your leading article is all right. A good write-up of the cottonbelt with plenty of photographs is a winner any time. New York is always interested in the cotton crop. And this sensational account of the Hatfield-McCoy feud, by a schoolmate of a niece of the Governor of Kentucky, isn't such a bad idea. It happened so long ago that most people have forgotten it. Now, here's a poem three pages long called 'The Tyrant's Foot,' by Lorella Lascelles. I've pawed around a good deal over manuscripts, but I never saw her name on a rejection slip.''

"Miss Lascelles," said the editor, "is one of our most widely recognized Southern poetesses. She is closely related to the Alabama Lascelles family, and made with her own hands the silken Confederate banner that was presented to the governor of that state at his inauguration.''

"But why," persisted Thacker, "is the poem illustrated with a view of the M. & O. Railroad depot at Tuscaloosa?''

"The illustration," said the colonel, with dignity, "shows a corner of the fence surrounding the old homestead where Miss Lascelles was born.''

"All right," said Thacker, "I read the poem, but I couldn't tell whether it was about the depot or the battle of Bull Run. Now, here's a short story called 'Rosie's Temptation,' by Fosdyke Piggott. It's rotten. What is a Piggott, anyway?''

"Mr. Piggott," said the editor, "is a brother of the principal stockholder of the magazine.''

"All's right with the world—Piggott passes," said Thacker. "Well, this article on Arctic exploration and the one on tarpon fishing might go. But how about this write-up of the Atlanta, New Orleans, Nashville, and Savannah breweries? It seems to consist mainly of statistics about their output and the quality of their beer. What's the chip over the bug?"

"If I understand your figurative language," answered Colonel Telfair, "it is this: the article you refer to was handed to me by the owners of the magazine with instructions to publish it. The literary quality of it did not appeal to me. But, in a measure, I feel impelled to conform, in certain matters, to the wishes of the gentlemen who are interested in the financial side of *The Rose*."

"I see," said Thacker. "Next we have two pages of selections from 'Lalla Rookh,' by Thomas Moore. Now, what Federal prison did Moore escape from, or what's the name of the F.F.V. family that he carries as a handicap?"

"Moore was an Irish poet who died in 1852," said Colonel Telfair, pityingly. "He is a classic. I have been thinking of reprinting his translation of Anacreon serially in the magazine."

"Look out for the copyright laws," said Thacker, flippantly. "Who's Bessie Belleclair, who contributes the essay on the newly completed waterworks plant in Milledgeville?"

"The name, sir," said Colonel Telfair, "is the *nom de guerre* of Miss Elvira Simpkins. I have not the honor of knowing the lady; but her contribution was sent us by Congressman Brower, of her native state. Congressman Brower's mother was related to the Polks of Tennessee."

"Now see here, Colonel," said Thacker, throwing down the magazine, "this won't do. You can't successfully run a magazine for one particular section of the country. You've got to make a universal appeal. Look how the Northern publications have catered to the South and encouraged the Southern writers. And you've got to go far and wide for your contributors. You've got to buy stuff according to its quality, without any regard to the pedigree of the author. Now, I'll bet a quart of ink that this Southern parlor organ you've been running has never played a note that originated above Mason & Hamlin's line. Am I right?''

''I have carefully and conscientiously rejected all contributions from that section of the country—if I understand your figurative language aright,'' replied the colonel.

''All right. Now, I'll show you something.''

Thacker reached for his thick manila envelope and dumped a mass of typewritten manuscript on the editor's desk.

''Here's some truck,'' said he, ''that I paid cash for, and brought along with me.''

One by one he folded back the manuscripts and showed their first pages to the colonel.

''Here are four short stories by four of the highest priced authors in the United States—three of 'em living in New York, and one commuting. There's a special article on Vienna-bred society by Tom Vampson. Here's an Italian serial by Captain Jack—no—it's the other Crawford. Here are three separate exposés of city governments by Sniffings, and here's a dandy entitled 'What Women Carry in Dress-Suit Cases'—a Chicago newspaper woman hired herself out for five years as a lady's maid to get that information. And here's a Synopsis of Preceding Chapters of Hall Caine's new serial to appear next June. And here's a couple of pounds of *vers de société* that I got at a rate from the clever magazines. That's the stuff that people everywhere want. And now here's a write-up with photographs at the ages of four, twelve, twenty-two, and thirty of George B. McClellan. It's a prognostication. He's bound to be elected Mayor of New York. It'll make a big hit all over the country. He——''

''I beg your pardon,'' said Colonel Telfair, stiffening in his chair. ''What was the name?''

''Oh, I see,'' said Thacker, with half a grin. ''Yes, he's a son of the General. We'll pass that manuscript up.

But, if you'll excuse me, Colonel, it's a magazine we're trying to make go off—not the first gun at Fort Sumter. Now, here's a thing that's bound to get next to you. It's an original poem by James Whitcomb Riley. J. W. himself. You know what that means to a magazine. I won't tell you what I had to pay for that poem; but I'll tell you this—Riley can make more money writing with a fountain-pen than you or I can with one that lets the ink run. I'll read you the last two stanzas:

"Pa lays around 'n' loafs all day,
  'N' reads and makes us leave him
    be.
He lets me do just like I please.
  'N' when I'm bad he laughs at me,
'N' when I holler loud 'n' say
  Bad words 'n' then begin to tease
The cat, 'n' pa just smiles, ma's mad
  'N' gives me Jesse crost her knees.
  I always wondered why that
    wuz—
  I guess it's cause
    Pa never does.

" 'N' after all the lights are out
  I'm sorry 'bout it; so I creep
Out of my trundle bed to ma's
  'N' say I love her a whole heap,
'N' kiss her, 'n' I hug her tight.
  'N' it's too dark to see her eyes,
But every time I do I know
  She cries 'n' cries 'n' cries 'n' cries.
  I always wondered why that
    wuz—
  I guess it's cause
    Pa never does.

"That's the stuff," continued Thacker. "What do you think of that?"

"I am not unfamiliar with the works of Mr. Riley," said the colonel deliberately. "I believe he lives in Indiana. For the last ten years I have been somewhat of a literary recluse, and am familiar with nearly all the books in the Cedar Heights library. I am also of the opinion that a magazine should contain a certain amount of poetry. Many of the sweetest singers of the South have already contributed to the pages of *The Rose of Dixie*. I, myself, have thought of translating from the original for publication in its pages the works of the great Italian poet Tasso. Have you ever drunk from the fountain of this immortal poet's lines, Mr. Thacker?"

"Not even a demi-Tasso," said Thacker. "Now, let's come to the point, Colonel Telfair. I've already invested some money in this as a flyer. That bunch of manuscripts cost me $4,000. My object was to try a number of them in the next issue—I believe you make up less than a month ahead—and see what effect it has on the circulation. I believe that by printing the best stuff we can get in the North, South, East, or West we can make the magazine go. You have there the letter from the owning company asking you to cooperate with me in the plan. Let's chuck out some of this slush that you've been publishing just because the writers are related to the Skoopdoodles of Skoopdoodle County. Are you with me?"

"As long as I continue to be the editor of *The Rose*," said Colonel Telfair, with dignity, "I shall be its editor. But I desire also to conform to the wishes of its owners if I can do so conscientiously."

"That's the talk," said Thacker, briskly. "Now, how much of this stuff I've brought can we get into the January number? We want to begin right away."

"There is yet space in the January number," said the editor, "for about eight thousand words, roughly estimated."

"Great!" said Thacker. "It isn't much, but it'll give the readers some change from goobers, governors, and Gettysburg. I'll leave the selection of the stuff I brought to fill the space to you, as it's all good. I've got to run back to New York, and I'll be down again in a couple of weeks."

Colonel Telfair slowly swung his eye-glasses by their broad, black ribbon.

"The space in the January number that I referred to," said he, measuredly, "has been held open purposely, pending a decision that I have not yet made. A short time ago a contribution was submitted to *The Rose of Dixie* that is one of the most remarkable literary efforts that has ever come under my observation. None but a master mind and talent could have produced it. It would about fill the space that I have reserved for its possible use."

Thacker looked anxious.

"What kind of stuff is it?" he asked. "Eight thousand words sounds suspicious. The oldest families must have been collaborating. Is there going to be another secession?"

"The author of the article," continued the colonel, ignoring Thacker's allusions, "is a writer of some reputation. He has also distinguished himself in other ways. I do no feel at liberty to reveal to you his name—at least not until I have decided whether or not to accept his contribution."

"Well," said Thacker, nervously, "is it a continued story, or an account of the unveiling of the new town pump in Whitmire, South Carolina, or a revised list of General Lee's body-servants, or what?"

"You are disposed to be facetious," said Colonel Telfair, calmly. "The article is from the pen of a thinker, a philosopher, a lover of mankind, a student, and a rhetorician of high degree."

"It must have been written by a syndicate," said Thacker. "But, honestly, Colonel, you want to go slow. I don't know of any eight-thousand-word single doses of written matter that are read by anybody these days, except Supreme Court briefs and reports of murder trials. You haven't by any accident gotten hold of a copy of one of Daniel Webster's speeches, have you?"

Colonel Telfair swung a little in his chair and looked steadily from under his bushy eyebrows at the magazine promoter.

"Mr. Thacker," he said, gravely, "I am willing to segregate the somewhat crude expression of your sense of humor from the solicitude that your business investments undoubtedly have conferred upon you. But I must ask you to cease your jibes and derogatory comments upon the South and the Southern people. They, sir, will not be tolerated in the office of *The Rose of Dixie* for one moment. And before you proceed with more of your covert insinuations that I, the editor of this magazine, am not a competent judge of the merits of the matter submitted to its consideration, I beg that you will first present some evidence or proof that you are my superior in any way, shape, or form relative to the question in hand."

"Oh, come, Colonel," said Thacker, good-naturedly, "I didn't do anything like that to you. It sounds like an indictment by the fourth assistant attorney-general. Let's get back to business. What's this 8,000 to 1 shot about?"

"The article," said Colonel Telfair, acknowledging the apology by a slight bow, "covers a wide area of knowledge. It takes up theories and questions that have puzzled the world for centuries, and disposes of them logically and concisely. One by one it holds up to view the evils of the world, points out the way of eradicating them, and then conscientiously and in detail commends the good. There is hardly a phase of human life that it does not discuss wisely, calmly, and equitably. The great policies of governments, the duties of private citizens, the obligations of home life, ethics, morality—all these important subjects are handled with a calm wisdom and confidence that I must confess has captured my admiration."

"It must be a crackerjack," said Thacker, impressed.

"It is a great contribution to the world's wisdom," said the colonel. "The only doubt remaining in my mind as to the tremendous advantage it would be to us to give it publication in *The Rose of Dixie* is that I have not yet sufficient information about the author to give his work publicity in our magazine."

"I thought you said he is a distinguished man," said Thacker.

"He is," replied the colonel, "both in literary and in other more diversified and extraneous fields. But I am extremely careful about the matter that I accept for publication. My contributors are people of unquestionable repute and connections, which fact can be verified at any time. As I said, I am holding this article until I can acquire more information about its author. I do not know whether I will publish it or not. If I decide against it, I shall be much pleased, Mr. Thacker, to substitute the matter that you are leaving with me in its place.''

Thacker was somewhat at sea.

"I don't seem to gather," said he, "much about the gist of that inspired piece of literature. It sounds more like a dark horse than Pegasus to me.''

"It is a human document," said the colonel-editor, confidently, "from a man of great accomplishments who, in my opinion, has obtained a stronger grasp on the world and its outcomes than that of any man living to-day.''

Thacker rose to his feet excitedly.

"Say!" he said. "It isn't possible that you've cornered John D. Rockefeller's memoirs, is it? Don't tell me that all at once.''

"No, sir," said Colonel Telfair. "I am speaking of mentality and literature, not of the less worthy intricacies of trade.''

"Well, what's the trouble about running the article," asked Thacker, a little impatiently, "if the man's well known and has got the stuff?''

Colonel Telfair sighed.

"Mr. Thacker," said he, "for once I have been tempted. Nothing has yet appeared in *The Rose of Dixie* that has not been from the pen of one of its sons or daughters. I know little about the author of this article except that he has acquired prominence in a section of the country that has always been inimical to my heart and mind. But I recognize his genius; and, as I have told you, I have instituted an investigation of his personality. Perhaps it will be futile. But I shall pursue the inquiry. Until that is finished, I must leave open the question of filling the vacant space in our January number.''

Thacker arose to leave.

"All right, Colonel," he said, as cordially as he could. "You use your own judgment. If you've really got a scoop or something that will make 'em sit up, run it instead of my stuff. I'll drop in again in about two weeks. Good luck!''

Colonel Telfair and the magazine promoter shook hands.

Returning a fortnight later, Thacker dropped off a very rocky Pullman at Toombs City. He found the January number of the magazine made up and the forms closed.

The vacant space that had been yawning for type was filled by an article that was headed thus:

SECOND MESSAGE TO CONGRESS

Written for

THE ROSE OF DIXIE

BY

A Member of the Well-Known
BULLOCH FAMILY, OF GEORGIA
T. ROOSEVELT

Two Renegades

In the Gate City of the south the Confederate Veterans were reuniting; and I stood to see them march, beneath the tangled flags of the great conflict, to the hall of their oratory and commemoration.

While the irregular and halting line was passing I made onslaught upon it and dragged forth from the ranks my friend Barnard O'Keefe, who had no right to be there. For he was a Northerner born and bred; and what should he be doing hallooing for the Stars and Bars among those gray and moribund veterans? And why should he be trudging, with his shining, martial, humorous, broad face, among those warriors of a previous and alien generation?

I say I dragged him forth, and held him till the last hickory leg and waving goatee had stumbled past. And then I hustled him out of the crowd into a cool interior; for the Gate City was stirred that day, and the hand-organs wisely eliminated "Marching Through Georgia" from their repertories.

"Now, what deviltry are you up to?" I asked of O'Keefe when there were a table and things in glasses between us.

O'Keefe wiped his heated face and instigated a commotion among the floating ice in his glass before he chose to answer.

"I am assisting at the wake," said he, "of the only nation on earth that ever did me a good turn. As one gentleman to another, I am ratifying and celebrating the foreign policy of the late Jefferson Davis, as fine a

79

statesman as ever settled the financial question of a country. Equal ratio—that was his platform—a barrel of money for a barrel of flour—a pair of $20 bills for a pair of boots—a hatful of currency for a new hat—say, ain't that simple compared with W.J.B.'s little old oxidized plank?"

"What talk is this?" I asked. "Your financial digression is merely a subterfuge. Why were you marching in the ranks of the Confederate Veterans?"

"Because, my lad," answered O'Keefe, "the Confederate Government in its might and power interposed to protect and defend Barnard O'Keefe against immediate and dangerous assassination at the hands of a bloodthirsty foreign country after the United States of America had overruled his appeal for protection, and had instructed Private Secretary Cortelyou to reduce his estimate of the Republican majority for 1905 by one vote."

"Come, Barney," said I, "the Confederate States of America had been out of existence nearly forty years. You do not look older yourself. When was it that the deceased government exerted its foreign policy in your behalf?"

"Four months ago," said O'Keefe, promptly. "The infamous foreign power I alluded to is still staggering from the official blow dealt it by Mr. Davis's contraband aggregation of states. That's why you see me cakewalking with the ex-rebs to the illegitimate tune about 'simmonseels and cotton. I vote for the Great Father in Washington, but I am not going back on Mars' Jeff. You say the Confederacy has been dead forty years? Well, if it hadn't been for it, I'd have been breathing today with soul so dead I couldn't have whispered a single cussword about my native land. The O'Keefes are not overburdened with ingratitude."

I must have looked bewildered. "The war was over," I said vacantly, "in——"

O'Keefe laughed loudly, scattering my thoughts.

"Ask old Doc Millikin if the war is over!" he shouted,

hugely diverted.''Oh, no! Doc hasn't surrendered yet. And the Confederate States! Well, I just told you they bucked officially and solidly and nationally against a foreign government four months ago and kept me from being shot. Old Jeff's country stepped in and brought me off under its wing while Roosevelt was having a gunboat painted and waiting for the National Campaign Committee to look up whether I had ever scratched the ticket.''

"Isn't there a story in this, Barney?" I asked.

"No," said O'Keefe; "but I'll give you the facts. You know I went down to Panama when this irritation about a canal began. I thought I'd get in on the ground floor. I did, and had to sleep on it, and drink water with little zoos in it; so, of course, I got the Chagres fever. That was in a little town called San Juan on the coast.

"After I got the fever hard enough to kill a Port-au-Prince nigger, I had a relapse in the shape of Doc Millikin.

"There was a doctor to attend a sick man! If Doc Millikin had your case, he made the terrors of death seem like an invitation to a donkey-party. He had the bedside manners of a Piute medicine-man and the soothing presence of a dray loaded with iron bridge-girders. When he laid his hand on your fevered brow you felt like Cap John Smith just before Pocahontas went his bail.

"Well, this old medical outrage floated down to my shack when I sent for him. He was built like a shad, and his eyebrows was black, and his white whiskers trickled down from his chin like milk coming out of a sprinkling-pot. He had a nigger boy along carrying an old tomato-can full of calomel, and a saw.

"Doc felt my pulse, and then he began to mess up some calomel with an agricultural implement that belonged to the trowel class.

" 'I don't want any death-mask made yet, Doc,' I says, 'nor my liver put in a plaster-of-paris cast. I'm sick; and it's medicine I need, not frescoing.'

" 'You're a blame Yankee, ain't you?' asked Doc, going on mixing up his Portland cement.

" 'I'm from the North,' says I, 'but I'm a plain man, and don't care for mural decorations. When you get the Isthmus all asphalted over with that boll-weevil prescription, would you mind giving me a dose of painkiller, or a little strychnine on toast to ease up this feeling of unhealthiness that I have got?'

" 'They was all sassy, just like you,' says old Doc, 'but we lowered their temperature considerable. Yes, sir, I reckon we sent a good many of ye over to old *mortuis nisi bonum*. Look at Antietam and Bull Run and Seven Pines and around Nashville! There never was a battle where we didn't lick ye unless you was ten to our one. I knew you were a blame Yankee the minute I laid eyes on you.'

" 'Don't reopen the chasm, Doc,' I begs him. 'Any Yankeeness I may have is geographical; and, as far as I am concerned a Southerner is as good as a Filipino any day. I'm feeling too bad to argue. Let's have secession without misrepresentation, if you say so; but what I need is more laudanum and less Lundy's Lane. If you're mixing that compound gefloxide of gefloxicum for me, please fill my ears with it before you get around to the battle of Gettysburg, for there is a subject full of talk.'

"By this time Doc Millikin had thrown up a line of fortifications on square pieces of paper; and he says to me: 'Yank, take one of these powders every two hours. They won't kill you. I'll be around again about sundown to see if you're alive.'

"Old Doc's powders knocked the chagres. I stayed in San Juan, and got to knowing him better. He was from Mississippi, and the red-hottest Southerner that ever smelled mint. He made Stonewall Jackson and R. E. Lee look like Abolitionists. He had a family somewhere down near Yazoo City; but he stayed away from the States on account of an uncontrollable liking he had for the absence of a Yankee government. Him and me got as thick personally as the Emperor of Russia and the dove of peace, but sectionally we didn't amalgamate.

" 'Twas a beautiful system of medical practice introduced by old Doc into that isthmus of land. He'd take that bracketsaw and the mild chloride and his hypodermic, and treat anything from yellow fever to a personal friend.

"Besides his other liabilities Doc could play a flute for a minute or two. He was guilty of two tunes—'Dixie' and another one that was mighty close to the 'Suwanee River'—you might say one of its tributaries. He used to come down and sit with me while I was getting well, and aggrieve his flute and say unreconstructed things about the North. You'd have thought the smoke from the first gun at Fort Sumter was still floating around in the air.

"You know that was bout the time they staged them property revolutions down there, that wound up in the fifth act with the thrilling canal scene where Uncle Sam has nine curtain-calls holding Miss Panama by the hand, while the bloodhounds keep Senator Morgan treed up in a cocoanut-palm.

"That's the way it wound up; but at first it seemed as if Colombia was going to make Panama look like one of the $3.98 kind, with dents made in it in the factory, like they wear at North Beach fish fries. For mine, I played the strawhat crowd to win; and they gave me a colonel's commission over a brigade of twenty-seven men in the left wing and second joint of the insurgent army.

"The Colombian troops were awfully rude to us. One day when I had my brigade in a sandy spot, with its shoes off doing a battalion drill by squads, the Government army rushed from behind a bush at us, acting as noisy and disagreeable as they could.

"My troops enfiladed, left-faced, and left the spot. After enticing the enemy for three miles or so we struck a brierpatch and had to sit down. When we were ordered to throw up our toes and surrender we obeyed. Five of my best staff-officers fell, suffering extremely with stone-bruised heels.

"Then and there those Colombians took your friend

Barney, sir, stripped him of the insignia of his rank, consisting of a pair of brass knuckles and a canteen of rum, and dragged him before a military court. The presiding general went through the usual legal formalities that sometimes cause a case to hang on the calendar of a South American military court as long as ten minutes. He asked me my age, and then sentenced me to be shot.

"They woke up the court interpreter, an American named Jenks, who was in the rum business and vice versa, and told him to translate the verdict.

"Jenks stretched himself and took a morphine tablet.

" 'You've got to back up against th' 'dobe, old man,' says he to me. 'Three weeks, I believe, you get. Haven't got a chew of fine-cut on you, have you?'

" 'Translate that again, with footnotes and a glossary,' says I. 'I don't know whether I'm discharged, condemned, or handed over to the Gerry Society.'

" 'Oh,' says Jenks, 'don't you understand? You're to be stood up against a 'dobe wall and shot in two or three weeks—three, I think, they said.'

" 'Would you mind asking 'em which?' says I. 'A week don't amount to much after you are dead, but it seems a real nice long spell while you are alive.'

" 'It's two weeks,' says the interpreter, after inquiring in Spanish of the court. 'Shall I ask 'em again?'

" 'Let be,' says I. 'Let's have a stationary verdict. If I keep on appealing this way they'll have me shot about ten days before I was captured. No, I haven't got any fine-cut.'

"They sends me over to the *calaboza* with a detachment of colored postal-telegraph boys carrying Enfield rifles, and I am locked up in a kind of brick bakery. The temperature in there was just about the kind mentioned in the cooking recipes that call for a quick oven

"Then I gives a silver dollar to one of the guards to send for the United States consul. He comes around in pajamas with a pair of glasses in his nose and a dozen or two inside of him.

" 'I'm to be shot in two weeks,' says I. 'And although I've made a memorandum of it, I don't seem to get it off my mind. You want to call up Uncle Sam on the cable as quick as you can and get him all worked up about it. Have 'em send the *Kentucky* and the *Kearsarge* and the *Oregon* down right away. That'll be about enough battle-ships; but it wouldn't hurt to have a couple of cruisers and a torpedo-boat destroyer, too. And—say, if Dewey isn't busy, better have him come along on the fastest one of the fleet.'

" 'Now, see here, O'Keefe,' says the consul, getting the best of a hiccup, 'what do you want to bother the State Department about this matter for?'

" 'Didn't you hear me?' says I; 'I'm to be shot in two weeks. Did you think I said I was going to a lawn-party? And it wouldn't hurt if Roosevelt could get the Japs to send down the *Yellowyamstiskookum* or the *Ogotosingsing* or some other first-class cruiser to help. It would make me feel safer.'

" 'Now, what you want,' says the consul, 'is not to get excited. I'll send you over some chewing tobacco and some banana fritters when I go back. The United States can't interfere in this. You know you were caught insurging against the government, and you're subject to the laws of this country. Tell you the truth, I've had an intimation from the State Department—unofficially, of course—that whenever a soldier of fortune demands a fleet of gun-boats in a case of revolutionary *katzenjammer*, I should cut the cable, give him all the tobacco he wants, and after he's shot take his clothes, if they fit me, for part payment of my salary.'

" 'Consul,' says I to him, 'this is a serious question. You are representing Uncle Sam. This ain't any little international tomfoolery, like a universal peace congress or the christening of the *Shamrock IV*. I'm an American citizen and I demand protection. I demand the Mosquito fleet, and Schley, and the Atlantic squadron, and Bob

Evans, and General E. Byrd Grubb, and two or three protocols. What are you doing to do about it?'

" 'Nothing doing,' says the consul.

" 'Be off with you, then,' says I, out of patience with him, 'and send me Doc Millikin. Ask Doc to come and see me.'

"Doc comes and looks through the bars at me, surrounded by dirty soldiers, with even my shoes and canteen confiscated, and he looks mightily pleased.

" 'Hello, Yank,' says he, 'getting a little taste of Johnson's Island, now, ain't ye?'

" 'Doc,' says I, "I've just had an interview with the U.S. consul. I gather from his remarks that I might just as well have been caught selling suspenders in Kishineff under the name of Rosenstein as to be in my present condition. It seems that the only maritime aid I am to receive from the United States is some navy-plug to chew. Doc,' says I, 'can't you suspend hostilities on the slavery question long enough to do something for me?'

" 'It ain't been my habit,' Doc Millikin answers, 'to do any painless dentistry when I find a Yank cutting an eyetooth. So the Stars and Stripes ain't landing any marines to shell the huts of the Colombian cannibals, hey? Oh, say, can you see by the dawn's early light the star-spangled banner has fluked in the fight? What's the matter with the War Department, hey? It's a great thing to be a citizen of a gold-standard nation, ain't it?'

" 'Rub it in, Doc, all you want,' says I. 'I guess we're weak on foreign policy.'

" 'For a Yank,' says Doc, putting on his specs and talking more mild, you ain't so bad. If you had come from below the line I reckon I would have liked you right smart. Now since your country has gone back on you, you have to come to the old doctor whose cotton you burned and whose mules you stole and whose niggers you freed to help you. Ain't that so, Yank?'

" 'It is,' says I heartily, 'and let's have a diagnosis of the case right away, for in two weeks' time all you can do is to hold an autopsy and I do't want to be amputated if I can help it.'

" 'Now,' says Doc, business-like, 'it's easy enough for you to get out of this scrape. Money'll do it. You've got to pay a long string of 'em from General Pomposo down to this anthropoid ape guarding your door. About $10,000 will do the trick. Have you got the money?'

" 'Me?' says I. 'I've got one Chili dollar, two *real* pieces, and a *medio*.'

" 'Then if you've any last words, utter 'em,' says that old reb. 'The roster of your financial budget sounds quite much to me like the noise of a requiem.'

" 'Change the treatment,' says I. 'I admit that I'm short. Call a consultation or use radium or smuggle me in some saws or something.'

" 'Yank,' says Doc Millikin, 'I've a good notion to help you. There's only one government in the world that can get you out of this difficulty; and that's the Confederate States of America, the grandest nation that ever existed.'

"Just as you said to me I says to Doc: 'Why, the Confederacy ain't a nation. It's been absolved forty years ago.'

" 'That's a campaign lie,' says Doc. 'She's running along as solid as the Roman Empire. She's the only hope you've got. Now, you, being a Yank, have got to go through with some preliminary obsequies before you can get official aid. You've got to take the oath of allegiance to the Confederate Government. Then I'll guarantee she does all she can for you. What do you say, Yank?— it's your last chance.'

" 'If you're fooling with me, Doc,' I answered, 'you're no better than the United States. But as you say it's the last chance, hurry up and swear me. I always did like corn whisky and 'possum anyhow. I believe I'm half Southerner by nature. I'm willing to try the Ku Klux in place of khaki. Get brisk.'

"Doc Millikin thinks awhile, and then he offers me

this oath of allegiance to take without any kind of a chaser:

" 'I, Barnard O'Keefe, Yank, being of sound body but a Republican mind, hereby swear to transfer my fealty, respect, and allegiance to the Confederate States of America, and the Government thereof, in consideration of said government, through its official acts and powers, obtaining my freedom and release from confinement and sentence of death brought about by the exuberance of my Irish proclivities and my general pizenness as a Yank.'

"I repeated these words after Doc, but they seemed to me a kind of hocus-pocus; and I don't believe any life-insurance company in the country would have issued me a policy on the strength of 'em.

"Doc went away saying he would communicate with his government immediately.

"Say—you can imagine how I felt—me to be shot in two weeks and my only hope for help being a government that's been dead so long that it isn't even remembered except on Decoration Day and when Joe Wheeler signs the voucher for his pay-check. But it was all there was in sight; and somehow I thought Doc Millikin had something up his old alpaca sleeve that wasn't all foolishness.

"Around to the jail comes old Doc again in about a week. I was flea-bitten, a mite sarcastic, and fundamentally hungry.

" 'Any Confederate ironclads in the offing?' I asks. 'Do you notice any sounds resembling the approach of Jeb Stewart's cavalry overland or Stonewall Jackson sneaking up in the rear? If you do, I wish you'd say so.'

" 'It's too soon yet for help to come,' says Doc.

" 'The sooner the better,' says I. 'I don't care if it gets in fully fifteen minutes before I am shot; and if you happen to lay eyes on Beauregard or Albert Sidney Johnson or any of the relief corps, wig-wag 'em to hike along.'

" 'There's been no answer received yet,' says Doc.

" 'Don't forget,' says I, 'that there's only four days more. I don't know how you propose to work this thing, Doc,' I says to him; 'but it seems to me I'd sleep better if you had got a government that was alive and on the map—like Afghanistan or Great Britain, or old man Kruger's kingdom, to take this matter up. I don't mean any disrespect to your Confederate States, but I can't help feeling that my chances of being pulled out of this scrape was decidedly weakened when General Lee surrendered.'

" 'It's your only chance,' said Doc; 'don't quarrel with it. What did your own country do for you?'

"It was only two days before the morning I was to be shot when Doc Millikin came around again.

" 'All right, Yank,' says he. 'Help's come. The Confederate States of America is going to apply for your release. The representatives of the government arrived on a fruit-steamer last night.'

" 'Bully!' says I—'bully for you, Doc! I suppose it's marines with a Gatling. I'm going to love your country all I can for this.'

" 'Negotiations,' says old Doc, 'will be opened between the two governments at once. You will know later on to-day if they are successful.'

"About four in the afternoon a soldier in red trousers brings a paper round to the jail, and they unlocks the door and I walks out. The guard at the door bows and I bows, and I steps into the grass and wades around to Doc Millikin's shack.

"Doc was sitting in his hammock playing 'Dixie,' soft and low and out of tune, on his flute. I interrupted him at 'Look away! look away!' and shook his hand for five minutes.

" 'I never thought,' says Doc, taking a chew fretfully, 'that I'd ever try to save any blame Yank's life. But, Mr. O'Keefe, I don't see but what you are entitled to be considered part human, anyhow. I never thought Yanks had any of the rudiments of decorum and laudability

about them. I reckon I might have been too aggregative
in my tabulation. But it ain't me you want to thank—it's
the Confederate States of America.'

" 'And I'm much obliged to 'em,' says I. 'It's a poor
man that wouldn't be patriotic with a country that's saved
his life. I'll drink to the Stars and Bars whenever there's
a flag-staff and a glass convenient. But where,' says I,
'are the rescuing troops? If there was a gun fired or a
shell burst, I didn't hear it.'

"Doc Millikin raises up and points out the window
with his flute at the banana-steamer loading with fruit.

" 'Yank,' says he, 'there's a steamer that's going to
sail in the morning. If I was you, I'd sail on it. The
Confederate Government's done all it can for you. There
wasn't a gun fired. The negotiations was carried on
secretly between the two nations by the purser of that
steamer. I got him to do it because I didn't want to
appear in it. Twelve thousand dollars was paid to the
officials in bribes to let you go.'

" 'Man!' says I, sitting down hard—'twelve thousand—
how will I ever—who could have—where did the money
come from?'

" 'Yazoo City,' says Doc Millikin; 'I've got a little bit
saved up there. Two barrels full. It looks good to these
Colombians. 'Twas Confederate money, every dollar of
it. Now do you see why you'd better leave before they
try to pass some of it on an expert?'

" 'I do,' says I.

" 'Now, let's hear you give the password,' says Doc
Millikin.

" 'Hurrah for Jeff Davis!' says I.

" 'Correct,' says Doc. 'And let me tell you something. The next tune I learn on my flute is going to be
"Yankee Doodle." I reckon there's some Yanks that are
not so pizen. Or, if you was me, would you try "The
Red, White, and Blue"?' "

The Skylight Room

First Mrs. Parker would show you the double parlors. You would not dare to interrupt her description of their advantages and of the merits of the gentleman who had occupied them for eight years. Then you would manage to stammer forth the confession that you were neither a doctor nor a dentist. Mrs. Parker's manner of receiving the admission was such that you could never afterward entertain the same feeling toward your parents, who had neglected to train you up in one of the professions that fitted Mrs. Parker's parlors.

Next you ascended one flight of stairs and looked at the second-floor-back at $8. Convinced by her second-floor manner that it was worth the $12 that Mr. Toosenberry always paid for it until he left to take charge of his brother's orange plantation in Florida near Palm Beach, where Mrs. McIntyre always spent the winters that had the double front room with private bath, you managed to babble that you wanted something still cheaper.

If you survived Mrs. Parker's scorn, you were taken to look at Mr. Skidder's large hall room on the third floor. Mr. Skidder's room was not vacant. He wrote plays and smoked cigarettes in it all day long. But every room-hunter was made to visit his room to admire the lambrequins. After each visit, Mr. Skidder, from the fright caused by possible eviction, would pay something on his rent.

Then—oh, then—if you still stood on one foot, with your hot hand clutching the three moist dollars in your pocket, and hoarsely proclaimed your hideous and culpable poverty, nevermore would Mrs. Parker be cicerone of yours. She would honk loudly the word "Clara," she would show you her back, and march downstairs. Then Clara, the colored maid, would escort you up the carpeted ladder that served for the fourth flight, and show you the Skylight Room. It occupied 7 x 8 feet of floor space in the middle of the hall. On each side of it was a dark lumber closet or storeroom.

In it was an iron cot, a washstand and a chair. A shelf was the dresser. Its four bare walls seemed to close in upon you like the sides of a coffin. Your hand crept to your throat, you gasped, you looked up as from a well—and breathed once more. Through the glass of the little skylight you saw a square of blue infinity.

"Two dollars, suh," Clara would say in her half-contemptuous, half-Tuskegeenial tones.

One day Miss Leeson came hunting for a room. She carried a typewriter made to be lugged around by a much larger lady. She was a very little girl, with eyes and hair that had kept on growing after she had stopped and that always looked as if they were saying: "Goodness me! Why didn't you keep up with us?"

Mrs. Parker showed her the double parlors. "In this closet," she said, "one could keep a skeleton or anæsthetic or coal——"

"But I am neither a doctor nor a dentist," said Miss Leeson, with a shiver.

Mrs. Parker gave her the incredulous, pitying, sneering, icy stare that she kept for those who failed to qualify as doctors or dentists, and led the way to the second-floor-back.

"Eight dollars?" said Miss Leeson. "Dear me! I'm not Hetty if I do look green. I'm just a poor little working girl. Show me something higher and lower."

Mr. Skidder jumped and strewed the floor with cigarette stubs at the rap on his door.

"Excuse me, Mr. Skidder," said Mrs. Parker, with

her demon's smile at his pale looks. "I didn't know you were in. I asked the lady to have a look at your lambrequins."

"They're too lovely for anything," said Miss Leeson, smiling in exactly the way the angels do.

After they had gone, Mr. Skidder got very busy erasing the tall, black-haired heroine from his latest (unproduced) play and inserted a small, roguish one with heavy, bright hair and vivacious features.

"Anna Held'll jump at it," said Mr. Skidder to himself, putting his feet up against the lambrequins and disappearing in a cloud of smoke like an aerial cuttlefish.

Presently the tocsin call of "Clara!" sounded to the world the state of Miss Leeson's purse. A dark goblin seized her, mounted a Stygian stairway, thrust her into a vault with a glimmer of light in its top and muttered the menacing and cabalistic words "two dollars!"

"I'll take it!" sighed Miss Leeson, sinking down upon the squeaky iron bed.

Every day Miss Leeson went out to work. At night she brought home papers with handwriting on them and made copies with her typewriter. Sometimes she had no work at night, and then she would sit on the steps of the high stoop with the other roomers. Miss Leeson was not intended for a skylight room when the plans were drawn for her creation. She was gay-hearted and full of tender, whimsical fancies. Once she let Mr. Skidder read to her three acts of his great (unpublished) comedy, "It's No Kid; or, The Heir of the Subway."

There was rejoicing among the gentlemen roomers whenever Miss Leeson had time to sit on the steps for an hour or two. But Miss Longnecker, the tall blonde who taught in a public school and said, "Well, really!" to everything you said, sat on the top step and sniffed. And Miss Dorn, who shot at the moving ducks at Coney every Sunday and worked in a department store, sat on the bottom step and sniffed. Miss Leeson sat on the middle step and the men would quickly group around her.

Especially Mr. Skidder, who had cast her in his mind
for the star part in a private, romantic (unspoken) drama
in real life. And especially Mr. Hoover, who was forty-
five, fat, flush and foolish. And especially very young
Mr. Evans, who set up a hollow cough to induce her to
ask him to leave off cigarettes. The men voted her "the
funniest and jolliest ever," but the sniffs on the top step
and the lower step were implacable.

I pray you let the drama halt while chorus stalks to the
footlights and drops an epicedian tear upon the fatness of
Mr. Hoover. Tune the pipes to the tragedy of tallow, the
bane of bulk, the calamity of corpulence. Tried out,
Falstaff might have rendered more romance to the ton
than would have Romeo's rickety ribs to the ounce. A
lover may sigh, but he must not puff. To the train of
Momus are the fat men remanded. In vain beats the
faithfullest heart above a 52-inch belt. Avaunt, Hoover!
Hoover, forty-five, flush and foolish, might carry off
Helen herself; Hoover, forty-five, flush, foolish and fat is
meat for perdition. There was never a chance for you,
Hoover.

As Mrs. Parker's roomers sat thus one summer's evening, Miss Leeson looked up into the firmament and
cried with her little gay laugh:

"Why, there's Billy Jackson! I can see him from down
here, too."

All looked up—some at the windows of skyscrapers,
some casting about for an airship, Jackson-guided.

"It's that star," explained Miss Leeson, pointing with
a tiny finger. "Not the big one that twinkles—the steady
blue one near it. I can see it every night through my
skylight. I named it Billy Jackson."

"Well, really!" said Miss Longnecker. "I didn't know
you were an astronomer, Miss Leeson."

"Oh, yes," said the small star gazer, "I know as

much as any of them about the style of sleeves they're going to wear next fall in Mars."

"Well, really!" said Miss Longnecker. "That star you refer to is Gamma, of the constellation Cassiopeia. It is nearly of the second magnitude, and its meridian passage is——"

"Oh," said the very young Mr. Evans, "I think Billy Jackson is a much better name for it."

"Same here," said Mr. Hoover, loudly breathing defiance to Miss Longnecker. "I think Miss Leeson has just as much right to name stars as any of those old astrologers had."

"Well, really!" said Miss Longnecker.

"I wonder whether it's a shooting star," remarked Miss Dorn. "I hit nine ducks and a rabbit out of ten in the gallery at Coney Sunday."

"He doesn't show up very well from down here," said Miss Leeson. "You ought to see him from my room. You know you can see stars even in the daytime from the bottom of a well. At night my room is like the shaft of a coal mine, and it makes Billy Jackson look like the big diamond pin that Night fastens her kimono with."

There came a time after that when Miss Leeson brought no formidable papers home to copy. And when she went out in the morning, instead of working, she went from office to office and let her heart melt away in the drip of cold refusals transmitted through insolent office boys. This went on.

There came an evening when she wearily climbed Mrs. Parker's stoop at the hour when she always returned from her dinner at the restaurant. But she had had no dinner.

As she stepped into the hall Mr. Hoover met her and seized his chance. He asked her to marry him, and his fatness hovered above her like an avalanche. She dodged, and caught the balustrade. He tried for her hand, and she raised it and smote him weakly in the face. Step by step she went up, dragging herself by the railing. She passed

Mr. Skidder's door as he was red-inking a stage direction for Myrtle Delorme (Miss Leeson) in his (unaccepted) comedy, to "pirouette across stage front from L to the side of the Count." Up the carpeted ladder she crawled at last and opened the door of the skylight room.

She was too weak to light the lamp or to undress. She fell upon the iron cot, her fragile body scarcely hollowing the worn springs. And in that Erebus of a room she slowly raised her heavy eyelids, and smiled.

For Billy Jackson was shining down on her, calm and bright and constant through the skylight. There was no world about her. She was sunk in a pit of blackness, with but that small square of pallid light framing the star that she had so whimsically and oh, so ineffectually, named. Miss Longnecker must be right: It was Gamma, of the constellation Cassiopeia, and not Billy Jackson. And yet she could not let it be Gamma.

As she lay on her back, she tried twice to raise her arm. The third time she got two thin fingers to her lips and blew a kiss out of the black pit to Billy Jackson. Her arm fell back limply.

"Good-bye, Billy," she murmured, faintly. "You're millions of miles away and you won't even twinkle once. But you kept where I could see you most of the time up there when there wasn't anything else but darkness to look at, didn't you? . . . Millions of miles. . . . Good-bye, Billy Jackson."

Clara, the colored maid, found the door locked at 10 the next day, and they forced it open. Vinegar, and the slapping of wrists and burnt feathers proving of no avail, some one ran to 'phone for an ambulance.

In due time it backed up to the door with much gong-clanging, and the capable young medico, in his white linen coat, ready, active, confident, with his smooth face half debonair, half grim, danced up the steps.

"Ambulance call to 49," he said, briefly. "What's the trouble?"

"Oh, yes, doctor," sniffed Mrs. Parker, as though her

trouble that there should be trouble in the house was the greater. "I can't think what can be the matter with her. Nothing we could do would bring her to. It's a young woman, a Miss Elsie—yes, a Miss Elsie Leeson. Never before in my house——"

"What room?" cried the doctor in a terrible voice, to which Mrs. Parker was a stranger.

"The skylight room. It——"

Evidently the ambulance doctor was familiar with the location of skylight rooms. He was gone up the stairs, four at a time. Mrs. Parker followed slowly, as her dignity demanded.

On the first landing she met him coming back bearing the astronomer in his arms. He stopped and let loose the practised scalpel of his tongue, not loudly. Gradually Mrs. Parker crumpled as a stiff garment that slips down from a nail. Ever afterwards there remained crumples in her mind and body. Sometimes her curious roomers would ask her what the doctor said to her.

"Let that be," she would answer. "If I can get forgiveness for having heard it I will be satisfied."

The ambulance physician strode with his burden through the pack of hounds that follow the curiosity chase, and even they fell back along the sidewalk abashed, for his face was that of one who bears his own dead.

They noticed that he did not lay down upon the bed prepared for it in the ambulance the form that he carried, and all that he said was: "Drive like h—l, Wilson," to the driver.

That is all. Is it a story? In the next morning's paper I saw a little news item, and the last sentence of it may help you (as it helped me) to weld the incidents together.

It recounted the reception into Bellevue Hospital of a young woman who had been removed from No. 49 East——Street, suffering from debility induced by starvation. It concluded with these words:

"Dr. William Jackson, the ambulance physician who attended the case says the patient will recover."

The Cop and
the Anthem

On his bench in Madison Square Soapy moved uneasily. When wild geese honk high of nights, and when women without sealskin coats grow kind to their husbands, and when Soapy moves uneasily on his bench in the park, you may know that winter is near at hand.

A dead leaf fell in Soapy's lap. That was Jack Frost's card. Jack is kind to the regular denizens of Madison Square, and gives fair warning of his annual call. At the corners of four streets he hands his pasteboard to the North Wind, footman of the mansion of All Outdoors, so that the inhabitants thereof may make ready.

Soapy's mind became cognizant of the fact that the time had come for him to resolve himself into a singular Committee of Ways and Means to provide against the coming rigor. And therefore he moved uneasily on his bench.

The hibernatorial ambitions of Soapy were not of the highest. In them were no considerations of Mediterranean cruises, of soporific Southern skies or drifting in the Vesuvian Bay. Three months on the Island was what his soul craved. Three months of assured board and bed and congenial company, safe from Boreas and bluecoats, seemed to Soapy the essence of things desirable.

For years the hospitable Blackwell's had been his winter quarters. Just as his more fortunate fellow New Yorkers had bought their tickets to Palm Beach and the Riviera each winter, so Soapy had made his humble arrangements for his annual hegira to the Island. And now the time was come. On the previous night three Sabbath newspapers, distributed beneath his coat, about his ankles and over his lap, had failed to repulse the cold as he slept on his bench near the spurting fountain in the ancient square. So the Island loomed big and timely in Soapy's mind. He scorned the provisions made in the name of charity for the city's dependents. In Soapy's opinion the Law was more benign than Philanthropy. There was an endless round of institutions, municipal and eleemosynary, on which he might set out and receive lodging and food accordant with the simple life. But to one of Soapy's proud spirit the gifts of charity are encumbered. If not in coin you must pay in humiliation of spirit for every benefit received at the hands of philanthropy. As Cæsar had his Brutus, every bed of charity must have its toll of a bath, every loaf of bread its compensation of a private and personal inquisition. Wherefore it is better to be a guest of the law, which, though conducted by rules, does not meddle unduly with a gentleman's private affairs.

Soapy, having decided to go to the Island, at once set about accomplishing his desire. There were many easy ways of doing this. The pleasantest was to dine luxuriously at some expensive restaurant; and then, after declaring insolvency, be handed over quietly and without uproar to a policeman. An accommodating magistrate would do the rest.

Soapy left his bench and strolled out of the square and across the level sea of asphalt, where Broadway and Fifth Avenue flow together. Up Broadway he turned, and halted at a glittering café, where are gathered together nightly the choicest products of the grape, the silkworm, and the protoplasm.

Soapy had confidence in himself from the lowest button of his vest upward. He was shaven, and his coat was decent and his neat black, ready-tied four-in-hand had been presented to him by a lady missionary on Thanksgiving Day. If he could reach a table in the restaurant unsuspected success would be his. The portion of him that would show above the table would raise no doubt in the waiter's mind. A roasted mallard duck, thought Soapy, would be about the thing—with a bottle of Chablis, and then Camembert, a demi-tasse and a cigar. One dollar for the cigar would be enough. The total would not be so high as to call forth any supreme manifestation of revenge from the café management; and yet the meat would leave him filled and happy for the journey to his winter refuge.

But as Soapy set foot inside the restaurant door the head waiter's eye fell upon his frayed trousers and decadent shoes. Strong and ready hands turned him about and conveyed him in silence and haste to the sidewalk and averted the ignoble fate of the menaced mallard.

Soapy turned off Broadway. It seemed that his route to the coveted Island was not to be an epicurean one. Some other way of entering limbo must be thought of.

At a corner of Sixth Avenue electric lights and cunningly displayed wares behind plate-glass made a shop window conspicuous. Soapy took a cobblestone and dashed it through the glass. People came running around the corner, a policeman in the lead. Soapy stood still, with his hands in his pockets, and smiled at the sight of brass buttons.

"Where's the man that done that?" inquired the officer, excitedly.

"Don't you figure out that I might have had something to do with it?" said Soapy, not without sarcasm, but friendly, as one greets good fortune.

The policeman's mind refused to accept Soapy even as a clue. Men who smash windows do not remain to parley with the law's minions. They take to their heels. The policeman saw a man halfway down the block running to catch a car. With drawn club he joined in the pursuit. Soapy, with disgust in his heart, loafed along, twice unsuccessful.

On the opposite side of the street was a restaurant of no great pretensions. It catered to large appetites and modest purses. Its crockery and atmosphere were thick; its soup and napery thin. Into this place Soapy took his accusive shoes and telltale trousers without challenge. At a table he sat and consumed beefsteak, flapjacks, doughnuts and pie. And then to the waiter he betrayed the fact that the minutest coin and himself were strangers.

"Now, get busy and call a cop," said Soapy. "And don't keep a gentleman waiting."

"No cop for youse," said the waiter, with a voice like butter cakes and an eye like the cherry in a Manhattan cocktail. "Hey, Con!"

Neatly upon his left ear on the callous pavement two waiters pitched Soapy. He arose joint by joint, as a carpenter's rule opens, and beat the dust from his clothes. Arrest seemed but a rosy dream. The Island seemed very far away. A policeman who stood before a drug store two doors away laughed and walked down the street.

Five blocks Soapy travelled before his courage permitted him to woo capture again. This time the opportunity presented what he fatuously termed to himself a "cinch." A young woman of a modest and pleasing guise was standing before a show window gazing with sprightly interest at its display of shaving mugs and ink-stands, and two yards from the window a large policeman of severe demeanor leaned against a water plug.

It was Soapy's design to assume the rôle of the despicable and execrated "masher." The refined and elegant appearance of his victim and the contiguity of the conscientious cop encouraged him to believe that he would soon feel the pleasant official clutch upon his arm that would insure his winter quarters on the right little, tight little isle.

Soapy straightened the lady missionary's ready-made tie, dragged his shrinking cuffs into the open, set his hat at a killing cant and sidled toward the young woman. He made eyes at her, was taken with sudden coughs and "hems," smiled, smirked and went brazenly through the impudent and contemptible litany of the "masher." With half an eye Soapy saw that the policeman was watching him fixedly. The young woman moved away a few steps, and again bestowed her absorbed attention upon the shaving mugs. Soapy followed, boldly stepping to her side, raised his hat and said:

"Ah there, Bedelia! Don't you want to come and play in my yard?"

The policeman was still looking. The persecuted young woman had but to beckon a finger and Soapy would be practically en route for his insular haven. Already he imagined he could feel the cozy warmth of the station-house. The young woman faced him and, stretching out a hand, caught Soapy's coat sleeve.

"Sure, Mike," she said, joyfully, "if you'll blow me to a pail of suds. I'd have spoke to you sooner, but the cop was watching."

With the young woman playing the clinging ivy to his oak Soapy walked past the policeman overcome with gloom. He seemed doomed to liberty.

At the next corner he shook off his companion and ran. He halted in the district where by night are found the lightest streets, hearts, vows and librettos. Women in furs and men in greatcoats moved gaily in the wintry air. A sudden fear seized Soapy that some dreadful enchantment had rendered him immune to arrest. The thought brought a little of panic upon it, and when he came upon another policeman lounging grandly in front of a transplendent theatre he caught at the immediate straw of "disorderly conduct."

On the sidewalk Soapy began to yell drunken gibberish at the top of his harsh voice. He danced, howled, raved, and otherwise disturbed the welkin.

The policeman twirled his club, turned his back to Soapy and remarked to a citizen.

" 'Tis one of them Yale lads celebratin' the goose egg

they give to the Hartford College. Noisy; but no harm. We've instructions to lave them be."

Disconsolate, Soapy ceased his unavailing racket. Would never a policeman lay hands on him? In his fancy the Island seemed an unattainable Arcadia. He buttoned his thin coat against the chilling wind.

In a cigar store he saw a well-dressed man lighting a cigar at a swinging light. His silk umbrella he had set by the door on entering. Soapy stepped inside, secured the umbrella and sauntered off with it slowly. The man at the cigar light followed hastily.

"My umbrella," he said, sternly.

"Oh, is it?" sneered Soapy, adding insult to petit larceny. "Well, why don't you call a policeman? I took it. Your umbrella! Why don't you call a cop? There stands one on the corner."

The umbrella owner slowed his steps. Soapy did likewise, with a presentiment that luck would again run against him. The policeman looked at the two curiously.

"Of course," said the umbrella man—"that is—well, you know how these mistakes occur—I—if it's your umbrella I hope you'll excuse me—I picked it up this morning in a restaurant—If you recognize it as yours, why—I hope you'll——"

"Of course it's mine," said Soapy, viciously.

The ex-umbrella man retreated. The policeman hurried to assist a tall blonde in an opera cloak across the street in front of a street car that was approaching two blocks away.

Soapy walked eastward through a street damaged by improvements. He hurled the umbrella wrathfully into an excavation. He muttered against the men who wear helmets and carry clubs. Because he wanted to fall into their clutches, they seemed to regard him as a king who could do no wrong.

At length Soapy reached one of the avenues to the east where the glitter and turmoil was but faint. He set his face down this toward Madison Square, for the homing instinct survives even when the home is a park bench.

But on an unusually quiet corner Soapy came to a standstill. Here was an old church, quaint and rambling and gabled. Through one violet-stained window a soft light glowed, where, no doubt, the organist loitered over the keys, making sure of his mastery of the coming Sabbath anthem. For there drifted out to Soapy's ears sweet music that caught and held him transfixed against the convolutions of the iron fence.

The moon was above, lustrous and serene; vehicles and pedestrians were few; sparrows twittered sleepily in the eaves—for a little while the scene might have been a country churchyard. And the anthem that the organist played cemented Soapy to the iron fence, for he had known it well in the days when his life contained such things as mothers and roses and ambitions and friends and immaculate thoughts and collars.

The conjunction of Soapy's receptive state of mind and the influences about the old church wrought a sudden and wonderful change in his soul. He viewed with swift horror the pit into which he had tumbled, the degraded days, unworthy desires, dead hopes, wrecked faculties and base motives that made up his existence.

And also in a moment his heart responded thrillingly to this novel mood. An instantaneous and strong impulse moved him to battle with his desperate fate. He would pull himself out of the mire; he would make a man of himself again; he would conquer the evil that had taken possession of him. There was time; he was comparatively young yet; he would resurrect his old eager ambitions and pursue them without faltering. Those solemn but sweet organ notes had set up a revolution in him. To-morrow he would go into the roaring downtown district and find work. A fur importer had once offered him a place as driver. He would find him to-morrow and ask for the position. He would be somebody in the world. He would——

Soapy felt a hand laid on his arm. He looked quickly around into the broad face of a policeman.

"What are you doin' here?" asked the officer.

"Nothin'," said Soapy.

"Then come along," said the policeman.

"Three months on the Island," said the Magistrate in the Police Court the next morning.

Memoirs of a Yellow Dog

I don't suppose it will knock any of you people off your perch to read a contribution from an animal. Mr. Kipling and a good many others have demonstrated the fact that animals can express themselves in remunerative English, and no magazine goes to press nowadays without an animal story in it, except the old-style monthlies that are still running pictures of Bryan and the Mont Pelée horror.

But you needn't look for any stuck-up literature in my piece, such as Bearoo, the bear, and Snakoo, the snake, and Tammanoo, the tiger, talk in the jungle books. A yellow dog that's spent most of his life in a cheap New York flat, sleeping in a corner on an old sateen underskirt (the one she spilled port wine on at the Lady Longshoremen's banquet), mustn't be expected to perform any tricks with the art of speech.

I was born a yellow pup; date, locality, pedigree and weight unknown. The first thing I can recollect, an old woman had me in a basket at Broadway and Twenty-third trying to sell me to a fat lady. Old Mother Hubbard was boosting me to beat the band as a genuine Pomeranian-Hambletonian-Red-Irish-Cochin-China-Stoke-Poges fox terrier. The fat lady chased a V around among the samples of grosgrain flannelette in her shopping bag till she cornered it, and gave up. From that moment I was a pet—a mamma's own wootsey squidlums. Say, gentle reader, did you ever have a 200-pound woman breathing a flavor of Camembert cheese and Peau d'Espagne pick you up and wallop her nose all over you, remarking all the time in an Emma Eames tone of voice: "Oh, oo's um oodlum, doodlum, woodlum, toodlum, bitsy-witsy skoodlums?"

From pedigreed yellow pup I grew up to be an anonymous yellow cur looking like a cross between an Angora cat and a box of lemons. But my mistress never tumbled. She thought that the two primeval pups that Noah chased into the ark were but a collateral branch of my ancestors. It took two policemen to keep her from entering me at the Madison Square Garden for the Siberian bloodhound prize.

I'll tell you about that flat. The house was the ordinary thing in New York, paved with Parian marble in the entrance hall and cobblestones above the first floor. Our flat was three—well, not flights—climbs up. My mistress rented it unfurnished, and put in the regular things—1903 antique upholstered parlor set, oil chromo of geishas in a Harlem tea house, rubber plant and husband.

By Sirius! there was a biped I felt sorry for. He was a little man with sandy hair and whiskers a good deal like mine. Henpecked?—well, toucans and flamingoes and pelicans all had their bills in him. He wiped the dishes and listened to my mistress tell about the cheap, ragged things the lady with the squirrel-skin coat on the second floor hung out on her line to dry. And every evening while she was getting supper she made him take me out on the end of a string for a walk.

If men knew how women pass the time when they are alone they'd never marry. Laura Lean Jibbey, peanut brittle, a little almond cream on the neck muscles, dishes unwashed, half an hour's talk with the iceman, reading a package of old letters, a couple of pickles and two bottles of malt extract, one hour peeking through a hole in the window shade into the flat across the airshaft—that's about all there is to it. Twenty minutes before time for him to come home from work she straightens up the house, fixes her rat so it won't show, and gets out a lot of sewing for a ten-minute bluff.

I led a dog's life in that flat. 'Most all day I lay there in my corner watching that fat woman kill time. I slept sometimes and had pipe dreams about being out chasing cats into basements and growling at old ladies with black mittens, as a dog was intended to do. Then she would pounce upon me with a lot of that drivelling poodle palaver and kiss me on the nose—but what could I do? A dog can't chew cloves.

I began to feel sorry for Hubby, dog my cats if I didn't. We looked so much alike that people noticed it when we went out; so we shook the streets that Morgan's cab drives down, and took to climbing the piles of last December's snow on the streets where cheap people live.

One evening when we were thus promenading, and I was trying to look like a prize St. Bernard, and the old man was trying to look like he wouldn't have murdered the first organ-grinder he heard play Mendelssohn's wedding-march, I looked up at him and said, in my way:

"What are you looking so sour about, you oakum trimmed lobster? She don't kiss you. You don't have to sit on her lap and listen to talk that would make the book of a musical comedy sound like the maxims of Epictetus. You ought to be thankful you're not a dog. Brace up, Benedick, and bid the blues begone."

The matrimonial mishap looked down at me with almost canine intelligence in his face.

"Why, doggie," says he, "good doggie. You almost look like you could speak. What is it, doggie—Cats."

Cats! Could speak!

But, of course, he couldn't understand. Humans were denied the speech of animals.; The only common ground of communication upon which dogs and men can get together is in fiction.

In the flat across the hall from us lived a lady with a black-and-tan terrier. Her husband strung it and took it out every evening, but he always came home cheerful and whistling. One day I touched noses with the black-and-tan in the hall, and I struck him for an elucidation.

"See here, Wiggle-and-Skip," I says, "you know that it ain't the nature of a real man to play dry nurse to a dog in public. I never saw one leashed to a bow-wow yet that didn't look like he'd like to lick every other man that looked at him. But your boss comes in every day as perky and set up as an amateur prestidigitator doing the egg trick. How does he do it? Don't tell me he likes it."

"Him?" says the black-and-tan. "Why, he uses Nature's Own Remedy. He gets spifflicated. At first when we go out he's as shy as the man on the steamer who would rather play pedro when they make 'em all jackpots. By the time we've been in eight saloons he don't care whether the thing on the end of his line is a dog or a catfish. I've lost two inches of my tail trying to sidestep those swinging doors."

The pointer I got from that terrier—vaudeville please copy—set me to thinking.

One evening about 6 o'clock my mistress ordered him to get busy and do the ozone act for Lovey. I have concealed it until now, but that is what she called me. The black-and-tan was called "Tweetness." I consider that I have the bulge on him as far as you could chase a rabbit. Still "Lovey" is something of a nomenclatural tin can on the tail of one's self-respect.

At a quiet place on a safe street I tightened the line of my custodian in front of an attractive, refined saloon. I made a dead-ahead scramble for the doors, whining like a dog in the press despatches that lets the family know that little Alice is bogged while gathering lilies in the brook.

"Why, darn my eyes," says the old man, with a grin; "darn my eyes if the saffron-colored son of a seltzer lemonade ain't asking me in to take a drink. Lemme see—how long's it been since I saved shoe leather by keeping one foot on the footrest? I believe I'll——"

I knew I had him. Hot Scotches he took, sitting at a table. For an hour he kept the Campbells coming. I sat by his side rapping for the waiter with my tail, and eating free lunch such as mamma in her flat never equalled with her homemade truck bought at a delicatessen store eight minutes before papa comes home.

When the products of Scotland were all exhausted except the rye bread the old man unwound me from the table leg and played me outside like a fisherman plays a salmon. Out there he took off my collar and threw it into the street.

"Poor doggie," says he; "good doggie. She shan't kiss you any more. 'S a darned shame. Good doggie, go away and get run over by a street car and be happy."

I refused to leave. I leaped and frisked around the old man's legs happy as a pug on a rug.

"You old flea-headed woodchuck-chaser," I said to him—"you moon-baying, rabbit-pointing, egg-stealing old beagle, can't you see that I don't want to leave you? Can't you see that we're both Pups in the Wood and the missis is the cruel uncle after you with the dish towel and me with the flea liniment and pink bow to tie on my tail. Why not cut that all out and be pards forever more?"

Maybe you'll say he didn't understand—maybe he didn't. But he kind of got a grip on the Hot Scotches, and stood still for a minute, thinking.

"Doggie," says he, finally, "we don't live more than a dozen lives on this earth, and very few of us live to be more than 300. If I ever see that flat any more I'm a flat, and if you do you're flatter; and that's no flattery. I'm offering 60 to 1 that Westward Ho wins out by the length of a dachshund."

There was no string, but I frolicked along with my master to the Twenty-third Street ferry. And the cats on the route saw reason to give thanks that prehensile claws had been given to them.

On the Jersey side my master said to a stranger who stood eating a currant bun:

"Me and my doggie, we are bound for the Rocky Mountains."

But what pleased me most was when my old man pulled both of my ears until I howled, and said:

"You common, monkey-headed, rat-tailed, sulphur-colored son of a door mat, do you know what I'm going to call you?"

I thought of "Lovey," and I whined dolefully.

"I'm going to call you 'Pete,' " says my master; and if I'd had five tails I couldn't have done enough wagging to do justice to the occasion.

The Green Door

Suppose you should be walking down Broadway after dinner, with ten minutes allotted to the consummation of your cigar while you are choosing between a diverting tragedy and something serious in the way of vaudeville. Suddenly a hand is laid upon your arm. You turn to look into the thrilling eyes of a beautiful woman, wonderful in diamonds and Russian sables. She thrusts hurriedly into your hand an extremely hot buttered roll, flashes out a tiny pair of scissors, snips off the second button of your overcoat, meaningly ejaculates the one word, "parallelogram!" and swiftly flies down a cross street, looking back fearfully over her shoulder.

That would be pure adventure. Would you accept it? Not you. You would flush with embarrassment; you would sheepishly drop the roll and continue down Broadway, fumbling feebly for the missing button. This you would do unless you are one of the blessed few in whom the pure spirit of adventure is not dead.

True adventurers have never been plentiful. They who are set down in print as such have been mostly business men with newly invented methods. They have been out after the things they wanted—golden fleeces, holy grails, lady loves, treasure, crowns and fame. The true adventurer goes forth aimless and uncalculating to meet and greet unknown fate. A fine example was the Prodigal Son—when he started back home.

Half-adventurers—brave and splendid figures—have been numerous. From the Crusades to the Palisades they

have enriched the arts of history and fiction and the trade
of historical fiction. But each of them had a prize to win,
a goal to kick, an axe to grind, a race to run, a new thrust
in tierce to deliver, a name to carve, a crow to pick—so
they were not followers of true adventure.

In the big city the twin spirits Romance and Adventure
are always abroad seeking worthy wooers. As we roam
the streets they slyly peep at us and challenge us in
twenty different guises. Without knowing why, we look
up suddenly to see in a window a face that seems to
belong to our gallery of intimate portraits; in a sleeping
thoroughfare we hear a cry of agony and fear coming
from an empty and shuttered house; instead of at our
familiar curb a cab-driver deposits us before a strange
door, which one, with a smile, opens for us and bids us
enter; a slip of paper, written upon, flutters down to our
feet from the high lattices of Chance; we exchange glances
of instantaneous hate, affection, and fear with hurrying
strangers in the passing crowds; a sudden souse of rain—
and our umbrella may be sheltering the daughter of the
Full Moon and first cousin of the Sidereal System; at
every corner handkerchiefs drop, fingers beckon, eyes
besiege, and the lost, the lonely, the rapturous, the mysterious, the perilous changing clues of adventure are
slipped into our fingers. But few of us are willing to hold
and follow them. We are grown stiff with the ramrod of
convention down our backs. We pass on; and some day
we come, at the end of a very dull life, to reflect that our
romance has been a pallid thing of a marriage or two, a
satin rosette kept in a safe-deposit drawer, and a lifelong
feud with a steam radiator.

Rudolf Steiner was a true adventurer. Few were the
evenings on which he did not go forth from his hall
bedchamber in search of the unexpected and the egre-
gious. The most interesting thing in life seemed to him to
be what might lie just around the next corner. Sometimes
his willingness to tempt fate led him into strange paths.
Twice he had spent the night in a station-house; again

and again he had found himself the dupe of ingenious and mercenary tricksters; his watch and money had been the price of one flattering allurement. But with undiminished ardor he picked up every glove cast before him into the merry lists of adventure.

One evening Rudolf was strolling along a cross-town street in the older central part of the city. Two streams of people filled the sidewalks—the home-hurrying, and that restless contingent that abandons home for the specious welcome of the thousand-candle-power *table d'hôte*.

The young adventurer was of pleasing presence, and moved serenely and watchfully. By daylight he was a salesman in a piano store. He wore his tie drawn through a topaz ring instead of fastened with a stick pin; and once he had written to the editor of a magazine that "Junie's Love Test," by Miss Libbey, had been the book that had most influenced his life.

During his walk a violent chattering of teeth in a glass case on the sidewalk seemed at first to draw his attention (with a qualm) to a restaurant before which it was set; but a second glance revealed the electric letters of a dentist's sign high above the next door. A giant Negro, fantastically dressed in a red embroidered coat, yellow trousers and a military cap, discreetly distributed cards to those of the passing crowd who consented to take them.

This mode of dentistic advertising was a common sight to Rudolf. Usually he passed the dispenser of the dentist's cards without reducing his store; but to-night the African slipped one into his hand so deftly that he retained it there smiling a little at the successful feat.

When he had travelled a few yards further he glanced at the card indifferently. Surprised, he turned it over and looked again with interest. One side of the card was blank; on the other was written in ink three words, "The Green Door." And then Rudolf saw, three steps in front of him, a man throw down the card the Negro had given him as he passed. Rudolf picked it up. It was printed with the dentist's name and address and the usual schedule of "plate work" and "bridge work" and "crowns," and specious promises of "painless" operations.

The adventurous piano salesman halted at the corner and considered. Then he crossed the street, walked down a block, recrossed and joined the upward current of people again. Without seeming to notice the Negro as he passed the second time, he carelessly took the card that was handed him. Ten steps away he inspected it. In the same handwriting that appeared on the first card "The Green Door" was inscribed upon it. Three or four cards were tossed to the pavement by pedestrians both following and leading him. These fell blank side up. Rudolf turned them over. Every one bore the printed legend of the dental "parlors."

Rarely did the arch sprite Adventure need to beckon twice to Rudolf Steiner, his true follower. But twice it had been done, and the quest was on.

Rudolf walked slowly back to where the giant Negro stood by the case of rattling teeth. This time as he passed he received no card. In spite of his gaudy and ridiculous garb, the Ethiopian displayed a natural barbaric dignity as he stood, offering the cards suavely to some, allowing others to pass unmolested. Every half minute he chanted a harsh, unintelligible phrase akin to the jabber of car conductors and grand opera. And not only did he withhold a card this time but it seemed to Rudolf that he received from the shining and massive black countenance a look of cold, almost contemptuous disdain.

The look stung the adventurer. He read in it a silent accusation that he had been found wanting. Whatever the mysterious written words on the cards might mean, the black had selected him twice from the throng for their recipient; and now seemed to have condemned him as deficient in the wit and spirit to engage the enigma.

Standing aside from the rush, the young man made a rapid estimate of the building in which he conceived that his adventure must lie. Five stories high it rose. A small restaurant occupied the basement.

The first floor, now closed, seemed to house millinery or furs. The second floor, by the winking electric letters, was the dentist's. Above this a polyglot babel of signs struggled to indicate the abodes of palmists, dressmakers, musicians, and doctors. Still higher up draped curtains and milk bottles white on the window sills proclaimed the regions of domesticity.

After concluding his survey Rudolf walked briskly up the high flight of stone steps into the house. Up two flights of the carpeted stairway he continued; and at its top paused. The hallway there was dimly lighted by two pale jets of gas—one far to his right, the other nearer, to his left. He looked toward the nearer light and saw, within its wan halo, a green door. For one moment he hesitated; then he seemed to see the contumelious sneer of the African juggler of cards; and then he walked straight to the green door and knocked against it.

Moments like those that passed before his knock was answered measure the quick breath of true adventure. What might not be behind those green panels! Gamesters at play; cunning rogues baiting their traps with subtle skill; beauty in love with courage, and thus planning to be sought by it; danger, death, love, disappointment, ridicule—any of these might respond to that temerarious rap.

A faint rustle was heard inside, and the door slowly opened. A girl not yet twenty stood there white-faced and tottering. She loosed the knob and swayed weakly, groping with one hand. Rudolf caught her and laid her on a faded couch that stood against the wall. He closed the door and took a swift glance around the room by the light of a flickering gas jet. Neat, but extreme poverty was the story that he read.

The girl lay still, as if in a faint. Rudolf looked around the room excitedly for a barrel. People must be rolled upon a barrel who—no, no; that was for drowned persons. He began to fan her with his hat. That was successful, for he struck her nose with the brim of his derby and she opened her eyes. And then the young man saw that hers, indeed, was the one missing face from his heart's gallery of intimate portraits. The frank, gray eyes, the little nose, turning pertly outward; the chestnut hair, curling like the tendrils of a pea vine, seemed the right end and reward of all his wonderful adventures. But the face was woefully thin and pale.

The girl looked at him calmly, and then smiled.

"Fainted, didn't I?" she asked, weakly. "Well, who wouldn't? You try going without anything to eat for three days and see!"

"Himmel!" exclaimed Rudolf, jumping up. "Wait till I come back."

He dashed out the green door and down the stairs. In twenty minutes he was back again kicking at the door with his toe for her to open it. With both arms he hugged an array of wares from the grocery and the restaurant. On the table he laid them—bread and butter, cold meats, cakes, pies, pickles, oysters, a roasted chicken, a bottle of milk and one of red-hot tea.

"This is ridiculous," said Rudolf, blusteringly, "to go without eating. You must quit making election bets of this kind. Supper is ready." He helped her to a chair at the table and asked: "Is there a cup for the tea?" "On the shelf by the window," she answered. When he turned again with the cup he saw her, with eyes shining rapturously, beginning upon a huge dill pickle that she had rooted out from the paper bags with a woman's unerring instinct. He took it from her, laughingly, and poured the cup full of milk. "Drink that first," he ordered, "and then you shall have some tea, and then a chicken wing. If you are very good you shall have a pickle to-morrow. And now, if you'll allow me to be your guest we'll have supper."

He drew up the other chair. The tea brightened the girl's eyes and brought back some of her color. She began to eat with a sort of dainty ferocity like some starved wild animal. She seemed to regard the young man's presence and the aid he had rendered her as a natural thing—not as though she undervalued the conventions; but as one whose great stress gave her the right to put aside the artificial for the human. But gradually, with the return of strength and comfort, came also a sense of the little conventions that belong; and she began to tell him her little story. It was one of a thousand such as the city yawns at every day—the shop girl's story of insufficient wages, further reduced by "fines" that go to swell the store's profits; of time lost through illness; and then of lost positions, lost hope, and—the knock of the adventurer upon the green door.

But to Rudolf the history sounded as big as the Iliad or the crisis in "Junie's Love Test."

"To think of you going through all that," he exclaimed.

"It was something fierce," said the girl, solemnly.

"And you have no relatives or friends in the city?"

"None whatever."

"I am all alone in the world, too," said Rudolf, after a pause.

"I am glad of that," said the girl, promptly; and somehow it pleased the young man to hear that she approved of his bereft condition.

Very suddenly her eyelids dropped and she sighed deeply.

"I'm awfully sleepy," she said, "and I feel so good."

Rudolf rose and took his hat.

"Then I'll say good-night. A long night's sleep will be fine for you."

He held out his hand, and she took it and said "good-night." But her eyes asked a question so eloquently, so frankly and pathetically that he answered it with words.

"Oh, I'm coming back to-morrow to see how you are getting along. You can't get rid of me so easily."

Then, at the door, as though the way of his coming had been so much less important than the fact that he had come, she asked: "How did you come to knock at my door?"

He looked at her for a moment, remembering the cards, and felt a sudden jealous pain. What if they had fallen into other hands as adventurous as his? Quickly he decided that she must never know the truth. He would never let her know that he was aware of the strange expedient to which she had been driven by her great distress.

"One of our piano tuners lives in this house," he said. "I knocked at your door by mistake."

The last thing he saw in the room before the green door closed was her smile.

At the head of the stairway he paused and looked curiously about him. And then he went along the hallway to its other end; and, coming back, ascended to the floor above and continued his puzzled explorations. Every door that he found in the house was painted green.

Wondering, he descended to the sidewalk. The fantastic African was still there. Rudolf confronted him with his two cards in his hand.

"Will you tell me why you gave me these cards and what they mean?" he asked.

In a broad, good-natured grin the Negro exhibited a splendid advertisement of his master's profession.

"Dar it is, boss," he said, pointing down the street. "But I 'spect you is a little late for de fust act."

Looking the way he pointed Rudolf saw above the entrance to a theatre the blazing electric sign of its new play, "The Green Door."

"I'm informed dat it's a fust-rate show, sah," said the Negro. "De agent what represents it pussented me with a dollar, sah, to distribute a few of his cards along with de doctah's. May I offer you one of de doctah's cards, sah?"

At the corner of the block in which he lived Rudolf stopped for a glass of beer and a cigar. When he had come out with his lighted weed he buttoned his coat, pushed back his hat and said, stoutly, to the lamp post on the corner:

"All the same, I believe it was the hand of Fate that doped out the way for me to find her."

Which conclusion, under the circumstances, certainly admits Rudolf Steiner to the ranks of the true followers of Romance and Adventure.

The Furnished Room

Restless, shifting, fugacious as time is a certain vast bulk of the population of the red brick district of the lower West Side. Homeless, they have a hundred homes. They flit from furnished room to furnished room, transients forever—transients in abode, transients in heart and mind. They sing "Home, Sweet Home" in ragtime; they carry their *lares et penates* in a bandbox; their vine is entwined about a picture hat; a rubber plant is their fig tree.

Hence the houses of this district, having had a thousand dwellers, should have a thousand tales to tell, mostly dull ones, no doubt; but it would be strange if there could not be found a ghost or two in the wake of all these vagrant guests.

One evening after dark a young man prowled among these crumbling red mansions, ringing their bells. At the twelfth he rested his lean hand-baggage upon the step and wiped the dust from his hatband and forehead. The bell sounded faint and far away in some remote, hollow depths.

To the door of this, the twelfth house whose bell he had rung, came a housekeeper who made him think of an unwholesome, surfeited worm that had eaten its nut to a hollow shell and now sought to fill the vacancy with edible lodgers.

He asked if there was a room to let.

"Come in," said the housekeeper. Her voice came from her throat; her throat seemed lined with fur. "I have the third-floor back, vacant since a week back. Should you wish to look at it?"

The young man followed her up the stairs. A faint light from no particular source mitigated the shadows of the halls. They trod noiselessly upon a stair carpet that its own loom would have forsworn. It seemed to have become vegetable; to have degenerated in that rank, sunless air to lush lichen or spreading moss that grew in patches to the stair-case and was viscid under the foot like organic matter. At each turn of the stairs were vacant niches in the wall. Perhaps plants had once been set within them. If so they had died in that foul and tainted air. It may be that statues of the saints had stood there, but it was not difficult to conceive that imps and devils had dragged them forth in the darkness and down to the unholy depths of some furnished pit below.

"This is the room," said the housekeeper, from her furry throat. "It's a nice room. It ain't often vacant. I had some most elegant people in it last summer—no trouble at all, and paid in advance to the minute. The water's at the end of the hall. Sprowls and Mooney kept it three months. They done a vaudeville sketch. Miss B'retta Sprowls—you may have heard of her—Oh, that was just the stage names—right there over the dresser is where the marriage certificate hung, framed. The gas is here, and you see there is plenty of closet room. It's a room everybody likes. It never stays idle long."

"Do you have many theatrical people rooming here?" asked the young man.

"They comes and goes. A good proportion of my lodgers is connected with the theatres. Yes, sir, this is the theatrical district. Actor people never stays long anywhere. I get my share. Yes, they comes and they goes."

He engaged the room, paying for a week in advance. He was tired, he said, and would take possession at once. He counted out the money. The room had been made ready, she said, even to towels and water. As the housekeeper moved away he put, for the thousandth time, the question that he carried at the end of his tongue.

"A young girl—Miss Vashner—Miss Eloise Vashner —do you remember such a one among your lodgers? She would be singing on the stage, most likely. A fair girl, of medium height and slender, with reddish, gold hair and a dark mole near her left eyebrow."

"No, I don't remember the name. Them stage people has names they change as often as their rooms. They comes and they goes. No, I don't call that one to mind."

No. Always no. Five months of ceaseless interrogation and the inevitable negative. So much time spent by day in questioning managers, agents, schools and choruses; by night among the audiences of theatres from all-star casts down to music halls so low that he dreaded to find what he most hoped for. He who had loved her best had tried to find her. He was sure that since her disappearance from home this great, water-girt city held her somewhere, but it was like a monstrous quicksand, shifting its particles constantly, with no foundation, its upper granules of to-day buried to-morrow in ooze and slime.

The furnished room received its latest guest with a first glow of pseudo-hospitality, a hectic, haggard, perfunctory welcome like the specious smile of a demirep. The sophistical comfort came in reflected gleams from the decayed furniture, the ragged brocade upholstery of a couch and two chairs, a foot-wide cheap pier glass between the two windows, from one or two gilt picture frames and a brass bedstead in a corner.

The guest reclined, inert, upon a chair, while the room, confused in speech as though it were an apartment in Babel, tried to discourse to him of its divers tenantry.

A polychromatic rug like some brilliant-flowered, rectangular, tropical islet lay surrounded by a billowy sea of soiled matting. Upon the gay-papered wall were those pictures that pursue the homeless one from house to house—The Huguenot Lovers, The First Quarrel, The Wedding Breakfast, Psyche at the Fountain. The mantel's chastely severe outline was ingloriously veiled behind some pert drapery drawn rakishly askew like the sashes of the Amazonian ballet. Upon it was some desolate flotsam cast aside by the room's marooned when a lucky sail had borne them to a fresh port—a trifling vase or two, pictures of actresses, a medicine bottle, some stray cards out of a deck.

One by one, as the characters of a cryptograph become explicit, the little signs left by the furnished room's procession of guests developed a significance. The threadbare space in the rug in front of the dresser told that lovely women had marched in the throng. The tiny fingerprints on the wall spoke of little prisoners trying to feel their way to sun and air. A splattered stain, raying like the shadow of a bursting bomb, witnessed where a hurled glass or bottle had splintered with its contents against the wall. Across the pier-glass had been scrawled with a diamond in staggering letters the name "Marie." It seemed that the succession of dwellers in the furnished room had turned in fury—perhaps tempted beyond forbearance by its garish coldness—and wreaked upon it their passions. The furniture was chipped and bruised; the couch, distorted by bursting springs, seemed a horrible monster that had been slain during the stress of some grotesque convulsion. Some more potent upheaval had cloven a great slice from the marble mantel. Each plank in the floor owned its particular cant and shriek as from a separate and individual agony. It seemed incredible that all this malice and injury had been wrought upon the room by those who had called it for a time their home; and yet it may have been the cheated home instinct surviving blindly, the resentful rage at false household gods that had kindled their wrath. A hut that is our own we can sweep and adorn and cherish.

The young tenant in the chair allowed these thoughts to file, soft-shod, through his mind, while there drifted into the room furnished sounds and furnished scents. He heard in one room a tittering and incontinent, slack laugh-

ter; in others the monologue of a scold, the rattling of
dice, a lullaby, and one crying dully; above him a banjo
tinkled with spirit. Doors banged somewhere; the ele-
vated trains roared intermittently; a cat yowled miserably
upon a back fence. And he breathed the breath of the
house—a dank savor rather than a smell—a cold, musty
effluvium as from underground vaults mingled with the
reeking exhalations of linoleum and mildewed and rotten
woodwork.

Then suddenly, as he rested there, the room was filled
with the strong, sweet odor of mignonette. It came as
upon a single buffet of wind with such sureness and
fragrance and emphasis that it almost seemed a living
visitant. And the man cried aloud: "What, dear?" as if
he had been called, and sprang up and faced about. The
rich odor clung to him and wrapped him around. He
reached out his arms for it, all his senses for the time
confused and commingled. How could one be perempto-
rily called by an odor? Surely it must have been a sound.
But, was it not the odor that had touched, that had
caressed him?

"She has been in this room," he cried, and he sprang
to wrest from it a token, for he knew he would recognize
the smallest thing that had belonged to her or that she had
touched. This enveloping scent of mignonette, the odor
that she had loved and made her own—whence came it?

The room had been but carelessly set in order. Scat-
tered upon the flimsy dresser scarf were half a dozen
hairpins—those discreet, indistinguishable friends of wom-
ankind, feminine of gender, infinite mood and uncommu-
nicative of tense. These he ignored, conscious of their
triumphant lack of identity. Ransacking the drawers of
the dresser he came upon a discarded, tiny, ragged handkerchief. He pressed it to his face. It was racy and
insolent with heliotrope; he hurled it to the floor. In
another drawer he found odd buttons, a theatre pro-
gramme, a pawnbroker's card, two lost marshmallows, a
book on the divination of dreams. In the last was a

woman's black satin hair bow, which halted him, poised between ice and fire. But the black satin hair bow also is femininity's demure, impersonal common ornament and tells no tales.

And then he traversed the room like a hound on the scent, skimming the walls, considering the corners of the bulging matting on his hands and knees, rummaging mantel and tables, the curtains and hangings, the drunken cabinet in the corner, for a visible sign, unable to perceive that she was there beside, around, against, within, above him, clinging to him, wooing him, calling him so poignantly through the finer senses that even his grosser ones became cognizant of the call. Once again he answered loudly: "Yes, dear!" and turned, wild-eyed, to gaze on vacancy, for he could not yet discern form and color and love and outstretched arms in the odor of mignonette. Oh, God! whence that odor, and since when have odors had a voice to call? Thus he groped.

He burrowed in crevices and corners, and found corks and cigarettes. These he passed in passive contempt. But once he found in a fold of the matting a half-smoked çigar, and this he ground beneath his heel with a green and trenchant oath. He sifted the room from end to end. He found dreary and ignoble small records of many a peripatetic tenant; but of her whom he sought, and who may have lodged there, and whose spirit seemed to hover there, he found no trace.

And then he thought of the housekeeper.

He ran from the haunted room downstairs and to a door that showed a crack of light. She came out to his knock. He smothered his excitement as best he could.

"Will you tell me, madam," he besought her, "who occupied the room I have before I came?"

"Yes, sir. I can tell you again. 'Twas Sprowls and Mooney, as I said. Miss B'retta Sprowls it was in the theatres, but Missis Mooney she was. My house is well known for respectability. The marriage certificate hung, framed, on a nail over——"

"What kind of a lady was Miss Sprowls—in looks, I mean?"

"Why, black-haired, sir, short, and stout, with a comical face. They left a week ago Tuesday."

"And before they occupied it?"

"Why, there was a single gentleman connected with the draying business. He left owing me a week. Before him was Missis Crowder and her two children, that stayed four months; and back of them was old Mr. Doyle, whose sons paid for him. He kept the room six months. That goes back a year, sir, and further I do not remember."

He thanked her and crept back to his room. The room was dead. The essence that had vivified it was gone. The perfume of mignonette had departed. In its place was the old, stale odor of mouldy house furniture, of atmosphere in storage.

The ebbing of his hope drained his faith. He sat staring at the yellow, swinging gaslight. Soon he walked to the bed and began to tear the sheets into strips. With the blade of his knife he drove them tightly into every crevice around windows and door. When all was snug and taut he turned out the light, turned the gas full on again and laid himself gratefully upon the bed.

It was Mrs. McCool's night to go with the can for beer. So she fetched it and sat with Mrs. Purdy in one of those subterranean retreats where housekeepers foregather and the worm dieth seldom.

"I rented out my third-floor-back this evening," said Mrs. Purdy, across a fine circle of foam. "A young man took it. He went up to bed two hours ago."

"Now, did ye, Mrs. Purdy, ma'am?" said Mrs. McCool, with intense admiration. "You do be a wonder for rentin' rooms of that kind. And did ye tell him, then?" she concluded in a husky whisper laden with mystery.

"Rooms," said Mrs. Purdy, in her furriest tones, "are furnished for to rent. I did not tell him, Mrs. McCool."

" 'Tis right ye are, ma'am; 'tis by renting rooms we kape alive. Ye have the rale sense for business, ma'am. There be many people will rayjict the rentin' of a room if they be tould a suicide has been after dyin' in the bed of it."

"As you say, we has our living to be making," remarked Mrs. Purdy.

"Yis, ma'am; 'tis true. 'Tis just one wake ago this day I helped ye lay out the third-floor-back. A pretty slip of a colleen she was to be killin' herself wid the gas—a swate little face she had, Mrs. Purdy, ma'am."

"She'd a-been called handsome, as you say," said Mrs. Purdy, assenting but critical, "but for that mole she had a'growin' by her left eyebrow. Do fill up your glass again, Mrs. McCool."

The Pimienta Pancakes

While we were rounding up a bunch of the Triangle-O cattle in the Frio bottoms a projecting branch of a dead mesquite caught my wooden stirrup and gave my ankle a wrench that laid me up in camp for a week.

On the third day of my compulsory idleness I crawled out near the grub wagon, and reclined helpless under the conversational fire of Judson Odom, the camp cook. Jud was a monologist by nature, whom Destiny, with customary blundering, had set in a profession wherein he was bereaved, for the greater portion of his time, of an audience.

Therefore, I was manna in the desert of Jud's obmutescence.

Betimes I was stirred by invalid longings for something to eat that did not come under the caption of "grub." I had visions of the maternal pantry "deep as first love, and wild with all regret," and then I asked:

"Jud, can you make pancakes?"

Jud laid down his sixshooter, with which he was preparing to pound an antelope steak, and stood over me in what I felt to be a menacing attitude. He further indorsed my impression that his pose was resentful by fixing upon me with his light blue eyes a look of cold suspicion.

"Say, you," he said, with candid, though not excessive, choler, "did you mean that straight, or was you trying to throw the gaff into me? Some of the boys been telling you about me and that pancake racket?"

"No, Jud," I said, sincerely, "I meant it. It seems to

me I'd swap my pony and saddle for a stack of buttered brown pancakes with some first crop, open kettle, New Orleans sweetening. Was there a story about pancakes?''

Jud was mollified at once when he saw that I had not been dealing in allusions. He brought some mysterious bags and tin boxes from the grub wagon and set them in the shade of the hackberry where I lay reclined. I watched him as he began to arrange them leisurely and untie their many strings.

"No, not a story," said Jud, as he worked, "but just the logical disclosures in the case of me and that pink-eyed snoozer from Mired Mule Cañada and Miss Willella Learight. I don't mind telling you.

"I was punching then for old Bill Toomey, on the San Miguel. One day I gets all ensnared up in aspirations for to eat some canned grub that hasn't ever mooed or baaed or grunted or been in peck measures. So, I gets on my bronc and pushes the wind for Uncle Emsley Telfair's store at the Pimienta Crossing on the Nueces.

"About three in the afternoon I threwed my bridle over a mesquite limb and walked the last twenty yards into Uncle Emsley's store. I got up on the counter and told Uncle Emsley that the signs pointed to the devastation of the fruit crop of the world. In a minute I had a bag of crackers and a long-handled spoon, with an open can each of apricots and pineapples and cherries and green-gages beside of me with Uncle Emsley busy chopping away with the hatchet at the yellow clings. I was feeling like Adam before the apple stampede, and was digging my spurs into the side of the counter and working with my twenty-four-inch spoon when I happened to look out of the window into the yard of Uncle Emsley's house, which was next to the store.

"There was a girl standing there—an imported girl with fixings on—philandering with a croquet maul and amusing herself by watching my style of encouraging the fruit canning industry.

"I slid off the counter and delivered up my shovel to Uncle Emsley.

" 'That's my niece,' says he; 'Miss Willella Learight, down from Palestine on a visit. Do you want that I should make you acquainted?'

" 'The Holy Land,' I says to myself, my thoughts milling some as I tried to run 'em into the corral. 'Why not? There was sure angels in Pales—— Why yes, Uncle Emsley,' I says out loud, 'I'd be awful edified to meet Miss Learight.'

"So Uncle Emsley took me out in the yard and gave us each other's entitlements.

"I never was shy about women. I never could understand why some men who can break a mustang before breakfast and shave in the dark, get all lefthanded and full of perspiration and excuses when they see a bolt of calico draped around what belongs in it. Inside of eight minutes me and Miss Willella was aggravating the croquet balls around as amiable as second cousins. She gave me a dig about the quantity of canned fruit I had eaten, and I got back at her, flat-footed, about how a certain lady named Eve started the fruit trouble in the first free-grass pasture—'Over in Palestine, wasn't it?' says I, as easy and pat as roping a one-year-old.

"That was how I acquired cordiality for the proximities of Miss Willella Learight; and the disposition grew larger as time passed. She was stopping at Pimienta Crossing for her health, which was very good, and for the climate, which was forty per cent. hotter than Palestine. I rode over to see her once every week for a while; and then I figured it out that if I doubled the number of trips I would see her twice as often.

"One week I slipped in a third trip; and that's where the pancakes and the pink-eyed snoozer busted into the game.

"That evening, while I set on the counter with a peach and two damsons in my mouth, I asked Uncle Emsley how Miss Willella was.

" 'Why,' says Uncle Emsley, 'she's gone riding with Jackson Bird, the sheep man from over at Mired Mule Cañada.'

"I swallowed the peach seed and the two damson seeds. I guess somebody held the counter by the bridle while I got off; and then I walked out straight ahead till I butted against the mesquite where my roan was tied.

" 'She's gone riding,' I whispered in my bronc's ear, 'with Birdstone Jack, the hired mule from Sheep Man's Cañada. Did you get that, old Leather-and-Gallops?'

"That bronc of mine wept, in his way. He'd been raised a cow pony and he didn't care for snoozers.

"I went back and said to Uncle Emsley: 'Did you say a sheep man?'

" 'I said a sheep man,' says Uncle again. 'You must have heard tell of Jackson Bird. He's got eight sections of grazing and four thousand head of the finest Merinos south of the Arctic Circle.'

"I went out and sat on the ground in the shade of the store and leaned against a prickly pear. I sifted sand into my boots with unthinking hands while I soliloquized a quantity about this bird with the Jackson plumage to his name.

"I never had believed in harming sheep men. I see one, one day, reading a Latin grammar on hossback, and I never touched him! They never irritated me like they do most cowmen. You wouldn't go to work now, and impair and disfigure snoozers, would you, that eat on tables and wear little shoes and speak to you on subjects? I had always let 'em pass, just as you would a jack-rabbit; with a polite word and a guess about the weather, but no stopping to swap canteens. I never thought it was worth while to be hostile with a snoozer. And because I'd been lenient, and let 'em live, here was one going around riding with Miss Willella Learight!

"An hour by sun they come loping back, and stopped at Uncle Emsley's gate. The sheep person helped her off; and they stood throwing each other sentences all sprightful and sagacious for a while. And then this feathered Jackson flies up in his saddle and raises his little stewpot of a hat, and trots off in the direction of his mutton ranch. By this time I had turned the sand out of my boots and unpinned myself from the prickly pear; and by the time he gets half a mile out of Pimienta, I singlefoots up beside him on my bronc.

"I said that snoozer was pink-eyed, but he wasn't. His seeing arrangement was gray enough, but his eyelashes was pink and his hair was sandy, and that gave you the idea. Sheep man—he wasn't more than a lamb man, anyhow—a little thing with his neck involved in a yellow silk handkerchief, and shoes tied up in bowknots.

" 'Afternoon!' says I to him. 'You now ride with a equestrian who is commonly called Dead-Moral-Certainty Judson, on account of the way I shoot. When I want a stranger to know me I always introduce myself before the draw, for I never did like to shake hands with ghosts.'

" 'Ah,' says he, just like that—'Ah, I'm glad to know you, Mr. Judson. I'm Jackson Bird, from over at Mired Mule Ranch.'

"Just then one of my eyes saw a roadrunner skipping down the hill with a young tarantula in his bill, and the other eye noticed a rabbit-hawk sitting on a dead limb in a water-elm. I popped over one after the other with my forty-five, just to show him. 'Two out of three,' says I. 'Birds just naturally seem to draw my fire wherever I go.'

" 'Nice shooting,' says the sheep man, without a flutter. 'But don't you sometimes ever miss the third shot? Elegant fine rain that was last week for the young grass, Mr. Judson,' says he.

" 'Willie,' says I, riding over close to his palfrey, 'your infatuated parents may have denounced you by the name of Jackson, but you sure moulted into a twittering Willie—let us slough off this here analysis of rain and the elements, and get down to talk that is outside the vocabulary of parrots. That is a bad habit you have got of riding with young ladies over at Pimienta. I've known birds,' says I, 'to be served on toast for less than that. Miss Willella,' says I, 'don't ever want any nest made out of sheep's wool by a tomtit of the Jacksonian branch of ornithology. Now, are you going to quit, or do you wish for to gallop up against this Dead-Moral-Certainty attachment to my name, which is good for two hyphens and at least one set of funeral obsequies?'

"Jackson Bird flushed up some, and then he laughed.

" 'Why, Mr. Judson,' says he, 'you've got the wrong idea. I've called on Miss Learight a few times; but not for the purpose you imagine. My object is purely a gastronomical one.'

"I reached for my gun.

" 'Any coyote,' says I, 'that would boast of dishonorable——'

" 'Wait a minute,' says this bird, 'till I explain. What would I do with a wife? If you ever saw that ranch of mine! I do my own cooking and mending. Eating—that's all the pleasure I get out of sheep raising. Mr. Judson, did you ever taste the pancakes that Miss Learight makes?'

" 'Me? No,' I told him. 'I never was advised that she was up to any culinary maneuvers.'

" 'They're golden sunshine,' says he, 'honey-browned by the ambrosial fires of Epicurus. I'd give two years of my life to get the recipe for making them pancakes. That's what I went to see Miss Learight for,' says Jackson Bird, 'but I haven't been able to get it from her. It's an old recipe that's been in the family for seventy-five years. They hand it down from one generation to another, but they don't give it away to outsiders. If I could get that recipe, so I could make them pancakes for myself on my ranch, I'd be a happy man,' says Bird.

" 'Are you sure,' I says to him, 'that it ain't the hand that mixes the pancakes that you're after?'

" 'Sure,' says Jackson. 'Miss Learight is a mighty nice girl, but I can assure you my intentions go no further than the gastro—' but he seen my hand going down to my holster and he changed his similitude—'than the desire to produce a copy of the pancake recipe,' he finishes.

" 'You ain't such a bad little man,' says I, trying to be fair. 'I was thinking some of making orphans of your sheep, but I'll let you fly away this time. But you stick to pancakes,' says I, 'as close as the middle one of a stack; and don't go and mistake sentiments for syrup, or there'll be singing at your ranch, and you won't hear it.'

" 'To convince you that I am sincere,' says the sheep man, 'I'll ask you to help me. Miss Learight and you being closer friends, maybe she would do for you what she wouldn't for me. If you will get me a copy of that pancake recipe, I give you my word that I'll never call upon her again.'

" 'That's fair,' I says, and I shook hands with Jackson Bird. 'I'll get it for you if I can, and glad to oblige.' And he turned off down the big pear flat on the Piedra, in the direction of Mired Mule; and I steered northwest for old Bill Toomey's ranch.

"It was five days afterward when I got another chance to ride over to Pimienta. Miss Willella and me passed a gratifying evening at Uncle Emsley's. She sang some, and exasperated the piano quite a lot with quotations from the operas. I gave imitations of a rattlesnake, and told her about Snaky McFee's new way of skinning cows, and described the trip I made to Saint Louis once. We was getting along in one another's estimations fine. Thinks I, if Jackson can now be persuaded to migrate, I win. I recollect his promise about the pancake receipt, and I thinks I will persuade it from Miss Willella and give it to him; and then if I catches Birdie off of Mired Mule again, I'll make him hop the twig.

"So, along about ten o'clock, I put on a wheedling smile and says to Miss Willella: 'Now, if there's anything I do like better than the sight of a red steer on green grass it's the taste of a nice hot pancake smothered in sugarhouse molasses.'

"Miss Willella gives a little jump on the piano stool, and looked at me curious.

" 'Yes,' says she, 'they're real nice. What did you say was the name of that street in Saint Louis, Mr. Odom, where you lost your hat?'

" 'Pancake Avenue,' says I, with a wink, to show her that I was on about the family receipt, and couldn't be side-corralled off of the subject. 'Come, now Miss Willella,' I says; 'let's hear how you make 'em. Pancakes is just whirling in my head like wagon wheels. Start her off, now—pound of flour, eight dozen eggs, and so on. How does the catalogue of constituents run?'

" 'Excuse me for a moment, please,' says Miss Willella, and she gives me a quick kind of sideways look, and slides off the stool. She ambled out into the other room, and directly Uncle Emsley comes in in his shirt sleeves, with a pitcher of water. He turns around to get a glass on the table, and I see a forty-five in his hip pocket. 'Great post-holes!' thinks I, 'but here's a family thinks a heap of cooking receipts, protecting it with firearms. I've known outfits that wouldn't do that much by a family feud.'

" 'Drink this here down,' says Uncle Emsley, handing me the glass of water. 'You've rid too far to-day, Jud, and got yourself over-excited. Try to think about something else now.'

" 'Do you know how to make them pancakes, Uncle Emsley?' I asked.

" 'Well, I'm not as apprised in the anatomy of them as some,' says Uncle Emsley, 'but I reckon you take a sifter of plaster of paris and a little dough and saleratus and corn meal, and mix 'em with eggs and buttermilk as usual. Is old Bill going to ship beeves to Kansas City again this spring, Jud?'

"That was all the pancake specifications I could get that night. I didn't wonder that Jackson Bird found it uphill work. So I dropped the subject and talked with Uncle Emsley a while about hollow-horn and cyclones.

And then Miss Willella came and said 'Goodnight,' and I hit the breeze for the ranch.

"About a week afterward I met Jackson Bird riding out of Pimienta as I rode in, and we stopped in the road for a few frivolous remarks.

" 'Got the bill of particulars for them flapjacks yet?' I asked him.

" 'Well, no,' says Jackson. 'I don't seem to have any success in getting hold of it. Did you try?'

" 'I did,' says I, 'and 'twas like trying to dig a prairie dog out of his hole with a peanut hull. That pancake receipt must be a jooka-lorum, the way they hold on to it.'

" 'I'm 'most ready to give it up,' says Jackson, so discouraged in his pronunciations that I felt sorry for him; 'but I did want to know how to make them pancakes to eat on my lonely ranch,' says he. 'I lie awake at nights thinking how good they are.'

" 'You keep on trying for it,' I tells him, 'and I'll do the same. One of us is bound to get a rope over its horns before long. Well, so-long, Jacksy.'

"You see, by this time we was on the peacefullest of terms. When I saw that he wasn't after Miss Willella I had more endurable contemplations of that sandy-haired snoozer. In order to help out the ambitions of his appetite I kept on trying to get that receipt from Miss Willella. But every time I would say 'pancakes' she would get sort of remote and fidgety about the eye, and try to change the subject. If I held her to it she would slide out and round up Uncle Emsley with his pitcher of water and hip-pocket howitzer.

"One day I galloped over to the store with a fine bunch of blue verbenas that I cut out of a herd of wild flowers over on Poisoned Dog Prairie. Uncle Emsley looked at 'em with one eye shut and says:

" 'Haven't ye heard the news?'

" 'Cattle up?' I asks.

" 'Willella and Jackson Bird was married in Palestine yesterday,' says he. 'Just got a letter this morning.'

"I dropped them flowers in a cracker-barrel, and let the news trickle in my ears and down toward my upper left-hand shirt pocket until it got to my feet.

" 'Would you mind saying that over again once more, Uncle Emsley?' says I. 'Maybe my hearing has got wrong, and you only said that prime heifers was 4.80 on the hoof, or something like that.'

" 'Married yesterday,' says Uncle Emsley, 'and gone to Waco and Niagara Falls on a wedding tour. Why, didn't you see none of the signs all along? Jackson Bird has been courting Willella ever since that day he took her out riding.'

" 'Then,' says I, in a kind of a yell, 'what was all this zizzaparoola he gives me about pancakes? Tell me *that*.'

"When I said 'pancakes' Uncle Emsley sort of dodged and stepped back.

" 'Somebody's been dealing me pancakes from the bottom of the deck,' I says, 'and I'll find out. I believe you know. Talk up,' says I, 'or we'll mix a panful of batter right here.'

"I slid over the counter after Uncle Emsley. He grabbed at his gun, but it was in a drawer, and he missed it two inches. I got him by the front of his shirt and shoved him in a corner.

" 'Talk pancakes,' says I, 'or be made into one. Does Miss Willella make 'em?'

" 'She never made one in her life and I never saw one,' says Uncle Emsley, soothing. 'Calm down now, Jud—calm down. You've got excited, and that wound in your head is contaminating your sense of intelligence. Try not to think about pancakes.'

" 'Uncle Emsley,' says I, "I'm not wounded in the head except so far as my natural cogitative instincts run to runts. Jackson Bird told me he was calling on Miss Willella for the purpose of finding out her system of producing pancakes, and he asked me to help him get the bill of lading of the ingredients. I done so, with the results as you see. Have I been sodded down with Johnson grass by a pink-eyed snoozer, or what?'

" 'Slack up your grip on my dress shirt,' says Uncle Emsley, 'and I'll tell you. Yes, it looks like Jackson Bird has gone and humbugged you some. The day after he went riding with Willella he came back and told me and her to watch out for you whenever you got to talking about pancakes. He said you was in camp once where they was cooking flapjacks, and one of the fellows cut you over the head with a frying pan. Jackson said that whenever you got over-hot or excited that wound hurt you and made you kind of crazy, and you went raving about pancakes. He told us to just get you worked off of the subject and soothed down, and you wouldn't be dangerous. So, me and Willella done the best by you we knew how. Well, well,' says Uncle Emsley, 'that Jackson Bird is sure a seldom kind of a snoozer.' "

During the progress of Jud's story he had been slowly but deftly combining certain portions of the contents of his sacks and cans. Toward the close of it he set before me the finished product—a pair of red-hot, rich-hued pancakes on a tin plate. From some secret hoarding place he also brought a lump of excellent butter and a bottle of golden syrup.

"How long ago did these things happen?" I asked him.

"Three years," said Jud. "They're living on the Mired Mule Ranch now. But I haven't seen either of 'em since. They say Jackson Bird was fixing his ranch up fine with rocking chairs and window curtains all the time he was putting me up the pancake tree. Oh, I got over it after a while. But the boys kept the racket up."

"Did you make these cakes by the famous recipe?" I asked.

"Didn't I tell you there wasn't no receipt?" said Jud. "The boys hollered pancakes till they got pancake hungry, and I cut this receipt out of a newspaper. How does the truck taste?''

''They're delicious,'' I answered. ''Why don't you have some, too, Jud?'' I was sure I heard a sigh.

''Me?'' said Jud. ''I don't never eat 'em.''

The Passing of
Black Eagle

For some months of a certain year a grim bandit infested the Texas border along the Rio Grande. Peculiarly striking to the optic nerve was this notorious marauder. His personality secured him the title of "Black Eagle, the Terror of the Border." Many fearsome tales are on record concerning the doings of him and his followers. Suddenly, in the space of a single minute, Black Eagle vanished from earth. He was never heard of again. His own band never even guessed the mystery of his disappearance. The border ranches and settlements feared he would come again to ride and ravage the mesquite flats. He never will. It is to disclose the fate of Black Eagle that this narrative is written.

The initial movement of the story is furnished by the foot of a bartender in St. Louis. His discerning eye fell upon the form of Chicken Ruggles as he pecked with avidity at the free lunch. Chicken was a "hobo." He had a long nose like the bill of a fowl, an inordinate appetite for poultry, and a habit of gratifying it without expense, which accounts for the name given him by his fellow vagrants.

Physicians agree that the partaking of liquors at meal times is not a healthy practice. The hygiene of the saloon promulgates the opposite. Chicken had neglected to purchase a drink to accompany his meal. The bartender rounded the counter, caught the injudicious diner by the ear with a lemon squeezer, led him to the door and kicked him into the street.

Thus the mind of Chicken was brought to realize the signs of coming winter. The night was cold; the stars shone with unkindly brilliancy; people were hurrying along the streets in two egotistic, jostling streams. Men had donned their overcoats, and Chicken knew to an exact percentage the increased difficulty of coaxing dimes from those buttoned-in vest pockets. The time had come for his annual exodus to the south.

A little boy, five or six years old, stood looking with covetous eyes in a confectioner's window. In one small hand he held an empty two-ounce vial; in the other he grasped tightly something flat and round, with a shining milled edge. The scene presented a field of operations commensurate to Chicken's talents and daring. After sweeping the horizon to make sure that no official tug was cruising near, he insidiously accosted his prey. The boy, having been early taught by his household to regard altruistic advances with extreme suspicion, received the overtures coldly.

Then Chicken knew that he must make one of those desperate, nerve-shattering plunges into speculation that fortune sometimes requires of those who would win her favor. Five cents was his capital, and this he must risk against the chance of winning what lay within the close grasp of the youngster's chubby hand. It was a fearful lottery, Chicken knew. But he must accomplish his end by strategy, since he had a wholesome terror of plundering infants by force. Once, in a park, driven by hunger, he had committed an onslaught upon a bottle of peptonized infant's food in the possession of an occupant of a baby carriage. The outraged infant had so promptly opened its mouth and pressed the button that communicated with the welkin that help arrived, and Chicken did his thirty days in a snug coop. Wherefore he was, as he said, "leary of kids."

Beginning artfully to question the boy concerning his choice of sweets, he gradually drew out the information he wanted. Mamma said he was to ask the drug-store man for ten cents' worth of paregoric in the bottle; he was to keep his hand shut tight over the dollar; he must not stop to talk to any one in the street; he must ask the drug-store man to wrap up the change and put it in the pocket of his trousers. Indeed, they had pockets—two of them! And he liked chocolate creams best.

Chicken went into the store and turned plunger. He invested his entire capital in C. A. N. D. Y. stocks, simply to pave the way to the greater risk following.

He gave the sweets to the youngster, and had the satisfaction of perceiving that confidence was established. After that it was easy to obtain leadership of the expedition, to take the investment by the hand and lead it to a nice drug store he knew of in the same block. There Chicken, with a parental air, passed over the dollar and called for the medicine, while the boy crunched his candy, glad to be relieved of the responsibility of the purchase. And then the successful investor, searching his pockets, found an overcoat button—the extent of his winter trousseau—and, wrapping it carefully, placed the ostensible change in the pocket of confiding juvenility. Setting the youngster's face homeward, and patting him benevolently on the back—for Chicken's heart was as soft as those of his feathered namesakes—the speculator quit the market with a profit of 1,700 per cent. on his invested capital.

Two hours later an Iron Mountain freight engine pulled out of the railroad yards, Texas bound, with a string of empties. In one of the cattle cars, half buried in excelsior, Chicken lay at ease. Beside him in his nest was a quarter bottle of very poor whisky and a paper bag of bread and cheese. Mr. Ruggles, in his private car, was on his trip south for the winter season.

For a week that car was trundled southward, shifted, laid over, and manipulated after the manner of rolling stock, but Chicken stuck to it, leaving it only at necessary times to satisfy his hunger and thirst. He knew it must go down to the cattle country, and San Antonio, in

the heart of it, was his goal. There the air was salubrious
and mild; the people indulgent and long-suffering. The
bartenders there would not kick him. If he should eat too
long or too often at one place they would swear at him as
if by rote and without heat. They swore so drawlingly,
and they rarely paused short of their full vocabulary,
which was copious, so that Chicken had often gulped a
good meal during the process of the vituperative prohibi-
tion. The season there was always spring-like; the plazas
were pleasant at night, with music and gayety: except
during the slight and infrequent cold snaps one could
sleep comfortably out of doors in case the interiors should
develop inhospitality.

At Texarkana his car was switched to the I. and G. N.
Then still southward it trailed until, at length, it crawled
across the Colorado bridge at Austin, and lined out,
straight as an arrow, for the run to San Antonio.

When the freight halted at that town Chicken was fast
asleep. In ten minutes the train was off again for Laredo,
the end of the road. Those empty cattle cars were for
distribution along the line at points from which the ranches
shipped their stock.

When Chicken awoke his car was stationary. Looking
out between the slats he saw it was a bright, moonlit
night. Scrambling out, he saw his car with three others
abandoned on a little siding in a wild and lonesome
country. A cattle pen and chute stood on one side of the
track. The railroad bisected a vast, dim ocean of prairie,
in the midst of which Chicken, with his futile rolling
stock, was as completely stranded as was Robinson with
his land-locked boat.

A white post stood near the rails. Going up to it,
Chicken read the letters at the top, S. A. 90. Laredo was
nearly as far to the south. He was almost a hundred miles
from any town. Coyotes began to yelp in the mysterious
sea around him. Chicken felt lonesome. He had lived in
Boston without an education, in Chicago without nerve,
in Philadelphia without a sleeping place, in New York

without a pull, and in Pittsburgh sober, and yet he had never felt so lonely as now.

Suddenly through the intense silence, he heard the whicker of a horse. The sound came from the side of the track toward the east, and Chicken began to explore timorously in that direction. He stepped high along the mat of curly mesquite grass, for he was afraid of everything there might be in this wilderness—snakes, rats, brigands, centipedes, mirages, cowboys, fandangoes, tarantulas, tamales—he had read of them in the story papers. Rounding a clump of prickly pear that reared high its fantastic and menacing array of rounded heads, he was struck to shivering terror by a snort and a thunderous plunge, as the horse, himself startled, bounded away some fifty yards, and then resumed his grazing. But here was the one thing in the desert that Chicken did not fear. He had been reared on a farm; he had handled horses, understood them, and could ride.

Approaching slowly and speaking soothingly, he followed the animal, which, after its first flight, seemed gentle enough, and secured the end of the twenty-foot lariat that dragged after him in the grass. It required him but a few moments to contrive the rope into an ingenious nose-bridle, after the style of the Mexican *borsal*. In another he was upon the horse's back and off at a splendid lope, giving the animal free choice of direction. "He will take me somewhere," said Chicken to himself.

It would have been a thing of joy, that untrammelled gallop over the moonlit prairie, even to Chicken, who loathed exertion, but that his mood was not for it. His head ached; a growing thirst was upon him; the "somewhere" whither his lucky mount might convey him was full of dismal peradventure.

And now he noted that the horse moved to a definite goal. Where the prairie lay smooth he kept his course straight as an arrow's toward the east. Deflected by hill or arroyo or impracticable spinous brakes, he quickly flowed again into the current, charted by his unerring instinct. At last, upon the side of a gentle rise, he suddenly subsided to a complacent walk. A stone's cast away stood a little mott of coma trees; beneath it a *jacal* such as the Mexicans erect—a one-room house of upright poles daubed with clay and roofed with grass or tule reeds. An experienced eye would have estimated the spot as the headquarters of a small sheep ranch. In the moonlight the ground in the nearby corral showed pulverized to a level smoothness by the hoofs of the sheep. Everywhere was carelessly distributed the paraphernalia of the place—ropes, bridles, saddles, sheep pelts, wool sacks, feed troughs, and camp litter. The barrel of drinking water stood in the end of the two-horse wagon near the door. The harness was piled, promiscuous, upon the wagon tongue, soaking up the dew.

Chicken slipped to earth, and tied the horse to a tree. He halloed again and again, but the house remained quiet. The door stood open, and he entered cautiously. The light was sufficient for him to see that no one was at home. He struck a match and lighted a lamp that stood on a table. The room was that of a bachelor ranchman who was content with the necessaries of life. Chicken rummaged intelligently until he found what he had hardly dared hope for—a small brown jug that still contained something near a quart of his desire.

Half an hour later, Chicken—now a gamecock of hostile aspect—emerged from the house with unsteady steps. He had drawn upon the absent ranchman's equipment to replace his own ragged attire. He wore a suit of coarse brown ducking, the coat being a sort of rakish bolero, jaunty to a degree. Boots he had donned, and spurs that whirred with every lurching step. Buckled around him was a belt full of cartridges with a six-shooter in each of its two holsters.

Prowling about, he found blankets, a saddle and bridle with which he caparisoned his steed. Again mounting, he rode swiftly away, singing a loud and tuneless song.

Bud King's band of desperadoes, outlaws and horse

and cattle thieves were in camp at a secluded spot on the bank of the Frio. Their depredations in the Rio Grande country, while no bolder than usual, had been advertised more extensively, and Captain Kinney's company of rangers had been ordered down to look after them. Consequently, Bud King, who was a wise general, instead of cutting out a hot trail for the upholders of the law, as his men wished to do, retired for the time to the prickly fastnesses of the Frio valley.

Though the move was a prudent one, and not incompatible with Bud's well-known courage, it raised dissension among the members of the band. In fact, while they thus lay ingloriously *perdu* in the brush, the question of Bud King's fitness for the leadership was argued, with closed doors, as it were, by his followers. Never before had Bud's skill or efficiency been brought to criticism; but his glory was waning (and such is glory's fate) in the light of a newer star. The sentiment of the band was crystallizing into the opinion that Black Eagle could lead them with more luster, profit, and distinction.

This Black Eagle—sub-titled the "Terror of the Border" —had been a member of the gang about three months.

One night while they were in camp on the San Miguel water-hole a solitary horseman on the regulation fiery steed dashed in among them. The newcomer was of a portentous and devastating aspect. A beak-like nose with a predatory curve projected above a mass of bristling, blue-black whiskers. His eye was cavernous and fierce. He was spurred, sombreroed, booted, garnished with revolvers, abundantly drunk, and very much unafraid. Few people in the country drained by the Rio Bravo would have cared thus to invade alone the camp of Bud King. But this fell bird swooped fearlessly upon them and demanded to be fed.

Hospitality in the prairie country is not limited. Even if your enemy pass your way you must feed him before you shoot him. You must empty your larder into him before you empty your lead. So the stranger of undeclared intentions was set down to a mighty feast.

A talkative bird he was, full of most marvellous loud tales and exploits, and speaking a language at times obscure but never colorless. He was a new sensation to Bud King's men, who rarely encountered new types. They hung, delighted, upon his vainglorious boasting, the spicy strangeness of his lingo, his contemptuous familiarity with life, the world, and remote places, and the extravagant frankness with which he conveyed his sentiments.

To their guest the band of outlaws seemed to be nothing more than a congregation of country bumpkins whom he was "stringing for grub" just as he would have told his stories at the back door of a farmhouse to wheedle a meal. And, indeed, his ignorance was not without excuse, for the "bad man" of the Southwest does not run to extremes. Those brigands might justly have been taken for a little party of peaceable rustics assembled for a fish-fry or pecan gathering. Gentle of manner, slouching of gait, soft-voiced, unpicturesquely clothed; not one of them presented to the eye any witness of the desperate records they had earned.

For two days the glittering stranger within the camp was feasted. Then, by common consent, he was invited to become a member of the band. He consented, presenting for enrollment the prodigious name of "Captain Montressor." This was immediately overruled by the band, and "Piggy" substituted as a compliment to the awful and insatiate appetite of its owner.

Thus did the Texas border receive the most spectacular brigand that ever rode its chaparral.

For the next three months Bud King conducted business as usual, escaping encounters with law officers and being content with reasonable profits. The band ran off some very good companies of horses from the ranges, and a few bunches of fine cattle which they got safely across the Rio Grande and disposed of to fair advantage.

Often the band would ride into the little villages and Mexican settlements, terrorizing the inhabitants and plundering for the provisions and ammunition they needed. It was during these bloodless raids that Piggy's ferocious aspect and frightful voice gained him a renown more widespread and glorious than those other gentle-voiced and sad-faced desperadoes could have acquired in a lifetime.

The Mexicans, most apt in nomenclature, first called him The Black Eagle, and used to frighten the babes by threatening them with tales of the dreadful robber who carried off little children in his great beak. Soon the name extended, and Black Eagle, the Terror of the Border, became a recognized factor in exaggerated newspaper reports and ranch gossip.

The country from the Nueces to the Rio Grande was a wild but fertile stretch, given over to the sheep and cattle ranches. Range was free; the inhabitants were few; the law was mainly a letter, and the pirates met with little opposition until the flaunting and garish Piggy gave the band undue advertisement. Then Kinney's ranger company headed for those precincts, and Bud King knew that it meant grim and sudden war or else temporary retirement. Regarding the risk to be unnecessary, he drew off his band to an almost inaccessible spot on the bank of the Frio. Wherefore, as has been said, dissatisfaction arose among the members, and impeachment proceedings against Bud were premeditated, with Black Eagle in high favor for the succession. Bud King was not unaware of the sentiment, and he called aside Cactus Taylor, his trusted lieutenant, to discuss it.

"If the boys," said Bud, "ain't satisfied with me, I'm willin' to step out. They're buckin' against my way of handlin' 'em. And 'specially because I concludes to hit the brush while Sam Kinney is ridin' the line. I saves 'em from bein' shot or sent up on a state contract, and they up and says I'm no good."

"It ain't so much that," explained Cactus, "as it is

they're plum locoed about Piggy. They want them whiskers and that nose of his to split the wind at the head of the column.''

"There's somethin' mighty seldom about Piggy,'' declared Bud, musingly. "I never yet see anything on the hoof that he exactly grades up with. He can shore holler a plenty, and he straddles a hoss from where you laid the chunk. But he ain't never been smoked yet. You know, Cactus, we ain't had a row since he's been with us. Piggy's all right for skearin' the greaser kids and layin' waste a cross-roads store. I reckon he's the finest canned oyster buccaneer and cheese pirate that ever was, but how's his appetite for fightin'? I've knowed some citizens you'd think was starvin' for trouble get a bad case of dyspepsy the first dose of lead they had to take.''

"He talks all spraddled out,'' said Cactus, " 'bout the rookuses he's been in. He claims to have saw the elephant and hearn the owl.''

"I know,'' replied Bud, using the cow-puncher's expressive phrase of skepticism, "but it sounds to me!''

This conversation was held one night in camp while the other members of the band—eight in number—were sprawling around the fire, lingering over their supper. When Bud and Cactus ceased talking they heard Piggy's formidable voice holding forth to the others as usual while he was engaged in checking, though never satisfying, his ravening appetite.

"Wat's de use,'' he was saying, "of chasin' little red cowses and hosses 'round for t'ousands of miles? Dere ain't nuttin' in it. Gallopin' t'rough dese bushes and briers, and gettin' a t'irst dat a brewery couldn't put out, and missin' meals! Say! You know what I'd do if I was main finger of dis bunch? I'd stick up a train. I'd blow de express car and make hard dollars where you guys get wind. Youse makes me tired. Dis sook-cow kind of cheap sport gives me a pain.''

Later on, a deputation waited on Bud. They stood on one leg, chewed mesquite twigs and circumlocuted, for they hated to hurt his feelings. Bud foresaw their business, and made it easy for them. Bigger risks and larger profits was what they wanted.

The suggestion of Piggy's about holding up a train had fired their imagination and increased their admiration for the dash and boldness of the instigator. They were such simple, artless, and custom-bound bush-rangers that they had never before thought of extending their habits beyond the running off of livestock and the shooting of such of their acquaintances as ventured to interfere.

Bud acted "on the level," agreeing to take a subordinate place in the gang until Black Eagle should have been given a trial as leader.

After a great deal of consultation, studying of timetables and discussion of the country's topography, the time and place for carrying out their new enterprise was decided upon. At that time there was a feedstuff famine in Mexico and a cattle famine in certain parts of the United States, and there was a brisk international trade. Much money was being shipped along the railroads that connected the two republics. It was agreed that the most promising place for the contemplated robbery was at Espina, a little station on the I. and G. N., about forty miles north of Laredo. The train stopped there one minute; the country around was wild and unsettled; the station consisted of but one house in which the agent lived.

Black Eagle's band set out, riding by night. Arriving in the vicinity of Espina they rested their horses all day in a thicket a few miles distant.

The train was due at Espina at 10:30 P.M. They could rob the train and be well over the Mexican border with their booty by daylight the next morning.

To do Black Eagle justice, he exhibited no signs of flinching from the responsible honors that had been conferred upon him.

He assigned his men to their respective posts with discretion, and coached them carefully as to their duties. On each side of the track four of the band were to lie concealed in the chaparral. Gotch-Ear Rodgers was to stick up the station agent. Bronco Charlie was to remain with the horses, holding them in readiness. At a spot where it was calculated the engine would be when the train stopped, Bud King was to lie hidden on one side, and Black Eagle himself on the other. The two would get the drop on the engineer and fireman, force them to descend and proceed to the rear. Then the express car would be looted, and the escape made. No one was to move until Black Eagle gave the signal by firing his revolver. The plan was perfect.

At ten minutes to train time every man was at his post, effectually concealed by the thick chaparral that grew almost to the rails. The night was dark and lowering, with a fine drizzle falling from the flying gulf clouds. Black Eagle crouched behind a bush within five yards of the track. Two six-shooters were belted around him. Occasionally he drew a large black bottle from his pocket and raised it to his mouth.

A star appeared far down the track which soon waxed into the headlight of the approaching train. It came on with an increasing roar; the engine bore down upon the ambushing desperadoes with a glare and a shriek like some avenging monster come to deliver them to justice. Black Eagle flattened himself upon the ground. The engine, contrary to their calculations, instead of stopping between him and Bud King's place of concealment, passed fully forty yards farther before it came to a stand.

The bandit leader rose to his feet and peered around the bush. His men all lay quiet, awaiting the signal. Immediately opposite Black Eagle was a thing that drew his attention. Instead of being a regular passenger train it was a mixed one. Before him stood a box car, the door of which, by some means, had been left slightly open. Black Eagle went up to it and pushed the door farther open. An odor came forth—a damp, rancid, familiar, musty, intoxicating, beloved odor stirring strongly at old memories of happy days and travels. Black Eagle sniffed at the witching smell as the returned wanderer smells of the rose that twines his boyhood's cottage home. Nostalgia seized him. He put his hand inside. Excelsior—dry, springy, curly, soft, enticing, covered the floor. Outside the drizzle had turned to a chilling rain.

The train bell clanged. The bandit chief unbuckled his belt and cast it, with its revolvers, upon the ground. His spurs followed quickly, and his broad sombrero. Black Eagle was moulting. The train started with a rattling jerk. The ex-Terror of the Border scrambled into the box car and closed the door. Stretched luxuriously upon the excelsior, with the black bottle clasped closely to his breast, his eyes closed, and a foolish, happy smile upon his terrible features Chicken Ruggles started upon his return trip.

Undisturbed, with the band of desperate bandits lying motionless, awaiting the signal to attack, the train pulled out from Espina. As its speed increased, and the black masses of chaparral went whizzing past on either side, the express messenger, lighting his pipe, looked through his window and remarked, feelingly:

"What a jim-dandy place for a hold-up!"

Makes the Whole World Kin

The burglar stepped inside the window quickly, and then he took his time. A burglar who respects his art always takes his time before taking anything else.

The house was a private residence. By its boarded front door and untrimmed Boston ivy the burglar knew that the mistress of it was sitting on some oceanside piazza telling a sympathetic man in a yachting cap that no one had ever understood her sensitive, lonely heart. He knew by the light in the third-story front windows, and by the lateness of the season, that the master of the house had come home, and would soon extinguish his light and retire. For it was September of the year and of the soul, in which season the house's good man comes to consider roof gardens and stenographers as vanities, and to desire the return of his mate and the more durable blessings of decorum and the moral excellencies.

The burglar lighted a cigarette. The guarded glow of the match illuminated his salient points for a moment. He belonged to the third type of burglars.

This third type has not yet been recognized and accepted. The police have made us familiar with the first and second. Their classification is simple. The collar is the distinguishing mark.

When a burglar is caught who does not wear a collar he is described as a degenerate of the lowest type, singularly vicious and depraved, and is suspected of being the desperate criminal who stole the handcuffs out of Patrolman Hennessy's pocket in 1878 and walked away to escape arrest.

The other well-known type is the burglar who wears a collar. He is always referred to as a Raffles in real life. He is invariably a gentleman by daylight, breakfasting in a dress suit, and posing as a paperhanger, while after dark he plies his nefarious occupation of burglary. His mother is an extremely wealthy and respected resident of Ocean Grove, and when he is conducted to his cell he asks at once for a nail file and the *Police Gazette*. He always has a wife in every State in the Union and fiancées in all the Territories, and the newspapers print his matrimonial gallery out of their stock of cuts of the ladies who were cured by only one bottle after having been given up by five doctors, experiencing great relief after the first dose.

The burglar wore a blue sweater. He was neither a Raffles nor one of the chefs from Hell's Kitchen. The police would have been baffled had they attempted to classify him. They have not yet heard of the respectable, unassuming burglar who is neither above nor below his station.

This burglar of the third class began to prowl. He wore no masks, dark lanterns, or gum shoes. He carried a 38-calibre revolver in his pockets, and he chewed peppermint gum thoughtfully.

The furniture of the house was swathed in its summer dust protectors. The silver was far away in safe-deposit vaults. The burglar expected no remarkable "haul." His objective point was that dimly lighted room where the master of the house should be sleeping heavily after whatever solace he had sought to lighten the burden of his loneliness. A "touch" might be made there to the extent of legitimate, fair professional profits—loose money, a watch, a jeweled stickpin—nothing exorbitant or beyond reason. He had seen the window left open and had taken the chance.

The burglar softly opened the door of the lighted room.

The gas was turned low. A man lay in the bed asleep. On the dresser lay many things in confusion—a crumpled roll of bills, a watch, keys, three poker chips, crushed cigars, a pink silk hair bow, and an unopened bottle of bromo-seltzer for a bulwark in the morning.

The burglar took three steps toward the dresser. The man in the bed suddenly uttered a squeaky groan and opened his eyes. His right hand slid under his pillow, but remained there.

"Lay still," said the burglar in conversational tone. Burglars of the third type do not hiss. The citizen in the bed looked at the round end of the burglar's pistol and lay still.

"Now hold up both your hands," commanded the burglar.

The citizen had a little, pointed, brown-and-gray beard, like that of a painless dentist. He looked solid, esteemed, irritable, and disgusted. He sat up in bed and raised his right hand above his head.

"Up with the other one," ordered the burglar. "You might be amphibious and shoot with your left. You can count two, can't you? Hurry up, now."

"Can't raise the other one," said the citizen with a contortion of his lineaments.

"What's the matter with it?"

"Rheumatism in the shoulder."

"Inflammatory?"

"Was. The inflammation has gone down."

The burglar stood for a moment or two, holding his gun on the afflicted one. He glanced at the plunder on the dresser and then, with a half-embarrassed air back at the man in the bed. Then he, too, made a sudden grimace.

"Don't stand there making faces," snapped the citizen, bad-humoredly. "If you've come to burgle why don't you do it? There's some stuff lying around."

" 'Scuse me," said the burglar, with a grin; "but it just socked me one, too. It's good for you that rheumatism and me happens to be old pals. I got it in my left arm, too. Most anybody but me would have popped you when you wouldn't hoist that left claw of yours.''

"How long have you had it?" inquired the citizen.

"Four years. I guess that ain't all. Once you've got it, it's you for a rheumatic life—that's my judgment."

"Ever try rattlesnake oil?" asked the citizen interestedly.

"Gallons," said the burglar. "If all the snakes I've used the oil of was strung out in a row they'd reach eight times as far as Saturn, and the rattles could be heard at Valparaiso, Indiana, and back."

"Some use Chiselum's Pills," remarked the citizen.

"Fudge!" said the burglar. "Took 'em five months. No good. I had some relief the year I tried Finkelham's Extract, Balm of Gilead poultices, and Pott's Pain Pulverizer; but I think it was the buckeye I carried in my pocket what done the trick.

"Is yours worse in the morning or at night?" asked the citizen.

"Night," said the burglar; "just when I'm busiest. Say, take down that arm of yours—I guess you won't—Say! did you ever try Blickerstaff's Blood Builder?"

"I never did. Does yours come in paroxysms or is it a steady pain?"

The burglar sat down on the foot of the bed and rested his gun on his crossed knees.

"It jumps," said he. "It strikes me when I ain't looking for it. I had to give up second-story work because I got stuck sometimes half-way up. Tell you what—I don't believe the bloomin' doctors know what is good for it."

"Same here. I've spent a thousand dollars without getting any relief. Yours swell any?"

"Of mornings. And when it's goin' to rain—great Christopher!"

"Me, too," said the citizen. "I can tell when a streak of humidity the size of a tablecloth starts from Florida on its way to New York. And if I pass a theatre where there's an 'East Lynne' matinée going on, the moisture starts my left arm jumping like a toothache."

"It's undiluted—hades!" said the burglar.

"You're dead right," said the citizen.

The burglar looked down at his pistol and thrust it into his pocket with an awkward attempt at ease.

"Say, old man," he said, constrainedly, "ever try opodeldoc?"

"Slop!" said the citizen angrily. "Might as well rub on restaurant butter."

"Sure," concurred the burglar. "It's a salve suitable for little Minnie when the kitty scratches her finger. I'll tell you what! We're up against it. I only find one thing that eases her up. Hey? Little old sanitary, ameliorating, lest-we-forget Booze. Say—this job's off—'scuse me—get on your clothes and let's go out and have some. 'Scuse the liberty, but—ouch! There she goes again!"

"For a week," said the citizen, "I haven't been able to dress myself without help. I'm afraid Thomas is in bed, and——"

"Climb out," said the burglar, "I'll help you get into your duds."

The conventional returned as a tidal wave and flooded the citizen. He stroked his brown-and-gray beard.

"It's very unusual——" he began.

"Here's your shirt," said the burglar, "fall out. I know a man who said Omberry's Ointment fixed him in two weeks so he could use both hands in tying his four-in-hand."

As they were going out the door the citizen turned and started back.

" 'Liked to forgot my money," he explained; "laid it on the dresser last night."

The burglar caught him by the right sleeve.

"Come on," he said, bluffly. "I ask you. Leave it alone. I've got the price. Ever try witch hazel and oil of wintergreen?"

The Whirligig of Life

Justice-of-the-peace Benaja Widdup sat in the door of his office smoking his elder-stem pipe. Halfway to the Zenith the Cumberland range rose blue-gray in the afternoon haze. A speckled hen swaggered down the main street of the "settlement," cackling foolishly.

Up the road came a sound of creaking axles, and then a slow cloud of dust, and then a bull-cart bearing Ransie Bilbro and his wife. The cart stopped at the Justice's door, and the two climbed down. Ransie was a narrow six feet of sallow brown skin and yellow hair. The imperturbability of the mountains hung upon him like a suit of armor. The woman was calicoed, angled, snuff-brushed, and weary with unknown desires. Through it all gleamed a faint protest of cheated youth unconscious of its loss.

The Justice of the Peace slipped his feet into his shoes, for the sake of dignity, and moved to let them enter.

"We-all," said the woman, in a voice like the wind blowing through pine boughs, "wants a divo'ce." She looked at Ransie to see if he noted any flaw or ambiguity or evasion or partiality or self-partisanship in her statement of their business.

"A divo'ce," repeated Ransie, with a solemn nod. "We-all can't git along together nohow. It's lonesome enough fur to live in the mount'ins when a man and a woman keers fur one another. But when she's a-spittin' like a wildcat or a-sullenin' like a hoot-owl in the cabin, a man ain't got no call to live with her."

"When he's a no-'count varmint," said the woman, without any especial warmth, "a-traipsin' along of scalawags and moonshiners and a-layin' on his back pizen 'ith co'n whiskey, and a-pesterin' folks with a pack o'hungry, triflin' houn's to feed!"

"When she keeps a-throwin' skillet lids," came Ransie's antiphony, "and slings b'ilin' water on the best coon-dog in the Cumberlands, and sets herself again' cookin' a man's victuals, and keeps him awake o' nights accusin' him of a sight of doin's!"

"When he's al'ays a-fightin' the revenuers, and gits a hard name in the mount'ins fur a mean man, who's gwine to be able fur to sleep o' nights?"

The Justice of the Peace stirred deliberately to his duties. He placed his one chair and a wooden stool for his petitioners. He opened his book of statutes on the table and scanned the index. Presently he wiped his spectacles and shifted his inkstand.

"The law and the statues," said he, "air silent on the subjeck of divo'ce as fur as the jurisdiction of this co't air concerned. But, accordin' to equity and the Constitution and the golden rule, it's a bad barg'in that can't run both ways. If a justice of the peace can marry a couple, it's plain that he is bound to be able to divo'ce 'em. This here office will issue a decree of divo'ce and abide by the decision of the Supreme Co't to hold it good."

Ransie Bilbro drew a small tobacco-bag from his trousers pocket. Out of this he shook upon the table a five-dollar note. "Sold a b'arskin and two foxes fur that," he remarked. "It's all the money we got."

"The regular price of a divo'ce in this co't," said the Justice, "air five dollars." He stuffed the bill into the pocket of his homespun vest with a deceptive air of indifference. With much bodily toil and mental travail he wrote the decree upon half a sheet of foolscap, and then copied it upon the other. Ransie Bilbro and his wife listened to his reading of the document that was to give them freedom:

* * *

Know all men by these presents that Ransie Bilbro and his wife, Ariela Bilbro, this day personally appeared before me and promises that hereinafter they will neither love, honor, nor obey each other, neither for better nor worse, being of sound mind and body, and accept summons for divorce according to the peace and dignity of the State. Herein fail not, so help you God. Benaja Widdup, justice of the peace in and for the county of Piedmont, State of Tennessee.

The Justice was about to hand one of the documents to Ransie. The voice of Ariela delayed the transfer. Both men looked at her. Their dull masculinity was confronted by something sudden and unexpected in the woman.

"Judge, don't you give him that air paper yit. 'Tain't all settled, nohow. I got to have my rights first. I got to have my ali-money. 'Tain't no kind of a way to do fur a man to divo'ce his wife 'thout her havin' a cent fur to do with. I'm a-layin' off to be a-goin' up to brother Ed's up on Hogback Mount'in. I'm bound fur to hev a pa'r of shoes and some snuff and things besides. Ef Rance kin affo'd a divo'ce, let him pay me ali-money."

Ransie Bilbro was stricken to dumb perplexity. There had been no previous hint of alimony. Women were always bringing up startling and unlooked-for issues.

Justice Benaja Widdup felt that the point demanded judicial decision. The authorities were also silent on the subject of alimony. But the woman's feet were bare. The trail to Hogback Mountain was steep and flinty.

"Ariela Bilbro," he asked, in official tones, "how much did you 'low would be good and sufficient alimoney in the case befo' the co't?"

"I 'lowed," she answered, "fur the shoes and all, to say five dollars. That ain't much fur ali-money, but I reckon that'll git me up to brother Ed's."

"The amount," said the Justice, "air not onreasonable. Ransie Bilbro, you air ordered by the co't to pay the plaintiff the sum of five dollars befo' the decree of divo'ce air issued.''

"I hain't no mo' money," breathed Ransie, heavily. "I done paid you all I had.''

"Otherwise," said the Justice, looking severely over his spectacles, "you air in contempt of co't.''

"I reckon if you gimme till to-morrow," pleaded the husband, "I mout be able to rake or scrape it up somewhars. I never looked for to be a-payin' no ali-money.''

"The case air adjourned," said Benaja Widdup, "till to-morrow, when you-all will present yo'selves and obey the order of the co't. Followin' of which the decrees of divo'ce will be delivered." He sat down in the door and began to loosen a shoestring.

"We mout as well go down to Uncle Ziah's," decided Ransie, "and spend the night." He climbed into the cart on one side, and Ariela climbed in on the other. Obeying the flap of his rope, the little red bull slowly came around on a tack, and the cart crawled away in the nimbus arising from its wheels.

Justice-of-the-peace Benaja Widdup smoked his elder-stem pipe. Late in the afternoon he got his weekly paper, and read it until the twilight dimmed its lines. Then he lit the tallow candle on his table, and read until the moon rose, marking the time for supper. He lived in the double log cabin on the slope near the girdled poplar. Going home to supper he crossed a little branch darkened by a laurel thicket. The dark figure of a man stepped from the laurels and pointed a rifle at his breast. His hat was pulled down low, and something covered most of his face.

"I want yo' money," said the figure, " 'thout any talk, I'm gettin' nervous, and my finger's a-wabblin' on this here trigger.''

"I've only got f-f-five dollars," said the Justice, producing it from his vest pocket.

"Roll it up," came the order, "and stick it in the end of this here gun-bar'l.''

The bill was crisp and new. Even fingers that were clumsy and trembling found little difficulty in making a spill of it and inserting it (this with less ease) into the muzzle of the rifle.

"Now I reckon you kin be goin' along," said the robber.

The Justice lingered not on his way.

The next day came the little red bull, drawing the cart to the office door. Benaja Widdup had his shoes on, for he was expecting the visit. In his presence Ransie Bilbro handed to his wife a five-dollar bill. The official's eye sharply viewed it. It seemed to curl up as though it had been rolled and inserted into the end of a gun-barrel. But the Justice refrained from comment. It is true that other bills might be inclined to curl. He handed each one a decree of divorce. Each stood awkwardly silent, slowly folding the guarantee of freedom. The woman cast a shy glance full of constraint at Ransie.

"I reckon you'll be goin' back up to the cabin," she said, "along 'ith the bull-cart. There's bread in the tin box settin' on the shelf. I put the bacon in the b'ilin'-pot to keep the hounds from gettin' it. Don't forget to wind the clock to-night."

"You air a-goin' to your brother Ed's?" asked Ransie, with fine unconcern.

"I was 'lowin' to get along up thar afore night. I ain't sayin' as they'll pester theyselves any to make me welcome, but I hain't nowhar else fur to go. It's a right smart ways, and I reckon I better be goin'. I'll be a-sayin' good-bye, Ranse—that is, if you keer fur to say so."

"I don't know as anybody's a hound dog," said Ransie, in a martyr's voice, "fur to not want to say good-bye—'less you air so anxious to git away that you don't want me to say it."

Ariela was silent. She folded the five-dollar bill and her decree carefully, and placed them in the bosom of her dress. Benaja Widdup watched the money disappear with mournful eyes behind his spectacles.

And then with his next words he achieved rank (as his thoughts ran) with either the great crowd of the world's sympathizers or the little crowd of its great financiers.

"Be kind o' lonesome in the old cabin to-night, Ransie," she said.

Ransie Bilbro stared out at the Cumberlands, clear blue now in the sunlight. He did not look at Ariela.

"I 'low it might be lonesome," he said; "but when folks gits mad and wants a divo'ce, you can't make folks stay."

"There's others wanted a divo'ce," said Ariela, speaking to the wooden stool. "Besides, nobody don't want nobody to stay."

"Nobody never said they didn't."

"Nobody never said they did. I reckon I better start on now to brother Ed's."

"Nobody can't wind that old clock."

"Want me to go along 'ith you in the cart and wind it fur you, Ranse?"

The mountaineer's countenance was proof against emotion. But he reached out a big hand and enclosed Ariela's thin brown one. Her soul peeped out once through her impassive face, hallowing it.

"Them hounds sha'n't pester you no more," said Ransie. "I reckon I been mean and low down. You wind that clock, Ariela."

"My heart hit's in that cabin, Ranse," she whispered, "along 'ith you. I ain't a-goin' to git mad no more. Le's be startin', Ranse, so's we kin git home by sundown."

Justice-of-the-peace Benaja Widdup interposed as they started for the door, forgetting his presence.

"In the name of the State of Tennessee," he said, "I forbid you-all to be a-defyin' of its laws and statues. This co't is mo' than willin' and full of joy to see the clouds of discord and misunderstandin' rollin' away from two lovin' hearts, but it air the duty of the co't to p'eserve the morals and integrity of the State. The co't reminds you that you air no longer man and wife, but air divo'ced by regular decree, and as such air not entitled to the benefits and 'purtenances of the mattermonal estate.''

Ariela caught Ransie's arm. Did those words mean that she must lose him now when they had just learned the lesson of life?

"But the co't air prepared," went on the Justice, "fur to remove the disabilities set up by the decree of divo'ce. The co't air on hand to perform the solemn ceremony of marri'ge, thus fixin' things up and enablin' the parties in the case to resume the honor'ble and elevatin' state of mattermony which they desires. The fee fur performin' said ceremony will be, in this case, to wit, five dollars.''

Ariela caught the gleam of promise in his words. Swiftly her hand went to her bosom. Freely as an alighting dove the bill fluttered to the Justice's table. Her sallow cheek colored as she stood hand in hand with Ransie and listened to the reuniting words.

Ransie helped her into the cart, and climbed in beside her. The little red bull turned once more, and they set out, hand-clasped, for the mountains.

Justice-of-the-peace Benaja Widdup sat in his door and took off his shoes. Once again he fingered the bill tucked down in his vest pocket. Once again he smoked his elder-stem pipe. Once again the speckled hen swaggered down the main street of the "settlement," cackling foolishly.

The Voice of
the City

Twenty-five years ago the school children used to chant their lessons. The manner of their delivery was a sing-song recitative between the utterance of an Episcopal minister and the drone of a tired sawmill. I mean no disrespect. We must have lumber and sawdust.

I remember one beautiful and instructive little lyric that emanated from the physiology class. The most striking line of it was this:

"The shin-bone is the long-est bone in the human bod-y."

What an inestimable boon it would have been if all the corporeal and spiritual facts pertaining to man had thus been tunefully and logically inculcated in our youthful minds! But what we gained in anatomy, music, and philosophy was meagre.

The other day I became confused. I needed a ray of light. I turned back to those school days for aid. But in all the nasal harmonies we whined forth from those hard benches I could not recall one that treated of the voice of agglomerated mankind.

In other words, of the composite vocal message of massed humanity.

In other words, of the Voice of a Big City.

Now, the individual voice is not lacking. We can understand the song of the poet, the ripple of the brook, the meaning of the man who wants $5 until next Monday, the inscriptions on the tombs of the Pharaohs, the language of flowers, the "step lively" of the conductor, and the prelude of the milk cans at 4 A.M. Certain large-eared ones even assert that they are wise to the vibrations of the tympanum produced by concussion of the air emanating from Mr. H. James. But who can comprehend the meaning of the voice of the city?

I went out for to see.

First, I asked Aurelia. She wore white Swiss and a hat with flowers on it, and ribbons and ends of things fluttered here and there.

"Tell me," I said, stammeringly, for I have no voice of my own, "what does this big—er—enormous—er—whopping city say? It must have a voice of some kind. Does it ever speak to you? How do you interpret its meaning? It is a tremendous mass, but it must have a key."

"Like a Saratoga trunk?" asked Aurelia.

"No," said I. "Please do not refer to the lid. I have a fancy that every city has a voice. Each one has something to say to the one who can hear it. What does the big one say to you?"

"All cities," said Aurelia, judiciously, "say the same thing. When they get through saying it there is an echo from Philadelphia. So, they are unanimous."

"Here are 4,000,000 people," said I, scholastically, "compressed upon an island, which is mostly lamb surrounded by Wall Street water. The conjunction of so many units into so small a space must result in an identity—or, or rather a homogeneity—that finds its oral expression through a common channel. It is, as you might say, a consensus of translation, concentrating in a crystallized, general idea which reveals itself in what may be termed the Voice of the City. Can you tell me what it is?"

Aurelia smiled wonderfully. She sat on the high stoop. A spray of insolent ivy bobbed against her right ear. A ray of impudent moonlight flickered upon her nose. But I was adamant, nickel-plated.

"I must go and find out," I said, "what is the Voice

of this City. Other cities have voices. It is an assignment. I must have it. New York," I continued, in a rising tone, "had better not hand me a cigar and say: 'Old man, I can't talk for publication.' No other city acts in that way. Chicago says, unhesitatingly, 'I will'; Philadelphia says, 'I should'; New Orleans says, 'I used to'; Louisville says, 'Don't care if I do'; St. Louis says, 'Excuse me'; Pittsburgh says, 'Smoke up.' Now, New York——"

Aurelia smiled.

"Very well," said I, "I must go elsewhere and find out."

I went into a palace, tile-floored, cherub-ceilinged, and square with the cop. I put my foot on the brass rail and said to Billy Magnus, the best bartender in the diocese:

"Billy, you've lived in New York a long time—what kind of a song-and-dance does this old town give you? What I mean is, doesn't the gab of it seem to kind of bunch up and slide over the bar to you in a sort of amalgamated tip that hits off the burg in a kind of an epigram with a dash of bitters and a slice of——"

"Excuse me a minute," said Billy, "somebody's punching the button at the side door."

He went away; came back with an empty tin bucket; again vanished with it full; returned and said to me:

"That was Mame. She rings twice. She likes a glass of beer for supper. Her and the kid. If you ever saw that little skeesicks of mine brace up in his high chair and take his beer and—— But, say, what was yours? I get kind of excited when I hear them two rings—was it the baseball score or gin fizz you asked for?"

"Ginger ale," I answered.

I walked up to Broadway. I saw a cop on the corner. The cops take kids up, women across, and men in. I went up to him.

"If I'm not exceeding the spiel limit," I said, "let me ask you. You see New York during its vocative hours. It is the function of you and your brother cops to preserve the acoustics of the city. There must be a civic voice that is intelligible to you. At night during your lonely rounds you must have heard it. What is the epitome of its turmoil and shouting? What does the city say to you?''

"Friend," said the policeman, spinning his club, "it don't say nothing. I get my orders from the man higher up. Say, I guess you're all right. Stand here for a few minutes and keep an eye open for the roundsman.''

The cop melted into the darkness of the side street. In ten minutes he had returned.

"Married last Tuesday," he said, half gruffly. "You know how they are. She comes to that corner at nine every night for a—comes to say 'hello!' I generally manage to be there. Say, what was it you asked me a bit ago—what's doing in the city? Oh, there's a roof-garden or two just opened, twelve blocks up.''

I crossed a crow's-foot of street-car tracks, and skirted the edge of an umbrageous park. An artificial Diana, gilded, heroic, poised, wind-ruled, on the tower, shimmered in the clear light of her namesake in the sky. Along came my poet, hurrying, hatted, haired, emitting dactyls, spondees and dactylis. I seized him.

"Bill," said I (in the magazine he is Cleon), "give me a lift. I am on an assignment to find out the Voice of the City. You see, it's a special order. Ordinarily a symposium comprising the views of Henry Clews, John L. Sullivan, Edwin Markham, May Irwin and Charles Schwab would be about all. But this is a different matter. We want a broad, poetic, mystic vocalization of the city's soul and meaning. You are the very chap to give me a hint. Some years ago a man got at the Niagara Falls and gave us its pitch. The note was about two feet below the lowest G on the piano. Now, you can't put New York into a note unless it's better indorsed than that. But give me an idea of what it would say if it should speak. It is bound to be a mighty and far-reaching utterance. To arrive at it we must take the tremendous crash of the chords of the day's traffic, the laughter and music of the night, the solemn tones of Dr. Parkhurst, the rag-time, the weeping, the stealthy hum of cab-wheels, the shout of the press agent, the tinkle of fountains on the roof-gardens, the hullabaloo of the strawberry vender and the covers of *Everybody's Magazine*, the whispers of the lovers in the parks—all these sounds must go into your Voice—not combined, but mixed, and of the mixture an essence made; and of the essence an extract—an audible extract, of which one drop shall form the thing we seek.''

''Do you remember,'' asked the poet, with a chuckle, ''that California girl we met at Stiver's studio last week? Well, I'm on my way to see her. She repeated that poem of mine, 'The Tribute of Spring,' word for word. She's the smartest proposition in this town just at present. Say, how does this confounded tie look? I spoiled four before I got one to set right.''

''And the Voice that I asked you about?'' I inquired.

''Oh, she doesn't sing,'' said Cleon. ''But you ought to hear her recite my 'Angel of the Inshore Wind.' ''

I passed on. I cornered a newsboy and he flashed at me prophetic pink papers that outstripped the news by two revolutions of the clock's longest hand.

''Son,'' I said, while I pretended to chase coins in my penny pocket, ''doesn't it sometimes seem to you as if the city ought to be able to talk? All these ups and downs and funny business and queer things happening every day—what would it say, do you think, if it could speak?''

''Quit yer kiddin','' said the boy. ''Wot paper yer want? I got no time to waste. It's Mag's birthday, and I want thirty cents to git her a present.''

Here was no interpreter of the city's mouth-piece. I bought a paper, and consigned its undeclared treaties, its premeditated murders and unfought battles to an ash can.

Again I repaired to the park and sat in the moon shade. I thought and thought, and wondered why none could tell me what I asked for.

And then, as swift as light from a fixed star, the answer came to me. I arose and hurried—hurried as so many reasoners must, back around my circle. I knew the answer and I hugged it in my breast as I flew, fearing lest someone would stop me and demand my secret.

Aurelia was still on the stoop. The moon was higher and the ivy shadows were deeper. I sat at her side and we watched a little cloud tilt at the drifting moon and go asunder quite pale and discomfited.

And then, wonder of wonders and delight of delights! our hands somehow touched, and our fingers closed together and did not part.

After half an hour Aurelia said, with that smile of hers:

"Do you know, you haven't spoken a word since you came back!"

"That," said I, nodding wisely, "is the Voice of the City."

The Trimmed Lamp

O f course there are two sides to the question. Let us look at the other. We often hear ''shop-girls'' spoken of. No such persons exist. There are girls who work in shops. They make their living that way. But why turn their occupation into an adjective? Let us be fair. We do not refer to the girls who live on Fifth Avenue as ''marriage-girls.''

Lou and Nancy were chums. They came to the big city to find work because there was not enough to eat at their homes to go around. Nancy was nineteen; Lou was twenty. Both were pretty, active country girls who had no ambition to go on the stage.

The little cherub that sits up aloft guided them to a cheap and respectable boarding-house. Both found positions and became wage earners. They remained chums. It is at the end of six months that I would beg you to step forward and be introduced to them. Meddlesome Reader: My Lady Friends, Miss Nancy and Miss Lou. While you are shaking hands please take notice—cautiously—of their attire. Yes, cautiously; for they are as quick to resent a stare as a lady in a box at the horse show is.

Lou is a piece-work ironer in a hand laundry. She is clothed in a badly fitting purple dress, and her hat plume is four inches too long; but her ermine muff and scarf cost $25, and its fellow beasts will be ticketed in the windows at $7.98 before the season is over. Her cheeks are pink, and her light blue eyes bright. Contentment radiates from her.

Nancy you would call a shop-girl—because you have the habit. There is no type; but a perverse generation is always seeking a type; so this is what the type should be. She has the high-ratted pompadour and the exaggerated straight-front. Her skirt is shoddy, but has the correct flare. No furs protect her against the bitter spring air, but she wears her short broadcloth jacket as jauntily as though it were Persian lamb! On her face and in her eyes, remorseless type-seeker, is the typical shop-girl expression. It is a look of silent but contemptuous revolt against cheated womanhood; of sad prophecy of the vengeance to come. When she laughs her loudest the look is still there. The same look can be seen in the eyes of Russian peasants; and those of us left will see it some day on Gabriel's face when he comes to blow us up. It is a look that should wither and abash man; but he has been known to smirk at it and offer flowers—with a string tied to them.

Now lift your hat and come away, while you receive Lou's cheery "See you again," and the sardonic, sweet smile of Nancy that seems, somehow, to miss you and go fluttering like a white moth up over the housetops to the stars.

The two waited on the corner for Dan. Dan was Lou's steady company. Faithful? Well, he was on hand when Mary would have had to hire a dozen subpœna servers to find her lamb.

"Ain't you cold, Nancy?" said Lou. "Say, what a chump you are for working in that old store for $8 a week! I made $18.50 last week. Of course ironing isn't as swell work as selling lace behind a counter, but it pays. None of us ironers make less than $10. And I don't know that it's any less respectful work, either."

"You can have it," said Nancy, with uplifted nose. "I'll take my eight a week and hall bedroom. I like to be among nice things and swell people. And look what a chance I've got! Why, one of our glove girls married a Pittsburgh—a steel maker, or blacksmith or something—

the other day, worth a million dollars. I'll catch a swell
myself some time. I ain't bragging on my looks or
anything; but I'll take my chances where there's big
prizes offered. What show would a girl have in a laundry?''

"Why, that's where I met Dan," said Lou, trium-
phantly. "He came in for his Sunday shirt and collars
and saw me at the first board, ironing. We all try to get
to work at the first board. Ella Maginnis was sick that
day, and I had her place. He said he noticed my arms
first, how round and white they was. I had my sleeves
rolled up. Some nice fellows come into laundries. You
can tell 'em by their bringing their clothes in suit cases,
and turning in the door sharp and sudden.''

"How can you wear a waist like that, Lou?" said
Nancy, gazing down at the offending article with sweet
scorn in her heavy-lidded eyes. "It shows fierce taste."

"This waist!" said Lou, with wide-eyed indignation.
"Why, I paid $16 for this waist. It's worth twenty-five.
A woman left it to be laundered, and never called for it.
The boss sold it to me. It's got yards and yards of hand
embroidery on it. Better talk about that ugly, plain thing
you've got on.''

"This ugly, plain thing," said Nancy, calmly, "was
copied from one that Mrs. Van Alstyne Fisher was wearing. The girls say her bill in the store last year was
$12,000. I made mine, myself. It cost me $1.50. Ten
feet away you couldn't tell it from hers.''

"Oh, well," said Lou, good-naturedly, "if you want
to starve and put on airs, go ahead. But I'll take my job
and good wages; and after hours give me something as
fancy and attractive to wear as I am able to buy.''

But just then Dan came—a serious young man with a
ready-made necktie, who had escaped the city's brand of
frivolity—an electrician earning $30 per week who looked
upon Lou with the sad eyes of Romeo, and thought her
embroidered waist a web in which any fly should delight
to be caught.

"My friend, Mr. Owens—shake hands with Miss Danforth," said Lou.

"I'm mighty glad to know you, Miss Danforth," said Dan, with outstretched hand. "I've heard Lou speak of you so often."

"Thanks," said Nancy, touching his fingers with the tips of her cool ones, "I've heard her mention you—a few times."

Lou giggled.

"Did you get that handshake from Mrs. Van Alstyne Fisher, Nance?" she asked.

"If I did, you can feel safe in copying it," said Nancy.

"Oh, I couldn't use it at all. It's too stylish for me. It's intended to set off diamond rings, that high shake is. Wait till I get a few and then I'll try it."

"Learn it first," said Nancy, wisely, "and you'll be more likely to get the rings."

"Now, to settle this argument," said Dan, with his ready, cheerful smile, "let me make you a proposition. As I can't take both of you up to Tiffany's and do the right thing, what do you say to a little vaudeville? I've got the tickets. How about looking at stage diamonds since we can't shake hands with the real sparklers?"

The faithful squire took his place close to the curb; Lou next, a little peacocky in her bright and pretty clothes; Nancy on the inside, slender, and soberly clothed as the sparrow, but with the true Van Alstyne Fisher walk—thus they set out for their evening's moderate diversion.

I do not suppose that many look upon a great department store as an educational institution. But the one in which Nancy worked was something like that to her. She was surrounded by beautiful things that breathed of taste and refinement. If you live in an atmosphere of luxury, luxury is yours whether your money pays for it, or another's.

The people she served were mostly women whose

dress, manners, and position in the social world were
quoted as criterions. From them Nancy began to take
toll—the best from each according to her view.

From one she would copy a practise or gesture, from
another an eloquent lifting of an eyebrow, from others, a
manner of walking, of carrying a purse, of smiling, of
greeting a friend, of addressing "inferiors in station."
From her best beloved model, Mrs. Van Alstyne Fisher,
she made requisition for that excellent thing, a soft, low
voice as clear as silver and as perfect in articulation as
the notes of a thrush. Suffused in the aura of this high
social refinement and good breeding, it was impossible
for her to escape a deeper effect of it. As good habits are
said to be better than good principles, so, perhaps, good
manners are better than good habits. The teachings of
your parents may not keep alive your New England
conscience; but if you sit on a straight-back chair and
repeat the words "prisms and pilgrims" forty times the
devil will flee from you. And when Nancy spoke in the
Van Alstyne Fisher tones she felt the thrill of *noblesse
oblige* to her very bones.

There was another source of learning in the great
departmental school. Whenever you see three or four
shop-girls gather in a bunch and jingle their wire brace-
lets as an accompaniment to apparently frivolous conversation, do not think that they are there for the purpose of
criticizing the way Ethel does her back hair. The meeting
may lack the dignity of the deliberative bodies of man;
but it has all the importance of the occasion on which
Eve and her first daughter first put their heads together to
make Adam understand his proper place in the household. It is Woman's Conference for Common Defense
and Exchange of Strategical Theories of Attack and Repulse upon and against the World, which is a Stage, and
Man, its Audience who Persists in Throwing Bouquets
Thereupon. Woman, the most helpless of the young of
any animal—with the fawn's grace but without its fleet-
ness; with the bird's beauty but without its power of

flight; with the honey-bee's burden of sweetness but without its—— Oh, let's drop that simile—some of us may have been stung.

During this council of war they pass weapons one to another, and exchange stratagems that each has devised and formulated out of the tactics of life.

"I says to 'im," says Sadie, "ain't you the fresh thing! Who do you suppose I am, to be addressing such a remark to me? And what do you think he says back to me?"

The heads, brown, black, flaxen, red, and yellow bob together; the answer is given; and the parry to the thrust is decided upon, to be used by each thereafter in passages-at-arms with the common enemy, man.

Thus Nancy learned the art of defense; and to women successful defense means victory.

The curriculum of a department store is a wide one. Perhaps no other college could have fitted her as well for her life's ambition—the drawing of a matrimonial prize.

Her station in the store was a favored one. The music room was near enough for her to hear and become familiar with the works of the best composers—at least to acquire the familiarity that passed for appreciation in the social world in which she was vaguely trying to set a tentative and aspiring foot. She absorbed the educating influence of art wares, of costly and dainty fabrics, of adornments that are almost culture to women.

The other girls soon became aware of Nancy's ambition. "Here comes your millionaire, Nancy," they would call to her whenever any man who looked the rôle approached her counter. It got to be a habit of men, who were hanging about while their women folks were shopping, to stroll over to the handkerchief counter and dawdle over the cambric squares. Nancy's imitation high-bred air and genuine dainty beauty was what attracted. Many men thus came to display their graces before her. Some of them may have been millionaires; others were certainly no more than their sedulous apes, Nancy learned to discriminate. There was a window at the end of the handkerchief counter; and she could see the rows of vehicles waiting for the shoppers in the street below. She looked and perceived that automobiles differ as well as do their owners.

Once a fascinating gentleman bought four dozen handkerchiefs, and wooed her across the counter with a King Cophetua air. When he had gone one of the girls said:

"What's wrong, Nance, that you didn't warm up to that fellow? He looks the swell article, all right, to me."

"Him?" said Nancy, with her coolest, sweetest, most impersonal, Van Alstyne Fisher smile; "not for mine. I saw him drive up outside. A 12 H. P. machine and an Irish chauffeur! And you saw what kind of handkerchiefs he bought—silk! And he's got dactylis on him. Give me the real thing or nothing, if you please."

Two of the most "refined" women in the store—a forelady and a cashier—had a few "swell gentlemen friends" with whom they now and then dined. Once they included Nancy in an invitation. The dinner took place in a spectacular café whose tables are engaged for New Year's Eve in advance. There were two "gentlemen friends"—one without any hair on his head—high living ungrew it; and we can prove it—the other a young man whose worth and sophistication he pressed upon you in two convincing ways—he swore that all the wine was corked; and he wore diamond cuff buttons. This young man perceived irresistible excellencies in Nancy. His taste ran to shop-girls; and here was one that added the voice and manners of his high social world to the franker charms of her own caste. So, on the following day, he appeared in the store and made her a serious proposal of marriage over a box of hemstitched, grass-bleached Irish linens. Nancy declined. A brown pompadour ten feet away had been using her eyes and ears. When the rejected suitor had gone she heaped carboys of upbraidings and horror upon Nancy's head.

"What a terrible little fool you are! That fellow's a

millionaire—he's a nephew of old Van Skittles himself. And he was talking on the level, too. Have you gone crazy, Nance?"

"Have I?" said Nancy. "I didn't take him, did I? He isn't a millionaire so hard that you could notice it, anyhow. His family only allows him $20,000 a year to spend. The bald-headed fellow was guying him about it the other night at supper."

The brown pompadour came nearer and narrowed her eyes.

"Say, what do you want?" she inquired, in a voice hoarse for lack of chewing-gum. "Ain't that enough for you? Do you want to be a Mormon, and marry Rockefeller and Gladstone Dowie and the King of Spain and the whole bunch? Ain't $20,000 a year good enough for you?"

Nancy flushed a little under the level gaze of the black, shallow eyes.

"It wasn't altogether the money, Carrie," she explained. "His friend caught him in a rank lie the other night at dinner. It was about some girl he said he hadn't been to the theater with. Well, I can't stand a liar. Put everything together—I don't like him; and that settles it. When I sell out it's not going to be on any bargain day. I've got to have something that sits up in a chair like a man, anyhow. Yes, I'm looking out for a catch; but it's got to be able to do something more than make a noise like a toy bank."

"The physiopathic ward for yours!" said the brown pompadour, walking away.

These high ideas, if not ideals—Nancy continued to cultivate on $8 per week. She bivouacked on the trail of the great unknown "catch" eating her dry bread and tightening her belt day by day. On her face was the faint, soldierly, sweet, grim smile of the preordained manhunter. The store was her forest; and many times she raised her rifle at game that seemed broad-antlered and big; but always some deep unerring instinct—perhaps of the huntress, perhaps of the woman—made her hold her fire and take up the trail again.

Lou flourished in the laundry. Out of her $18.50 per week she paid $6 for her room and board. The rest went mainly for clothes. Her opportunities for bettering her taste and manners were few compared with Nancy's. In the steaming laundry there was nothing but work, work and her thoughts of the evening pleasures to come. Many costly and showy fabrics passed under her iron; and it may be that her growing fondness for dress was thus transmitted to her through the conducting metal.

When the day's work was over Dan awaited her outside, her faithful shadow in whatever light she stood.

Sometimes he cast an honest and troubled glance at Lou's clothes that increased in conspicuity rather than in style; but this was no disloyalty; he deprecated the attention they called to her in the streets.

And Lou was no less faithful to her chum. There was a law that Nancy should go with them on whatsoever outings they might take. Dan bore the extra burden heartily and in good cheer. It might be said that Lou furnished the color, Nancy the tone, and Dan the weight of the distraction-seeking trio. The escort, in his neat but obviously ready-made suit, his ready-made tie and unfailing, genial, ready-made wit never startled or clashed. He was of that good kind that you are likely to forget while they are present, but remember distinctly after they are gone.

To Nancy's superior taste the flavor of these ready-made pleasures was sometimes a little bitter; but she was young; and youth is a gourmand, when it cannot be a gourmet.

"Dan is always wanting me to marry him right away," Lou told her once. "But why should I? I'm independent. I can do as I please with the money I earn; and he never would agree for me to keep on working afterward. And say, Nance, what do you want to stick to that old store for, and half starve and half dress yourself? I could get you a place in the laundry right now if you'd come. It seems to me that you could afford to be a little less stuck-up if you could make a good deal more money.''

"I don't think I'm stuck-up, Lou," said Nancy, "but I'd rather live on half rations and stay where I am. I suppose I've got the habit. It's the chance that I want. I don't expect to be always behind a counter. I'm learning something new every day. I'm right up against refined and rich people all the time—even if I do only wait on them; and I'm not missing any pointers that I see passing around.''

"Caught your millionaire yet?" asked Lou with her teasing laugh.

"I haven't selected one yet," answered Nancy. "I've been looking them over.''

"Goodness! the idea of picking over 'em! Don't you ever let one get by you, Nancy—even if he's a few dollars shy. But of course you're joking—millionaires don't think about working girls like us.''

"It might be better for them if they did," said Nancy, with cool wisdom. "Some of us could teach them how to take care of their money.''

"If one was to speak to me," laughed Lou, "I know I'd have a duck-fit.''

"That's because you don't know any. The only difference between swells and other people is you have to watch 'em closer. Don't you think that red silk lining is just a little bit too bright for that coat, Lou?''

Lou looked at the plain, dull olive jacket of her friend.

"Well, no, I don't—but it may seem so beside that faded-looking thing you've got on.''

"This jacket," said Nancy, complacently, "has exactly the cut and fit of one that Mrs. Van Alstyne Fisher was wearing the other day. The material cost me $3.98. I suppose hers cost about $100 more.''

"Oh, well," said Lou, lightly, "it don't strike me as millionaire bait. Shouldn't wonder if I catch one before you do, anyway.''

Truly it would have taken a philosopher to decide upon

the values of the theories held by the two friends. Lou, lacking that certain pride and fastidiousness that keeps stores and desks filled with girls working for the barest living, thumped away gaily with her iron in the noisy and stifling laundry. Her wages supported her even beyond the point of comfort; so that her dress profited until sometimes she cast a sidelong glance of impatience at the neat but inelegant apparel of Dan—Dan the constant, the immutable, the undeviating.

As for Nancy, her case was one of tens of thousands. Silk and jewels and laces and ornaments and the perfume and music of the fine world of good-breeding and taste— these were made for woman; they are her equitable portion. Let her keep near them if they are a part of life to her, and if she will. She is no traitor to herself, as Esau was; for she keeps her birthright and the pottage she earns is often very scant.

In this atmosphere Nancy belonged; and she throve in it and ate her frugal meals and schemed over her cheap dresses with a determined and contented mind. She already knew woman; and she was studying man, the animal, both as to his habits and eligibility. Some day she would bring down the game that she wanted; but she promised herself it would be what seemed to her the biggest and the best, and nothing smaller.

Thus she kept her lamp trimmed and burning to receive the bridegroom when he should come.

But another lesson she learned, perhaps unconsciously. Her standard of values began to shift and change. Sometimes the dollar-mark grew blurred in her mind's eye, and shaped itself into letters that spelled such words as "truth" and "honor" and now and then just "kindness." Let us make a likeness of one who hunts the moose or elk in some mighty wood. He sees a little dell, mossy and embowered, where a rill trickles, babbling to him of rest and comfort. At these times the spear of Nimrod himself grows blunt.

So, Nancy wondered sometimes if Persian lamb was

always quoted at its market value by the hearts that it covered.

One Thursday evening Nancy left the store and turned across Sixth Avenue westward to the laundry. She was expected to go with Lou and Dan to a musical comedy.

Dan was just coming out of the laundry when she arrived. There was a queer, strained look on his face.

"I thought I would drop around to see if they had heard from her," he said.

"Heard from who?" asked Nancy. "Isn't Lou there?"

"I thought you knew," said Dan. "She hasn't been here or at the house where she lived since Monday. She moved all her things from there. She told one of the girls in the laundry she might be going to Europe."

"Hasn't anybody seen her anywhere?" asked Nancy.

Dan looked at her with his jaws set grimly, and a steely gleam in his steady gray eyes.

"They told me in the laundry," he said, harshly, "that they saw her pass yesterday—in an automobile. With one of the millionaires, I suppose, that you and Lou were forever busying your brains about."

For the first time Nancy quailed before a man. She laid her hand that trembled slightly on Dan's sleeve.

"You've no right to say such a thing to me, Dan—as if I had anything to do with it."

"I didn't mean it that way," said Dan, softening. He fumbled in his vest pocket.

"I've got the tickets for the show to-night," he said, with a gallant show of lightness. "If you——"

Nancy admired pluck whenever she saw it.

"I'll go with you, Dan," she said.

Three months went by before Nancy saw Lou again.

At twilight one evening the shop-girl was hurrying home along the border of a little quiet park. She heard her name called, and wheeled about in time to catch Lou rushing into her arms.

After the first embrace they drew their heads back as serpents do, ready to attack or to charm, with a thousand questions trembling on their swift tongues. And then Nancy noticed that prosperity had descended upon Lou, manifesting itself in costly furs, flashing gems, and creations of the tailor's art.

"You little fool!" cried Lou, loudly and affectionately. "I see you are still working in that store, and as shabby as ever. And how about that big catch you were going to make—nothing doing yet, I suppose?"

And then Lou looked, and saw that something better than prosperity had descended upon Nancy—something that shone brighter than gems in her eyes and redder than a rose in her cheeks, and that danced like electricity anxious to be loosed from the tip of her tongue.

"Yes, I'm still in the store," said Nancy, "but I'm going to leave it next week. I've made my catch—the biggest catch in the world. You won't mind now Lou, will you?—I'm going to be married to Dan—to Dan! —he's my Dan now—why, Lou!"

Around the corner of the park strolled one of those new-crop, smooth-faced young policemen that are making the force more endurable—at least to the eye. He saw a woman with an expensive fur coat, and diamond-ringed hands crouching down against the iron fence of the park sobbing turbulently, while a slender, plainly dressed working girl leaned close, trying to console her. But the Gibsonian cop, being of the new order, passed on, pretending not to notice, for he was wise enough to know that these matters are beyond help so far as the power he represents is concerned, though he rap the pavement with his nightstick till the sound goes up to the furthermost stars.

The Badge of Policeman O'Roon

It cannot be denied that men and women have looked upon one another for the first time and become instantly enamored. It is a risky process, this love at first sight, before she has seen him in Bradstreet or he has seen her in curl papers. But these things do happen; and one instance must form a theme for this story—though not, thank Heaven, to the overshadowing of more vital and important subjects, such as drink, policemen, horses, and earldoms.

During a certain war a troop calling itself the Gentle Riders rode into history and one or two ambuscades. The Gentle Riders were recruited from the aristocracy of the wild men of the West and the wild men of the aristocracy of the East. In khaki there is little telling them one from another, so they became good friends and comrades all around.

Ellsworth Remsen, whose old Knickerbocker descent atoned for his modest rating at only ten millions, ate his canned beef gayly by the campfires of the Gentle Riders. The war was a great lark to him, so that he scarcely regretted polo and planked shad.

One of the troopers was a well-set-up, affable, cool young man, who called himself O'Roon. To this young man Remsen took an especial liking. The two rode side by side during the famous mooted up-hill charge that was disputed so hotly at the time by the Spaniards and afterward by the Democrats.

After the war Remsen came back to his polo and shad.

One day a well-set-up, affable, cool young man disturbed him at his club, and he and O'Roon were soon pounding each other and exchanging opprobrious epithets after the manner of long-lost friends. O'Roon looked seedy and out of luck and perfectly contented. But it seemed that his content was only apparent.

"Get me a job, Remsen," he said. "I've just handed a barber my last shilling."

"No trouble at all," said Remsen. "I know a lot of men who have banks and stores and things downtown. Any particular line you fancy?"

"Yes," said O'Roon, with a look of interest. "I took a walk in your Central Park this morning. I'd like to be one of those bobbies on horseback. That would be about the ticket. Besides, it's the only thing I could do. I can ride a little and the fresh air suits me. Think you could land that for me?"

Remsen was sure that he could. And in a very short time he did. And they who were not above looking at mounted policemen might have seen a well-set-up, affable, cool young man on a prancing chestnut steed attending to his duties along the driveways of the park.

And now at the extreme risk of wearying old gentlemen who carry leather fob chains, and elderly ladies who—but no! grandmother herself yet thrills at foolish, immortal Romeo—there must be a hint of love at first sight.

It came just as Remsen was strolling into Fifth Avenue from his club a few doors away.

A motor car was creeping along foot by foot, impeded by a freshet of vehicles that filled the street. In the car was a chauffeur and an old gentleman with snowy side whiskers and a Scotch plaid cap which could not be worn while automobiling except by a personage. Not even a wine agent would dare do it. But these two were of no consequence—except, perhaps, for the guiding of the machine and the paying for it. At the old gentleman's side sat a young lady more beautiful than pomegranate blossoms, more exquisite than the first quarter moon viewed at twilight through the tops of oleanders. Remsen saw her and knew his fate. He could have flung himself under the very wheels that conveyed her, but he knew that would be the last means of attracting the attention of those who ride in motor cars. Slowly the auto passed, and, if we place the poets above the autoists, carried the heart of Remsen with it. Here was a large city of millions, and many women who at a certain distance appear to resemble pomegranate blossoms. Yet he hoped to see her again; for each one fancies that his romance has its own tutelary guardian and divinity.

Luckily for Remsen's peace of mind there came a diversion in the guise of a reunion of the Gentle Riders of the city. There were not many of them—perhaps a score—and there was wassail and things to eat, and speeches and the Spaniard was bearded again in recapitulation. And when daylight threatened them the survivors prepared to depart. But some remained upon the battlefield. One of these was Trooper O'Roon, who was not seasoned to potent liquids. His legs declined to fulfil the obligations they had sworn to the police department.

"I'm stewed, Remsen," said O'Roon to his friend. "Why do they build hotels that go round and round like catherine wheels? They'll take away my shield and break me. I can think and talk con-con-consec-sec-secutively, but I s-s-stammer with my feet. I've got to go on duty in three hours. The jig is up, Remsen. The jig is up, I tell you."

"Look at me," said Remsen, who was his smiling self, pointing to his own face; "whom do you see here?"

"Goo' fellow," said O'Roon, dizzily. "Goo' old Remsen."

"Not so," said Remsen. "You see Mounted Policeman O'Roon. Look at your face—no; you can't do that without a glass—but look at mine, and think of yours. How much alike are we? As two French *table d'hôte* dinners. With your badge, on your horse, in your uniform, will I charm nurse-maids and prevent the grass from growing under people's feet in the Park this day. I will have your badge and your honor, besides having the jolliest lark I've been blessed with since we licked Spain.''

Promptly on time the counterfeit presentment of Mounted Policeman O'Roon single-footed into the Park on his chestnut steed. In a uniform two men who are unlike will look alike; two who somewhat resemble each other in feature and figure will appear as twin brothers. So Remsen trotted down the bridle paths, enjoying himself hugely, so few real pleasures do ten-millionaires have.

Along the driveway in the early morning spun a victoria drawn by a pair of fiery bays. There was something foreign about the affair, for the Park is rarely used in the morning, except by unimportant people who love to be healthy, poor, and wise. In the vehicle sat an old gentleman with snowy side-whiskers and a Scotch plaid cap which could not be worn while driving except by a personage. At his side sat the lady of Remsen's heart—the lady who looked like pomegranate blossoms and the gibbous moon.

Remsen met them coming. At the instant of their passing her eyes looked into his, and but for the ever coward's heart of a true lover he could have sworn that she flushed a faint pink. He trotted on for twenty yards, and then wheeled his horse at the sound of runaway hoofs. The bays had bolted.

Remsen sent his chestnut after the victoria like a shot. There was work cut out for the impersonator of Policeman O'Roon. The chestnut ranged alongside the off bay thirty seconds after the chase began, rolled his eye back at Remsen, and said in the only manner open to policemen's horses:

''Well, you duffer, are you going to do your share? You're not O'Roon, but it seems to me if you'd lean to the right you could reach the reins of that foolish slow-running bay—ah! you're all right; O'Roon couldn't have done it more neatly!''

The runaway team was tugged to an inglorious halt by Remsen's tough muscles. The driver released his hands from the wrapped reins, jumped from his seat and stood at the heads of the team. The chestnut, approving his new rider, danced and pranced, reviling equinely the subdued bays. Remsen, lingering, was dimly conscious of a vague, impossible, unnecessary old gentleman in a Scotch cap who talked incessantly about something. And he was acutely conscious of a pair of violet eyes that would have drawn Saint Pyrites from his iron pillar—or whatever the allusion is—and of the lady's smile and look—a little frightened, but a look that, with the ever coward heart of a true lover, he could not yet construe. They were asking his name and bestowing upon him well-bred thanks for his heroic deed, and the Scotch cap was especially babbling and insistent. But the eloquent appeal was in the eyes of the lady.

A little thrill of satisfaction ran through Remsen, because he had a name to give which, without undue pride, was worthy of being spoken in high places, and a small fortune which, with due pride, he could leave at his end without disgrace.

He opened his lips to speak and closed them again.

Who was he? Mounted Policeman O'Roon. The badge and the honor of his comrade were in his hands. If Ellsworth Remsen, ten-millionaire and Knickerbocker, had just rescued pomegranate blossoms and Scotch cap from possible death, where was Policeman O'Roon? Off his beat, exposed, disgraced, discharged. Love had come, but before that there had been something that demanded precedence—the fellowship of men on battlefields fighting an alien foe.

Remsen touched his cap, looked between the chestnut's ears, and took refuge in vernacularity.

"Don't mention it," he said, stolidly. "We policemen are paid to do these things. It's our duty."

And he rode away—rode away cursing *noblesse oblige*, but knowing he could never have done anything else.

At the end of the day Remsen sent the chestnut to his stable and went to O'Roon's room. The policeman was again a well-set-up, affable, cool young man who sat by the window smoking cigars.

"I wish you and the rest of the police force and all badges, horses, brass buttons, and men who can't drink two glasses of *brut* without getting upset were at the devil," said Remsen, feelingly.

O'Roon smiled with evident satisfaction.

"Good old Remsen," he said, affably. "I know all about it. They trailed me down and cornered me here two hours ago. There was a little row at home, you know, and I cut sticks just to show them. I don't believe I told you that my Governor was the Earl of Ardsley. Funny you should bob against them in the Park. If you damaged that horse of mine I'll never forgive you. I'm going to buy him and take him back with me. Oh, yes, and I think my sister—Lady Angela, you know—wants particularly for you to come up to the hotel with me this evening. Didn't lose my badge, did you, Remsen? I've got to turn that in at Headquarters when I resign."

The Tale of a Tainted Tenner

Money talks, but you may think that the conversation of a little old ten-dollar bill in New York would be nothing more than a whisper. Oh, very well! Pass up this *sotto voce* autobiography of an X if you like. If you are one of the kind that prefers to listen to John D.'s checkbook roar at you through a megaphone as it passes by, all right. But don't forget that small change can say a word to the point now and then. The next time you tip your grocer's clerk a silver quarter to give you extra weight of his boss's goods read the four words above the lady's head. How are they for repartee?

I am a ten-dollar Treasury note, series of 1901. You may have seen one in a friend's hand. On my face, in the centre, is a picture of the bison Americanus, miscalled a buffalo by fifty or sixty millions of Americans. The heads of Capt. Lewis and Capt. Clark adorn the ends. On my back is the graceful figure of Liberty or Ceres or Maxine Elliott standing in the centre of the stage on a conservatory plant. My references is—or are—Section 3,588, Revised Statutes. Ten cold, hard dollars—I don't say whether silver, gold, lead or iron—Uncle Sam will hand you over his counter if you want to cash me in.

I beg you will excuse any conversational breaks that I make—thanks, I knew you would—got that sneaking little respect and agreeable feeling toward even an X, haven't you? You see, a tainted bill doesn't have much chance to acquire a correct form of expression. I never knew a really cultured and educated person that could afford to hold a ten-spot any longer than it would take to do an Arthur Duffy to the nearest That's All! sign or delicatessen store.

For a six-year-old, I've had a lively and gorgeous circulation. I guess I've paid as many debts as the man who dies. I've been owned by a good many kinds of people. But a little old ragged, damp, dingy five-dollar silver certificate gave me a jar one day. I was next to it in the fat and bad-smelling purse of a butcher.

"Hey, you Sitting Bull," says I, "don't scrouge so. Anyhow, don't you think it's about time you went in on a customs payment and got reissued? For a series of 1899 you're a sight."

"Oh, don't get crackly just because you're a Buffalo bill," says the fiver. "You'd be limp, too, if you'd been stuffed down in a thick cotton-and-lisle-thread under an elastic all day, and the thermometer not a degree under 85 in the store."

"I never heard of a pocketbook like that," says I. "Who carried you?"

"A shopgirl," says the five-spot.

"What's that?" I had to ask.

"You'll never know till their millennium comes," says the fiver.

Just then a two-dollar bill behind me with a George Washington head, spoke up to the fiver:

"Aw, cut out yer kicks. Ain't lisle thread good enough for yer? If you was under all cotton like I'd been to-day, and choked up with factory dust till the lady with the cornucopia on me sneezed half a dozen times, you'd have some reason to complain."

That was the next day after I arrived in New York. I came in a $500 package of tens to a Brooklyn bank from one of its Pennsylvania correspondents—and I haven't made the acquaintance of any of the five and two spots' friends' pocketbooks yet. Silk for mine, every time.

I was lucky money. I kept on the move. Sometimes I changed hands twenty times a day. I saw the inside of every business; I fought for my owner's every pleasure. It seemed that on Saturday nights I never missed being slapped down on a bar. Tens were always slapped down, while ones and twos were slid over to the bartenders folded. I got in the habit of looking for mine, and I managed to soak in a little straight or some spilled Martini or Manhattan whenever I could. Once I got tied up in a great greasy roll of bills in a pushcart peddler's jeans. I thought I never would get in circulation again, for the future department store owner lived on eight cents' worth of dog meat and onions a day. But this peddler got into trouble one day on account of having his cart too near a crossing, and I was rescued. I always will feel grateful to the cop that got me. He changed me at a cigar store near the Bowery that was running a crap game in the back room. So it was the Captain of the precinct, after all, that did me the best turn, when he got his. He blew me for wine and the next evening in a Broadway restaurant; and I really felt as glad to get back again as an Astor does when he sees the lights of Charing Cross.

A tainted ten certainly does get action on Broadway. I was alimony once, and got folded in a little dogskin purse among a lot of dimes. They were bragging about the busy times there were in Ossining whenever three girls got hold of one of them during the ice cream season. But its Slow Moving Vehicles Keep to the Right for the little Bok tips when you think of the way we bison plasters refuse to stick to anything during the rush lobster hour.

The first I ever heard of tainted money was one night when a good thing with a Van to his name threw me over with some other bills to buy a stack of blues.

About midnight a big, easy-going man with a fat face like a monk's and the eye of a janitor with his wages raised took me and a lot of other notes and rolled us into what is termed a "wad" among the money tainters.

"Ticket me for five hundred," said he to the banker, "and look out for everything, Charlie. I'm going out for a stroll in the glen before the moonlight fades from the brow of the cliff. If anybody finds the roof in their way there's $60,000 wrapped in a comic supplement in the upper left-hand corner of the safe. Be bold; everywhere be bold, but be not bowled over. 'Night.''

I found myself between two $20 gold certificates. One of 'em says to me:

"Well, old shorthorn, you're in luck to-night. You'll see something of life. Old Jack's going to make the Tenderloin look like a hamburg steak.''

"Explain,'' says I. "I'm used to joints, but I don't care for filet mignon with the kind of sauce you serve.''

" 'Xcuse me,'' said the twenty. "Old Jack is the proprietor of this gambling house. He's going on a whiz to-night because he offered $50,000 to a church and it refused to accept it because they said his money was tainted.''

"What is a church?'' I asked.

"Oh, I forgot,'' says the twenty, "that I was talking to a tenner. Of course you don't know. You're too much to put into the contribution basket, and not enough to buy anything at a bazaar. A church is—a large building in which penwipers and tidies are sold at $20 each.''

I don't care much about chinning with gold certificates. There's a streak of yellow in 'em. All is not gold that quitters.

Old Jack certainly was a gilt-edged sport. When it came his time to loosen up he never referred the waiter to an actuary.

By and by it got around that he was smiting the rock in the wilderness; and all along Broadway things with cold noses and hot gullets fell in on our trail. The third Jungle Book was there waiting for somebody to put covers on it. Old Jack's money may have had a taint to it, but all the same he had orders for his Camembert piling up on him every minute. First his friends rallied round him; and then the fellows that his friends knew by sight; and then a few of his enemies buried the hatchet; and finally he was buying souvenirs for so many Neapolitan fisher maidens and butterfly octettes that the head waiters were 'phoning all over town for Julian Mitchell to please come around and get them into some kind of order.

At last we floated into an uptown café that I knew by heart. When the hod-carriers' union in jackets and aprons saw us coming the chief goal kicker called out: "Six—eleven—forty-two—nineteen—twelve" to his men, and they put on nose guards till it was clear whether we meant Port Arthur or Portsmouth. But old Jack wasn't working for the furniture and glass factories that night. He sat down quiet and sang "Ramble" in a half-hearted way. His feelings had been hurt, so the twenty told me, because his offer to the church had been refused.

But the wassail went on; and Brady himself couldn't have hammered the thirst mob into a better imitation of the real penchant for the stuff that you screw out of a bottle with a napkin.

Old Jack paid the twenty above me for a round, leaving me on the outside of his roll. He laid the roll on the table and sent for the proprietor.

"Mike," says he, "here's money that the good people have refused. Will it buy of your wares in the name of the devil? They say it's tainted."

"It will," says Mike, "and I'll put it in the drawer next to the bills that was paid to the parson's daughter for kisses at the church fair to build a new parsonage for the parson's daughter to live in."

At 1 o'clock when the hod-carriers were making ready to close up the front and keep the inside open, a woman slips in the door of the restaurant and comes up to Old Jack's table. You've seen the kind—black shawl, creepy hair, ragged skirt, white face, eyes a cross between Gabriel's and a sick kitten's—the kind of woman that's always on the lookout for an automobile or the mendicancy squad—and she stands there without a word and looks at the money.

Old Jack gets up, peels me off the roll and hands me to her with a bow.

"Madam," says he, just like actors I've heard, "here is a tainted bill. I am a gambler. This bill came to me to-night from a gentleman's son. Where he got it I do not know. If you will do me the favor to accept it, it is yours."

The woman took me with a trembling hand.

"Sir," said she, "I counted thousands of this issue of bills into packages when they were virgin from the presses. I was a clerk in the Treasury Department. There was an official to whom I owed my position. You say they are tainted now. If you only knew—but I won't say any more. Thank you with all my heart, sir—thank you— thank you."

Where do you suppose that woman carried me almost at a run? To a bakery. Away from Old Jack and a sizzling good time to a bakery. And I got changed, and she does a Sheridan-twenty-miles-away with a dozen rolls and a section of jelly cake as big as a turbine water-wheel. Of course I lost sight of her then, for I was snowed up in the bakery, wondering whether I'd get changed at the drug store the next day in an alum deal or paid over to the cement works.

A week afterward I butted up against one of the one-dollar bills the baker had given the woman for change.

"Hello, E35039669," says I, "weren't you in the change for me in a bakery last Saturday night?"

"Yep," says the solitaire in his free and easy style.

"How did the deal turn out?" I asked.

"She blew E17051431 for milk and round steak," says the one-spot. "She kept me till the rent men came. It was a bum room with a sick kid in it. But you ought to have seen him go for the bread and tincture of formalde-hyde. Half-starved, I guess. Then she prayed some. Don't get stuck up, tenner. We one-spots hear ten prayers, when you hear one. She said something about 'who giveth to the poor.' Oh, let's cut out the slum talk. I'm certainly tired of the company that keeps me. I wish I was big enough to move in society with you tainted bills.''

''Shut up,'' says I, ''there's no such thing. I know the rest of it. There's a 'lendeth to the Lord'; somewhere in it. Now look on my back and read what you see there.''

''This note is a legal tender at its face value for all debts public and private.''

''This talk about tainted money makes me tired,'' says I.

Compliments of
the Season

There are no more Christmas stories to write. Fiction is exhausted; and newspaper items, the next best, are manufactured by clever young journalists who have married early and have an engagingly pessimistic view of life. Therefore, for seasonable diversion, we are reduced to two very questionable sources—facts and philosophy. We will begin with—whichever you choose to call it.

Children are pestilential little animals with which we have to cope under a bewildering variety of conditions. Especially when childish sorrows overwhelm them are we put to our wits' ends. We exhaust our paltry store of consolation; and then beat them, sobbing, to sleep. Then we grovel in the dust of a million years, and ask God why. Thus we crawl out of the rattrap. As for the children, no one understands them except old maids, hunchbacks, and shepherd dogs.

Now come the facts in the case of the Rag-Doll, the Tatterdemalion, and the Twenty-fifth of December.

On the tenth of that month the Child of the Millionaire lost her rag-doll. There were many servants in the Millionaire's palace on the Hudson, and these ransacked the house and grounds, but without finding the lost treasure. The Child was a girl of five, and one of those perverse little beasts that often wound the sensibilities of wealthy parents by fixing their affections upon some vulgar, inexpensive toy instead of upon diamond-studded automobiles and pony phaetons.

The Child grieved sorely and truly, a thing inexplica-

ble to the Millionaire, to whom the rag-doll market was
about as interesting as Bay State Gas; and to the Lady,
the Child's mother, who was all form—that is, nearly all,
as you shall see.

The Child cried inconsolably, and grew hollow-eyed,
knock-kneed, spindling, and cory-kilverty in many other
respects. The Millionaire smiled and tapped his coffers
confidently. The pick of the output of the French and
German toymakers was rushed by special delivery to the
mansion; but Rachel refused to be comforted. She was
weeping for her rag child, and was for a high protective
tariff against all foreign foolishness. Then doctors with
the finest bedside manners and stop-watches were called
in. One by one they chattered futilely about peptomanganate
of iron and sea voyages and hypophosphites until their
stopwatches showed that Bill Rendered was under the
wire for show or place. Then, as men, they advised that
the rag-doll be found as soon as possible and restored to
its mourning parent. The Child sniffed at therapeutics,
chewed a thumb, and wailed for her Betsy. And all this
time cablegrams were coming from Santa Claus saying
that he would soon be here and enjoining us to show a
true Christian spirit and let up on the poolrooms and
tontine policies and platoon systems long enough to give
him a welcome. Everywhere the spirit of Christmas was
diffusing itself. The banks were refusing loans, the pawn-
brokers had doubled their gang of helpers, people bumped
your shins on the streets with red sleds, Thomas and
Jeremiah bubbled before you on the bars while you waited
on one foot, holly-wreaths of hospitality were hung in
windows of the stores, they who had 'em were getting
out their furs. You hardly knew which was the best bet in
balls—three, high, moth, or snow. It was no time at
which to lose the rag-doll of your heart.

If Doctor Watson's investigating friend had been called
in to solve this mysterious disappearance he might have
observed on the Millionaire's wall a copy of "The Vam-
pire." That would have quickly suggested, by induction,

"A rag and a bone and a hank of hair." "Flip," a
Scotch terrier, next to the rag-doll in the Child's heart,
frisked through the halls. The hank of hair! Aha! X, the
unfound quantity, represented the rag-doll. But, the bone?
Well, when dogs find bones they—— Done! it were an
easy and a fruitful task to examine Flip's forefeet. Look,
Watson! Earth—dried earth between the toes. Of course,
the dog—but Sherlock was not there. Therefore it de-
volves. But topography and architecture must intervene.

The Millionaire's palace occupied a lordly space. In
front of it was a lawn close-mowed as a South Ireland
man's face two days after a shave. At one side of it, and
fronting on another street, was a pleasaunce trimmed to a
leaf, and the garage and stables. The Scotch pup had
ravished the rag-doll from the nursery, dragged it to a
corner of the lawn, dug a hole, and buried it after the
manner of careless undertakers. There you have the mystery solved, and no checks to write for the hypodermical
wizard or fi'-pun notes to toss to the sergeant. Then let's
get down to the heart of the thing, tiresome readers—the
Christmas heart of the thing.

Fuzzy was drunk—not riotously or helplessly or loqua-
ciously, as you or I might get, but decently, appropri-
ately, and inoffensively, as becomes a gentleman down
on his luck.

Fuzzy was a soldier of misfortune. The road, the
haystack, the park bench, the kitchen door, the bitter
round of eleemosynary beds-with-shower-bath-attachment,
the petty pickings and ignobly garnered largesse of great
cities—these formed the chapters of his history.

Fuzzy walked toward the river, down the street that
bounded one side of the Millionaire's house and grounds.
He saw a leg of Betsy, the lost rag-doll, protruding, like
the clue to a Lilliputian murder mystery, from its un-
timely grave in a corner of the fence. He dragged forth
the maltreated infant, tucked it under his arm, and went
on his way crooning a road song of his brethren that no
doll that has been brought up to the sheltered life should

hear. Well for Betsy that she had no ears. And well that she had no eyes save unseeing circles of black; for the faces of Fuzzy and the Scotch terrier were those of brothers, and the heart of no rag-doll could withstand twice to become the prey of such fearsome monsters.

Though you may not know it, Grogan's saloon stands near the river and near the foot of the street down which Fuzzy traveled. In Grogan's, Christmas cheer was already rampant.

Fuzzy entered with his doll. He fancied that as a mummer at the feast of Saturn he might earn a few drops from the wassail cup.

He set Betsy on the bar and addressed her loudly and humorously, seasoning his speech with exaggerated compliments and endearments as one entertaining his lady friend. The loafers and bibbers around caught the farce of it, and roared. The bartender gave Fuzzy a drink. Oh, many of us carry rag-dolls.

"One for the lady?" suggested Fuzzy, impudently, and tucked another contribution to Art beneath his waistcoat.

He began to see possibilities in Betsy. His first-night had been a success. Visions of a vaudeville circuit about town dawned upon him.

In a group near the stove sat "Pigeon" McCarthy, Black Riley, and "One-ear" Mike, well and unfavorably known in the tough shoe-string district that blackened the left bank of the river. They passed a newspaper back and forth among themselves. The item that each solid and blunt forefinger pointed out was an advertisement headed "One Hundred Dollars Reward." To earn it one must return the rag-doll lost, strayed, or stolen from the Millionaire's mansion. It seemed that grief still ravaged, unchecked, in the bosom of the too faithful Child. Flip, the terrier, capered and shook his absurd whisker before her, powerless to distract. She wailed for her Betsy in the faces of walking, talking, mamaing, and eye-closing French

Mabelles and Violettes. The advertisement was a last resort.

Black Riley came from behind the stove and approached Fuzzy in his one-sided parabolic way.

The Christmas mummer, flushed with success, had tucked Betsy under his arm, and was about to depart to the filling of impromptu dates elsewhere.

"Say, 'Bo," said Black Riley to him, "where did you cop out dat doll?"

"This doll?" asked Fuzzy, touching Betsy with his forefinger to be sure that she was the one referred to. "Why, this doll was presented to me by the Emperor of Beloochistan. I have seven hundred others in my country home in Newport. This doll—"

"Cheese the funny business," said Riley. "You swiped it or picked it up at de house on de hill where—but never mind dat. You want to take fifty cents for de rags, and take it quick. Me brother's kid at home might be wantin' to play wid it. Hey—what?"

He produced the coin.

Fuzzy laughed a gurgling, insolent, alcoholic laugh in his face. Go to the office of Sarah Bernhardt's manager and propose to him that she be released from a night's performance to entertain the Tackytown Lyceum and Literary Coterie. You will hear the duplicate of Fuzzy's laugh.

Black Riley gauged Fuzzy quickly with his blueberry eye as a wrestler does. His hand was itching to play the Roman and wrest the rag Sabine from the extemporaneous merry-andrew who was entertaining an angel unaware. But he refrained. Fuzzy was fat and solid and big. Three inches of well-nourished corporeity, defended from the winter winds by dingy linen, intervened between his vest and trousers. Countless small, circular wrinkles running around his coatsleeves and knees guaranteed the quality of his bone and muscle. His small, blue eyes, bathed in the moisture of altruism and wooziness, looked upon you kindly, yet without abashment. He was whiskerly, whiskyly, fleshily formidable. So, Black Riley temporized.

"Wot'll you take for it, den?" he asked.

"Money," said Fuzzy, with husky firmness, "cannot buy her."

He was intoxicated with the artist's first sweet cup of attainment. To set a faded-blue, earth-stained rag-doll on a bar, to hold mimic converse with it, and to find his heart leaping with the sense of plaudits earned and his throat scorching with free libations poured in his honor—could base coin buy him from such achievements? You will perceive that Fuzzy had the temperament.

Fuzzy walked out with the gait of a trained sea-lion in search of other cafés to conquer.

Though the dusk of twilight was hardly yet apparent, lights were beginning to spangle the city like popcorn bursting in a deep skillet. Christmas Eve, impatiently expected, was peeping over the brink of the hour. Millions had prepared for its celebration. Towns would be painted red. You, yourself, have heard the horns and dodged the capers of the Saturnalians.

"Pigeon" McCarthy, Black Riley, and "One-ear" Mike held a hasty converse outside Grogan's. They were narrow-chested, pallid striplings, not fighters in the open, but more dangerous in their ways of warfare than the most terrible of Turks. Fuzzy, in a pitched battle, could have eaten the three of them. In a go-as-you-please encounter he was already doomed.

They overtook him just as he and Betsy were entering Costigan's Casino. They deflected him, and shoved the newspaper under his nose. Fuzzy could read—and more.

"Boys," said he, "you are certainly damn true friends. Give me a week to think it over."

The soul of the real artist is quenched with difficulty.

The boys carefully pointed out to him that advertisements were soulless, and that the deficiencies of the day might not be supplied by the morrow.

"A cool hundred," said Fuzzy, thoughtfully and mushily.

"Boys," said he, "you are true friends. I'll go up and claim the reward. The show business is not what it used to be."

Night was falling more surely. The three tagged at his sides to the foot of the rise on which stood the Millionaire's house. There Fuzzy turned upon them acrimoniously.

"You are a pack of putty-faced beagle-hounds," he roared. "Go away."

They went away—a little way.

In "Pigeon" McCarthy's pocket was a section of one-inch gas-pipes eight inches long. In one end of it and in the middle of it was a lead slug. One-half of it was packed tight with solder. Black Riley carried a sling-shot, being a conventional thug. "One-ear" Mike relied upon a pair of brass knucks—an heirloom in the family.

"Why fetch and carry," said Black Riley, "when some one will do it for ye? Let him bring it out to us. Hey—what?"

"We can chuck him in the river," said "Pigeon" McCarthy, "with a stone tied to his feet."

"Youse guys make me tired," said "One-ear" Mike sadly. "Ain't progress ever appealed to none of yez? Sprinkle a little gasoline on 'im, and drop 'im on the Drive—well?"

Fuzzy entered the Millionaire's gate and zigzagged toward the softly glowing entrance of the mansion. The three goblins came up to the gate and lingered—one on each side of it, one beyond the roadway. They fingered their cold metal and leather, confident.

Fuzzy rang the door-bell, smiling foolishly and dreamily. An atavistic instinct prompted him to reach for the button of his right glove. But he wore no gloves; so his left hand dropped, embarrassed.

The particular menial whose duty it was to open doors to silks and laces shied at first sight of Fuzzy. But a second glance took in his passport, his card of admission,

his surety of welcome—the lost rag-doll of the daughter
of the house dangling under his arm.

Fuzzy was admitted into a great hall, dim with the
glow from unseen lights. The hireling went away and
returned with a maid and the Child. The doll was restored to the mourning one. She clasped her lost darling
to her breast; and then, with the inordinate selfishness
and candor of childhood, stamped her foot and whined
hatred and fear of the odious being who had rescued her
from the depths of sorrow and despair. Fuzzy wriggled
himself into an ingratiatory attitude and essayed the idi-
otic smile and blattering small talk that is supposed to
charm the budding intellect of the young. The Child
bawled, and was dragged away, hugging her Betsy close.

There came the Secretary, pale, poised, polished, glid-
ing in pumps, and worshipping pomp and ceremony. He
counted out into Fuzzy's hand ten ten-dollar bills; then
dropped his eye upon the door, transferred it to James, its
custodian, indicated the obnoxious earner of the reward
with the other, and allowed his pumps to waft him away
to secretarial regions.

James gathered Fuzzy with his own commanding optic
and swept him as far as the front door.

When the money touched Fuzzy's dingy palm his first
instinct was to take to his heels; but a second thought
restrained him from that blunder of etiquette. It was his;
it had been given him. It—and, oh, what an elysium it
opened to the gaze of his mind's eye! He had tumbled to
the foot of the ladder; he was hungry, homeless, friend-
less, ragged, cold, drifting; and he held in his hand the
key to a paradise of the mud-honey that he craved. The
fairy doll had waved a wand with her rag-stuffed hand;
and now wherever he might go the enchanted palaces
with shining foot-rests and magic red fluids in gleaming
glassware would be open to him.

He followed James to the door.

He paused there as the flunky drew open the great
mahogany portal for him to pass into the vestibule.

Beyond the wrought-iron gates in the dark highway Black Riley and his two pals casually strolled, fingering under their coats the inevitably fatal weapons that were to make the reward of the rag-doll theirs.

Fuzzy stopped at the Millionaire's door and bethought himself. Like little sprigs of mistletoe on a dead tree, certain living green thoughts and memories began to decorate his confused mind. He was quite drunk, mind you, and the present was beginning to fade. Those wreaths and festoons of holly with their scarlet berries making the great hall gay—where had he seen such things before? Somewhere he had known polished floors and odors of fresh flowers in winter, and—some one was singing a song in the house that he thought he had heard before. Some one singing and playing a harp. Of course, it was Christmas—Fuzzy thought he must have been pretty drunk to have overlooked that.

And then he went out of the present, and there came back to him out of some impossible, vanished, and irrevocable past a little, pure-white, transient, forgotten ghost—the spirit of *noblesse oblige*. Upon a gentleman certain things devolve.

James opened the outer door. A stream of light went down the graveled walk to the iron gate. Black Riley, McCarthy, and "One-ear" Mike saw, and carelessly drew their sinister cordon closer about the gate.

With a more imperious gesture than James's master had ever used or could ever use, Fuzzy compelled the menial to close the door. Upon a gentleman certain things devolve. Especially at the Christmas season.

"It is cust—customary," he said to James, the flustered, "when a gentleman calls on Christmas Eve to pass the compliments of the season with the lady of the house. You und'stand? I shall not move shtep till I pass compl'ments season with lady the house. Und'stand?"

There was an argument. James lost. Fuzzy raised his voice and sent it through the house unpleasantly. I did not say he was a gentleman. He was simply a tramp being visited by a ghost.

A sterling silver bell rang. James went back to answer it, leaving Fuzzy in the hall. James explained somewhere to some one.

Then he came and conducted Fuzzy to the library.

The Lady entered a moment later. She was more beautiful and holy than any picture that Fuzzy had seen. She smiled, and said something about a doll. Fuzzy didn't understand that; he remembered nothing about a doll.

A footman brought in two small glasses of sparkling wine on a stamped sterling-silver waiter. The Lady took one. The other was handed to Fuzzy.

As his fingers closed on the slender glass stem his disabilities dropped from him for one brief moment. He straightened himself; and Time, so disobliging to most of us, turned backward to accommodate Fuzzy.

Forgotten Christmas ghosts whiter than the false beards of the most opulent Kris Kringle were rising in the fumes of Grogan's whisky. What had the Millionaire's mansion to do with a long wainscoted Virginia hall, where the riders were grouped around a silver punch-bowl drinking the ancient toast of the House? And why should the patter of the cab horses' hoofs on the frozen street be in any wise related to the sound of the saddled hunters stamping under the shelter of the west veranda? And what had Fuzzy to do with any of it?

The Lady, looking at him over her glass, let her condescending smile fade away like a false dawn. Her eyes turned serious. She saw something beneath the rags and Scotch terrier whiskers that she did not understand. But it did not matter.

Fuzzy lifted his glass and smiled vacantly.

"P-pardon, lady," he said, "but couldn't leave without exchangin' comp'ments sheason with lady th' house. 'Gainst princ'ples gen'leman do sho."

And then he began the ancient salutation that was a

tradition in the House when men wore lace ruffles and powder.

"The blessings of another year—"

Fuzzy's memory failed him. The Lady prompted:

"—Be upon this hearth."

"—The guest——" stammered Fuzzy.

"—And upon her who——" continued the Lady, with a leading smile.

"Oh, cut it out," said Fuzzy, ill-manneredly. "I can't remember. Drink hearty."

Fuzzy had shot his arrow. They drank. The Lady smiled again the smile of her caste. James enveloped Fuzzy and reconducted him toward the front door. The harp music still softly drifted through the house.

Outside, Black Riley breathed on his cold hands and hugged the gate.

"I wonder," said the Lady to herself, musing, "who— but there were so many who came. I wonder whether memory is a curse or a blessing to them after they have fallen so low."

Fuzzy and his escort were nearly at the door. The Lady called: "James!"

James stalked back obsequiously, leaving Fuzzy waiting unsteadily, with his brief spark of the divine fire gone.

Outside, Black Riley stamped his cold feet and got a firmer grip on his section of gas-pipe.

"You will conduct this gentleman," said the Lady, "downstairs. Then tell Louis to get out the Mercedes and take him to whatever place he wishes to go."

Afterword

The critics would appreciate O. Henry a lot more if we had, or still had, the conception of artworks and the artist that is found, for example, in Japan. The Japanese take short poems and stories *much* more seriously than we. It's also felt that while they will have a long, arduous apprenticeship, true artists will write, or paint, their greatest works swiftly, effortlessly, and surely, in one concentrated burst of creativity, with the circumstances of composition and the very paper and pen strokes all a part of the act. Japanese art museums often display the original draft of revered poems, short stories, or letters; clearly, graceful but natural and fast calligraphy, and the story of how it was written, usually explained in helpful label, are all part of the artwork.

The contrary ideal—that of Professor Profundity—is exemplified in the critic's vision of James Joyce, who took two decades of writing and rewriting and rerewriting to produce *Finnegans' Wake*, reportedly on occasion spending an entire day on the choice of a single word. To complaints about length and the extreme difficulty of reading the work with understanding, Joyce replied that he expected the reader to devote several years if not a lifetime to reading it (a few English professors have).

In his prime, so observers tell us, O. Henry sat, "primly postured," at his desk and wrote his stories with elegant penmanship, going from the first word to the last with only a few brief hesitations, no slips of the pen, and without revising or crossing out a single word. We are told he wrote "The Gift of the Magi" exactly so, first to last word, with an impatient illustrator camped nearby. It took him less than two hours.

Surely somewhere he still wanders turn-of-the-century New York City, his beloved Bagdad on the Hudson, where blindered horses are giving way to subway and motor vehicle, and gaslamps to electricity. he strolls here and there, listening, watching, amidst the evening bustle along a misted, glittering Fourteenth Street, overhearing a harrange in Yiddish, smiling at the Irish cop, giving the graying newspaper lady his soft Southern thank you and ten times what the paper cost. He turns into Luchow's grandly plush German restaurant only to re-emerge, moving more quickly having seen the *New York World* editor who was owed a story last Monday (or was it Tuesday?). Perhaps he'll walk down to McSorley's Ale House. This early he might just be able to dash something off on one of the back room tables. If only he could hear what the skinny young woman in the black shawl was saying to the pale young man, who stood stiff as a cigar store Indian, staring away from her at the streetcar.

He feels a story coming on.

Four million lives swirl about him, four million stories, each equally precious. As the current *Soviet Encyclopedia* reminds us, in our today where college professors dismiss his stories as trite soapy trickery, "the real hero of O. Henry's stories is the ordinary American, with his right to happiness."

Surely, he is sentimental. Surely, he has the right to be, after all the guilt and pain and self-destruction. Surely, we do, too.

—Justin Leiber